Copyright 1999 Ray Fraser
Cover Design © 1999 Press-TIGE Publishing

All rights reserved, including the right to reproduce this book
or portions therein in any form whatsoever.

For information address:
Press-Tige Publishing
291 Main Street
Catskill, NY 12414
http://www.presstigebooks.com
Presstige9@aol.com

First Press-Tige Edition 1999

Printed in the United States of America

ISBN# 1-57532-147-5

Mike, I hope you enjoy my book. Ray 11/2001

CHAPTER 1

A cool breeze, filled with the hint of impending rain, rustled the Venetian blinds of my fourth floor walk-up, bringing a refreshing aroma to my smoke-filled office.

Once again, I was working late. Seems like I do very little else with my time these days. Fact is, I spend so much time in this dump, I sometimes wonder why I pay rent on an apartment.

But, when you're the sole proprietor, the C.E.O., and the lone employee of a PI business, you gotta do, what you gotta do.

Besides, I've always been one of those people that can't let things lay. I figure, if I'm gonna lose sleep anyway, I might as well be trying to get the monkey off my back, and make a few sheckles.

I leaned back in my chair, lit up a Red, took a deep hit, and looked out the half-open window of my office at San Francisco Bay. The ship lights in the bay twinkled and beckoned, the thick smell of the salt water filling the room and bringing to mind, my love of the sea.

Emotionally, I was too young to be away from home. But, my brother Cam and I decided we would be adventurous and join the Navy. "It's not just a job, it's an adventure", we used to laugh. Some adventure. God, Ma was pissed. The real adventure was tellin' her that we'd enlisted.

I grew up in the Navy, but I didn't like the formality and restraint it brought. I guess I've always been too much of a free spirit.

The only good thing about those days, was the fact that I got laid, traveled the world, and found a love for the open water.

I chuckled, thinking back to the good ol' days and some of the *bad* things that also came with the territory. For one, these damn cigarettes. I never smoked or drank until I joined up. I mean, how much can a preacher's kid from Detroit do when he's seventeen and living a sheltered life? Not much, until he gets away from home. The Navy offered Cam and I that opportunity.

So much for memory-lane, I thought. I snuffed out the Pall Mall and tried to put my mind back on the case before me.

* * * * * * * * * * * * * *

I had to get a new office. Something a little more classy. Uptown maybe, with central air and a new desk. And, bigger. I could use more space. Maybe even a secretary. I sighed. As always, these are only passing thoughts. I frequently talk about changing the office, but nothing ever changes.

If I could just get rid of the dark wood paneling and the old school smell, and maybe get someone to clean up once in a while, this place wouldn't be so bad. I made myself a mental note to look into it just as soon as I got the time.

I laughed to myself. Time. Time wasn't the problem, procrastination was. With things that involved personal issues, if there was a way to procrastinate, I'd find it. I guess I save all my best decision making power for my cases.

I swivelled around in my leather captain's chair and stared down at the scattered papers on my desk. I hate these cases. Some rich foreign bastard comes over here and marries some young honey. Everything is hunky-dorey for a while. Then one day she wakes up, realizes she's tired of screwing his greasy ass, and starts messing around with the butler, the chauffeur, the gardener or his brother, and I start making a living.

I was tired. Enough for one day, I thought. I figured I'd blow this place off and go grab a quick bite.

It's funny how your mind works when you reminisce. I hit the pack again. I could have gone to college like my twin brother Cam and made something of myself. Cam was always the ambitious one. I guess he was born with the professional ambitions for both of us.

Now, don't get me wrong. I love what I do. I'm somewhat respected, somewhat feared, and I earn a decent buck from time to time. But, it's not like I work for a living.

Cam and I are identicals. Being an identical twin does have its drawbacks. Parents of twins always think both of you should be the same.

As for Cam and I, we don't always follow that rule. The only things which we really have in common, are the same looks, an appreciation for a tight tush, and a love of life.

I sucked the smoke deep into my lungs, reached for the paper cup, and took a drink of long cold coffee. The coffee did little to wash out the slime of forty-five king-size, unfiltered cigarettes, from my mouth. I squeezed the coffee down and made a mental note to have a double shot of Cutty when I got to Jerry's. Hopefully, the scotch would wash out the taste of the coffee, and the smokes.

"Jerry's", is my kind of place. A little neighborhood bar, that serves cold beer, good scotch, and burgers that are just greasy enough to kill an all-day appetite.

I also like the "Emporium" because everyone knows me there. I get a lotta tips from the paying customers, and occasionally I get lucky.

When I reached to douse the rest of my butt in one of the empty coffee cups on my desk, the buzzer on my phone buzzed, loud and shrill. The night was so quiet and my thoughts so distant, that it startled the hell right out of me.

I took a deep breath and regained my composure. The phone shrilled on. I hated that phone. I reminded myself of my daily commitment to myself to throw the damned thing out the window and get one that wasn't so piercing. I made myself a mental note. I also let it buzz.

You see, I have business hours. At least they're posted on the door. When my phone rings at twelve-thirty in the morning, either it's a wrong number or somebody's desperate. It kept on buzzing, shrill and insistent.

The loud squealing continued until it finally got the best of me. After about twenty-five rings, I surrendered. I figured, what the hell, I was about done with this valley-girl case anyway, so I might as well put the poor bastard out of its misery. I reached to answer the phone.

* * * * * * * * * * * * *

"Yeah?" I said absently, into the fashion mouthpiece.

I hated this phone. It was nothing but a piece of cheap, imported crap.

"Sean?" came the reply.

It was my mother calling from Detroit. I coughed, cleared my throat and sat up.

"Yeah ma, how you doin'?"

My mind jogged back into reality before she could answer. What the hell was she doing calling me at this hour? Usually she was dead to the world by nine-thirty.

"I've been trying to reach you for hours Sean, but all I got was your machine."

"Yeah ma," I said. "I don't spend too much time at home these days."

Ma was always on my shit because I didn't lead a normal life. I got ready for another, what's wrong with your life, speeches. I loved my mom, but sometimes we just didn't see eye-to-eye on life. I figured this time, I would head her off.

"Look, Mom, you know you can't—"

"Sean," she interrupted. "Not now."

Mom's abruptness caught me off guard. I fell silent for a moment, hoping to change the mood.

"So, what's up, ma?"

"It's Cam. He's been in an accident."

"An accident? What kind of an accident?"

"A car accident. The doctors said it doesn't look good."

"How bad is it?" I asked, knowing before I did, that if ma was calling, it had to be serious.

Mom was crying softly and struggling to speak.

"It's bad Sean. He's not expected to live."

I leaned back in my chair and stared into the dim light of the overhead fluorescents. I couldn't help but think, shit, and I was gonna call him tomorrow. Then again, I was always gonna call him tomorrow, but I never did.

I guess I really never got over his normalcy. Successful business exec, married to his high school sweetheart, three cute kids. All settled down, or so I thought.

About the closest I ever came to settling down was Debra. Ah, Debbie. God knew what he was doing when he sent me to Frisco back in seventy. Now, don't get me wrong, Debbie was a great chick. Tall, blonde, good looking and tough as nails. She was probably the only woman I've ever known that had my number.

"How'd it happen, ma?" I asked.

Mom was still crying softly and struggling for words.

"It was his car, Sean. As near as we can tell, he lost control."

Lost control? That thought seemed ludicrous. I didn't tell you about the cars. Cam was to cars, what Michelangelo was to painting. He could make any car run, and if it ran already, he could do miracles with it.

The Navy had given us each something. Me, I got a love for the sea. Cam, he got cars. After his stint in the Navy, Cam had raced different kinds of cars from time to time. With his experience, it seemed a little odd that he would lose control of any vehicle.

"Are you sure it was an accident, ma?" I asked, my PI instincts pressing to the front of my logic.

Mom was solemn, "Yes, we're sure. They said he slid on the ice and hit a bridge abutment."

I had forgotten it was winter in Michigan. In Michigan, the winter snow, sleet, and freezing rain, make driving virtually impossible at times. Here in San Francisco, it doesn't snow or sleet in the winter, it just gets real shitty and rains all the time. Sometimes I think the snow would be a relief.

I turned my chair towards the window and stared hypnotically into the darkness, my reflection mirroring my image in the glass. My mind seemed to drift into a state of numbness. I heard ma's voice speaking to my subconscious mind.

"I need you here, Sean. They've got him on life support. They're only giving him hours. It'll take a miracle."

I sat quietly looking out the window, my mind racing, and said nothing. My only thought for the moment was, can this really be happening?"

"Did you hear me, Sean?" Ma asked.

"Yeah Ma, I heard you," I mumbled. "I'll catch the first flight out." I turned back around to my desk, and I hung up that damned phone.

CHAPTER 2

Getting a flight out of Frisco at this time of night isn't the easiest thing in the world to do. Especially when you're going to someplace everybody in the world wants to go to, like Detroit. That's a joke. Murder city, Motor city. It's all the same to most folks. I dialed the airport.

The first voice I heard, was the recording that all available operators were busy. Busy, my ass. I could envision people all over the bay area thinking in unison, by God Margaret, it's one a.m., we'd better call and book our flight to Tucson. In reality someone was on break, in the john, asleep, or just didn't feel like answering the phone. I decided I'd wait them out.

After about the twentieth play through, what sounded like a human being came on the line. "Hello and thank you for calling Northwest Air Lines. My name is Cindy, how may I help you?"

Cindy's voice sounded like one of my client's wives, if you know what I mean. I envisioned a skinny blonde with rat nest hair, too red lipstick, "Fabulous Fakes" fingernails, and a half-a-pack of "Juicy Fruit" gum in her mouth.

I could see her standing there with her plastic name tag that said "Northwest Air Lines", "Cyndi". I don't exactly know why, but I've always hated it when women bastardize their names to make them sound or look cute.

I did my best to keep from upchucking at that thought and gave her the benefit of the doubt.

"Cindy, I need the earliest flight possible to Detroit What have you got?"

There was a momentary silence. I heard the soft click of the computer keys in the background as Cindy checked the available flights.

I waited for what seemed like an eternity. While waiting, I thought of the phone again. Here I was talking on a piece of cheap foreign crap, listening to a dame that was probably also talking on some foreign intervention into our lives, while I waited for information on perhaps the most important plane ride of my life. Alexander Graham Bell would turn over in his grave if he could see us now.

After a moment or two, Cindy's voice echoed back on the line, sounding tinny and resonant.

"We have two flights out, both arrive in Detroit around eleven o'clock a.m.. One leaves at three-twenty-five, and stops in Chicago. There's a half an hour layover there, and then it arrives at Detroit Metro at eleven twenty-one, Detroit time. The other is a non-stop that leaves at four-oh-five and arrives in Detroit at eleven-seventeen."

All I wanted to do was get there the fastest and easiest way possible.

"Book me on the non-stop, honey," I said, before giving her my name.

Cindy surprised me. She was obviously a very bright girl. She either read the papers a lot, or really was one of my client's wives.

"Mr. Thomas, are you the famous private investigator?" she gushed, haloing the words, private investigator.

I began to think of Cindy in an entirely different light. You see, famous, is a word that has never been used in the same sentence with either my name or my job. So, if Cindy was trying to pique my interest, she was on the right track. I laughed, told her I was, and made a mental note to look her up when I got back from Motown.

Hey, I've misread a few broads in my time. Maybe I had misjudged Cindy. Besides, I decided I could use a little excitement.

I booked an aisle seat on the four-oh-five, and hung up the phone. I had about three hours to pack and get to San Francisco International before my flight left.

The quiet of my office offered a much needed solitude. I sat staring out the half-opened window, my mind drifting. The soft whirring of the cheap alarm clock on my desk, was interrupted by the mellow tone of the Bay Point fog horn and the occasional clang of a channel marker buoy.

As I listened to the fog horn's rhythmic cry, I thought to myself how quiet the night had become. No cars, no people, just the horn.

The still darkness of the night was broken only by the incessant passing of the light from the Alcatraz lighthouse, it's brilliant beam piercing the night like a broad white scythe.

I pulled the last cigarette from the pack, lit it, and mused back in time. Cam and I were real close growing up. In the beginning, our closeness was almost forced upon us by the others in our world.

Ma always bought us the same clothes, dressed us alike, and took joy in the fact that almost no one could tell us apart.

We learned early on, that we could get away with just about anything we wanted with very little effort.

You see, we really are identical. We're mirror images. The only difference between us is a small mole Cam has behind his right ear.Truth is, if you didn't know it was there, you'd never even see it.

We did all the things identicals do when we were growing up. One of us would cover classes while the other skipped. We played tricks on our relatives. And, we dated the same girls.

Usually, when we started dating a new girl, we would use each other's name. If the girl was hot, on the next date we would switch. I know that sounds crass, but what the hell, we were young, and wanted to sow some wild oats.

All that seemed to change when I met Angie. She was a doll. Seventeen, blonde, a cheer leader, and built like one.

I had just broken up with Bonnie, and Angie was transferring to our school. We met at registration, talked, and I asked her out. I told her I was Cam. That Friday, we went to the West Side Drive-In Theater, and I had the time of my life.

I told Cam about her and we laughed when she agreed to a second date. The next weekend I took Cam's girlfriend Linda to a "Welcome Back" party at school, and Cam took Angie to the West Side.

When Cam got home that night, I rushed to see how things went, if you know what I mean. Instead of being his jovial, light-hearted self, Cam was serious when we talked. He told me that he didn't want to play these games anymore, and that he didn't want me calling Angie again. The poor bastard had fallen in love.

At first I laughed it off. I figured his affection for Angie was a short-term thing. I was sure wrong about that. To keep him from getting shot in the ass by Linda, I filled in for him until he got the guts to tell Linda about Angie. When he did, I called Linda up, and she and I dated until we graduated.

I laugh to think about it now. For a long time, Cam and I thought the switch with Angie was our little joke. Cam was worried Angie would find out and swore me to secrecy. After he and Angie were married, she told me she had known all along. I guess the joke was on us, but I never told Cam.

I doused the last half-inch of my smoke in one of the cold, stale, cups of coffee that lined my desk and window sill. I stood up and pushed the window shut. The thought of returning to my apartment and going through the rigors of packing was less than appealing to me so, I decided that I wouldn't even screw with packing. I had my gold card, and I could wear some of Cam's clothes if push came to shove. Besides, right now, I felt like I needed some company.

On my way out the door, I dumped the half-dozen coffee cups that were empty into the trash, turned on my answering machine, and headed for "Jerry's".

* * * * * * * * * * * * *

It was a short walk to the corner where "Jerry's Bar and Emporium" stood. As I neared "Jerry's" I could hear Johnny Cash's "Ring of Fire" playing softly on the juke box. The smell of beer and food from the open windows of Jerry's kitchen reminded me that I hadn't eaten all day. I was starved.

I pushed the heavy wooden door open and peered into the semi-darkness. Jerry stood behind the bar talking to Raven. Raven, is a close friend and a regular at "The Emporium". She is also one very good-looking woman. Raven, is a Cajun girl, who will occasionally turn a trick to help raise cash to pay her rent.

I pulled up the stool next to her and sat down. I needed a smoke. My hand reached for the pack that wasn't there.

"Can I bum a smoke?" I asked, more for formality, than approval.

Raven turned and smiled when she saw me.

"Sean, how are you doin'?"

Her smile was infectious. I smiled back and reached for the pack of menthols that she slid over to me.

"Life's a bitch, doll," I answered . I shook one of the slim cigarettes out of the pack, broke off the filter, and lit it up.

Raven looked beautiful, I thought.

"You working tonight?" I asked.

Raven laughed. "No, not tonight," she answered contritely with a pout. Then she placed her hand on my cheek and smiled softly, "It's never work for you anyway."

I began to feel very warm.

I said that Raven hooked, and that is somewhat misleading. She doesn't go with just any Tom, Dick or Harry. She's selective. She only goes with people she knows or with someone referred by someone she knows. Unlike most ladies of the evening, she doesn't even have set rates.

We all figured that she knows what she needs to make ends meet, and then encourages the appropriate donations. Besides, if she charged what she was worth, none of us could afford her anyway.

Raven, is tall and almond skinned, with long black hair that hangs past the middle of her back. Her long shapely legs, crest at the tightest ass you could ever imagine. Her smile is broad, her lips pouty, and her eyes are formed in such a way as to make you think that you are the only man in the world when she looks at you. I suddenly wished I had a couple of extra hours before I had to leave.

Raven and I have had our moments. I met her when she was seventeen. She wandered into "Jerry's" one night, cold and broke. I set her up for a couple of nights at my place and the rest, as they say, is history.

I imagine that your first thought is that I'm some kind of dirty old man, but it's not like that at all. I was on my way to Philly for a few days, so I took a chance and let her stay at my place while I was gone.

She had told me that she was a hooker, and had been for a couple of years. I looked at this young thing and couldn't believe my eyes. Life was indeed a bitch.

When I got home from Philly, my place was immaculate. She had cleaned, dusted, vacuumed, and done my laundry.

After that, she stayed with me for a month or so, before she finally shared my bed. I won't tell you that I fought it, but I will say that she initiated our first encounter.

After having her as part of my life for that long, it just seemed like the most natural thing in the world the night she left the couch and joined me in the bedroom.

We were hot and did our thing for a couple of months, then one day, I came home to a rose and a note. She had taken a job in Redwood City, and wanted to try making it on her own.

Two years later, she was back. Oh, she had made it alright, but she missed the old neighborhood and the excitement of the world's oldest profession.

After she got back to San Francisco, we remained friends, but our relationship never got all the way back to the way it was in the early days. In spite of that fact, we always had something, special.

Jerry is a Navy buddy. He's the one that brought me to Frisco back in seventy. Back then, he was about to get married and wanted me to meet his fiance' Jan.

I came out from Detroit and we partied for a couple of weeks. Shortly before the wedding date, Jan was kidnaped, raped and murdered.

Jerry was devastated. I had never really wanted to be a private investigator. But, I was so pissed, that I vowed to find out who did it. After about a month of concerted effort, I tracked down the slime-ball that did it, and my career as a PI was born. Since then, my money's been no good at "Jerry's".

Jerry finished serving a customer at the other end of the bar and set me up with a double shot of Cutty and a draft. I ordered a burger and fries, a pack of smokes, and finished the menthol.

The "Cutty" ate through the staleness of the day, ridding my pallet of the smoke and coffee taste. The "Bud" was ice-cold and refreshing. After my second double, I sipped the beer to whet my whistle.

Raven noticed I was deep in thought and teased, "A penny for your thoughts."

I took a new Red from the pack, tamped it down, and fired it up before I answered.

"It's Cam. He's been in an accident," I said. "He's not expected to live."

Raven seemed stunned.

"Oh, Sean," she mouthed softly, then added, "Jerry, Cam's been in an accident."

Jerry came back to our end of the bar.

"Did you say Cam's been hurt?" he asked.

I nodded, "Yeah, car accident."

Jerry looked puzzled and shook his head.

"A car accident, huh?" he repeated, his voice trailing off in disbelief.

When Cam and Angie got married, Jerry and Raven flew to Detroit for the wedding. Jerry threw the bachelor party, and Raven gave Cam a wedding present that only she could give.

Cam, said that he never understood how I could allow Raven to shack up with him, but like I told him, I had no ties on her and asked for none. It was her choice.

Cam and I were brothers. What was mine, was his, too. Besides, it wasn't like Raven and I were married or anything. Anyway, I knew that once Cam said "I do", that he would never look at another woman.

I couldn't say the same about Angie. With her, it was always someone. Maybe just a tease here or a tease there. But, let me tell you, I've heard her make offers that almost no man could refuse.

As wholesome as Angie was, she was a kinky dame, too. She always wanted to get it on somewhere, with someone, where there was a heavy risk of being caught in the act. Cam never bought into that, and I think it frustrated her a lot.

After the wedding, we all flew back to Frisco to party for a few days, then Cam and Angie flew on to Hawaii for their honeymoon. Those few days together, created a bond of family, that has never been broken.

Jerry brought my food and let me eat in peace. Raven, had left to go to the head and stopped to talk to a client on the way back. I ate in silence.

After a thoughtful meal and a polite buzz, I looked at my watch. It was nearly time to leave. It was a fairly long drive to the airport and I didn't want to be late for this flight.

Jerry saw that I had finished eating and walked back to my end of the bar. By now, most of the regulars had left for the night. Jerry brought me another set-up. I tossed the Cutty and drained half the brew.

"What time's your flight?" he asked.

"Four," I answered.

"Goin' Northwest?"

I nodded, "Yeah, I got the "Red eye". I get in around eleven tomorrow."

Jerry wiped the bar. "Call me tomorrow and let me know how it's going."

I told him I would, and reached for my wallet to pay my tab. Jerry just laughed.

"Man, you never get it, do you?" he said, taking the paper plate and glasses, and turning his back on my attempt at payment. Then walking away, he continued over his shoulder, "Have a good flight, and don't forget, call me tomorrow."

I never figured finding Jan's killer was anything more than a friend, helping a friend. After they killed the bastard, Jerry came back to life. He said I had given him his life back. To me, any friend would have done the same thing.

I reached for my keys and turned to leave. Raven was there.

"I thought you were busy" I said.

"Not tonight, baby. You need a ride to the airport anyway, right?"

I nodded, "Yeah, I need a ride."

As we walked to my "two-forty-two", I thought how lucky I was to have friends like these. You're probably thinking, some friends; a part time hooker, and the owner of a small corner bar. But hell, I've never been one to worry about a person's background or occupation. I worry more about their character.

I let Raven in, got in the driver's side, and started to the airport. The night was foggy, and it was hard to see exactly where we were going at freeway speeds.

The polite buzz that I had started at "Jerry's", had also become more intense, so I slowed down a bit, focused my attentions on the road, hit the cigarette lighter and reached for the pack.

With all the flights being "No Smoking" flights, I had to stock up on some nicotine for the plane ride.

We rode in silence for a long while before Raven spoke.

"When are you coming back?"

I didn't really know, and I told her so. I had no idea what to expect when I got to Detroit. Of course, my mind was playing the, worst case scenario tapes, so I didn't think it would be soon. I asked her to look after my place and told her that I'd call her and let her know how things were going.

A few moments later, the lights for the airport became visible. I tooled up the ramp leading to the terminals. Man, it was foggy. I hoped my flight wouldn't be fogged in. The bright lights of the Northwest terminal chased the fog and allowed clear vision at last.

After a few moments of dodging cars, busses, taxis and people, we pulled up in front of the terminal, I put the car in park and turned to look at Raven. She smiled. "No bags?"

I laughed, "No. No bags. I forgot to pack."

Raven, knew me too well.

"You forgot to pack? Sean, sometimes you worry me to death."

I reached over and gave Raven a polite hug, a peck on the lips, and got out. Raven slid over and got under the wheel.

"I'll call you tomorrow."

"Don't forget," she reminded.

I nodded, "I won't," I said, and closed the door.

Raven hit the gear shift and turned the Volvo back towards the city. I watched silently as the taillights disappeared down the "Departing Flights" ramp, and then went inside to pick up my ticket.

As I approached the ticket counter, my mind shook off the thoughts of the last few hours. I thought I'd see if Cindy was still working. As luck would have it, she had clocked out at three. I took out a business card, underlined my phone number, and left it with Bette, to give to Cindy. Bette said she would give it to her when she came in to work again later in the day.

* * * * * * * * * * * * *

For me, the longest wait at an airport, seems to be the amount of time between "Check-in" and "Take-off". However, at long last, I was on the seven forty-seven, taxiing down the tarmac, heading towards the runway. I decided it was time for a little shut-eye.

As the plane climbed and banked, I reached up, clicked off the little light that always seems to shine in your face, and closed my eyes.

The next voice I heard was that of the flight attendant, reminding everyone to fasten their seat belts for the final descent into Detroit's Metropolitan Airport.

I suddenly had an urge for a Pall Mall, and I contemplated risking the $5,000 fine to light one up. I leaned over and looked out the window. The ground was coming up. I figured I could probably wait.

After a few moments, we finally landed and taxied to the terminal entrance. The pilot had told us in our final descent lecture, that the weather in Detroit was clear, but cold. He said, ten degrees, with a wind chill of minus eleven. Welcome to the frozen North.

The outdoor temperature and the piles of snow, which lined the runway, made my decision not to pack, seem more than a little asinine. I quickly realized, that if it was only ten degrees above zero, and I didn't have a coat, that I was going to freeze my ass off.

I had hoped for an Indian summer. This would have meant temperatures closer to 50 degrees, and plenty of sunshine. As luck would have it, Mother Nature was not interested in my wishes.

However, one of the good things about modern airports, is that you don't have to spend much time outside unless you really want to. It's heat lamps near the doors, shuttles to the parking lots, and shuttles to the rental cars.

At eleven o'clock on a Sunday morning in January, the Avis counter was deserted. I signed up for a Ford Escort, and hopped on the shuttle. When I got to the car, it was running and warm.

* * * * * * * * * * * * * *

Metro Airport is surrounded by freeway accesses. Unfortunately, most of them were created after I had already left Michigan for the coast. With no map in hand, I decided to play it safe and headed down the only freeway which I really knew, towards the Henry Ford Hospital in the heart of Detroit.

Michigan was having a cold winter. The snow was piled high along the freeway but the roadway was clear. As I drove past the many underpasses and viaducts, I found myself wondering if one of these might have been the one that Cam hit.

My curiosity was starting to nag at me. I knew there were facts that were left out of mom's telephone call. What exactly they were, was still a mystery to me.

I believe that everything happens for a reason. Cam's accident also happened for a reason. I was determined to find out just what that reason was. I always do. That's my job.

CHAPTER 3

Welcome to Detroit. For the past several decades, Detroit's murder rate has ranked near the top in the country.Decades of lousy administration and years of fiscal abuses, have left it one of the most undesirable cities in the country to live and work in.

I looked at this once friendly metropolis as I drove. Neighborhoods, that I remembered as friendly, which are now boarded up buildings or vacant lots. Whole neighborhoods were left to decay, and are now home to ghetto wars, and drug dealers. Businesses along once walkable streets such as Dexter, Livernois, and Woodward, were closed and gone.

Detroit has developed a reputation, and a bad one. The new administration is working hard to correct the past wrongs in the city, but the change certainly was not going to happen overnight.

Henry Ford Hospital was not in one of the best areas of Detroit, but then again, not much was. Detroit is a city that is falling apart faster than it can be renovated.

After about twenty-five minutes of driving, I jumped off the freeway at the West Grand Blvd exit and turned into the Ford Hospital complex. Henry Ford Hospital, so named after the auto pioneer, is a huge medical center, a real "General Hospital" in the traditional sense. I thought to myself, that it would make a perfect setting for virtually any emergency-medical TV show.

Fortunately for me, Ford Hospital had valet parking. This meant that once again, I would be spared the discomfort of freezing my ass off while I walked to the hospital. I tooled up to the "Valet Parking" area, disembarked, and slipped the kid a buck.

Inside the hospital, I was greeted by a forest green and mauve reception area. Sitting at a computer at the far end of the corridor was an elderly woman who sat under a sign that read "Visitor's Information". I walked in her direction.

"Cameron Thomas," I said, when I had finally reached her desk. Her attitude was stoic. She didn't look up at me, but typed Cam's name into her computer.

After a moment, she looked at the screen, took a visitor's pass and wrote a number on it. "Two-four-three East," then pointing down, she added, "Follow the yellow line to the elevator, take it to the second floor, and then again to the East I.C.U."

I mumbled a thanks and looked down at the rainbow of colored tape on the floor leading off like colored tentacles in all directions. I followed the yellow one.

As I looked down at the yellow line on the second floor, I was amazed to see that it started off in the exact spot where the one on the first floor ended.

From the elevator, it was a short walk to the end of the yellow line. I hit the "Door Open" panel on the outside the East intensive care unit, waited for the double doors to swing open, and then walked inside. The smell of medicine filled my nostrils, the rhythmic "beep" of the nursing station monitors, greeting my ears.

I looked up at the triangular lights above the glassed in units. Unit four-three was on the right, its curtains partially drawn and the lights dimmed. I could see my mother's feet propped up on a stool as I turned into the room. She was asleep.

I looked down at Cam. He looked bad. He lay flat on his back, uncovered except for a sheet draped across his loins.

In the dim lights of the room, I could clearly see the monitors. BP, one-seventy over one-twenty-five, heart rate one-oh-five. Cam's skin was pale, his face bloated.

Both of his legs were in bandages and swollen, his feet discolored, deep black and blue. His left arm was lightly gauzed, the row of stitches showing like a crossed-stitched tattoo, even in the darkness. A gauze and tape cap, covered his head.

I gripped his hand. The skin was cold and clammy. Cam had I.V.'s in both of his arms. A tube to drain his stomach was stuck into his nose and down his throat. A respirator tube was taped into his mouth. He appeared lifeless.

A lot of thoughts go through your mind at a time like this. As much as I had tried to condition myself for this moment, I now realized that I was seriously unprepared. For the first time since mom had called me, I fully realized that Cam was going to die.

Of course, for the moment, he was still alive. I remembered the old saying that says something like, "as long as you're alive, there's still hope". This time it was different. I felt no life energy in my brother's body.

CHAPTER 4

I sat down in the empty chair in Cam's room. As I did so, it moved, squeaking on the floor. Mom awoke with a start. She looked tired and drawn.

"Sean, why didn't you call?" mom said, stretching, "I could have had Angie pick you up."

Angie was missing, and noticeably so.

"Where is Angie?" I asked, emphasizing the word is.

"She had to pick-up the kids and take them to Sandy's," mom answered.

Sandy was one of Angie's sisters. I always thought she was a bitch. Sandy had this smart-ass air about her. She was always domineering, bossy and arrogant. I often wondered if she just didn't like me. I blew it off, because she treated everyone just as poorly. For whatever reason, there were always bad vibes between us.

Sandy and her husband Jeff were into a bunch of weird things like talking to the dead, attending seances and stuff. They even had a church that they attended, which preached about life after death. Our family went to a service there once when I was home, and frankly it scared the hell right out of me, no pun intended.

The way Cam and I were raised, once you were dead, you were dead. You had to wait for the resurrection to continue your spirit life in heaven or hell.

I know after dad died, Cam began exploring spirit communication with Angie. I guess it was his open mindedness that made it possible for him to do that. Me, I was just a little square on some things.

When we were growing up, we went to the show to see movies like "The Curse of the Mummies Tomb", and other horror movies like it. Cam loved it. Me, I had nightmares. I can remember many nights laying in bed at nine or ten o'clock at night, and dozing off for a few minutes, only to wake up at midnight and not be able to go back to sleep for the rest of the night.

Last I heard, Cam and Angie were regulars at the church, and did spirit messages and healings and weird crap like that.

As you can tell, just talking about these things gives me the willies. I'm always afraid some ghost is gonna sneak up and bite me in the ass when I'm not looking.

Mom wasn't very supportive of it either. But then again, she was raised to be a preacher's wife, and 35 years of Pentecostal indoctrination can leave a heavy mark on your thought processes.

Cam and Angie used to laugh at ma though. Mom would preach biblical damnation for people that talked to the dead, or believed in fortune tellers, but when dad would go out of town, she and the girls would take a ride to Canada to see a medium there to have their fortunes told.

I think she even went to Jeff and Sandy's church once. When she went, some young guy stood up and gave her an irrefutable message from her dead brother. After that, she never went back.

Cam and dad were always closer than dad and I were. Cam was a singer. He had a great voice and was very musically inclined. Dad always thought I had a great voice too. The truth was, I couldn't carry a tune in a bushel basket.

Dad frequently made Cam and I sing together. Most of the time, I just lip synced and let Cam do his thing. Dad also, thought that one of us would follow in his footsteps as a minister.

For a while we all thought it would be Cam. When Cam met Angie, things changed. Cam was smitten by Angie, and rearranged his priorities. When he did, dad and the church took a back seat to young love, and lust. I think it broke dad's heart.

When dad finally bought it with a heart attack, the whole family clung to their basic Christian theories for a while. After a few months, Jeff and Sandy invited Cam to their church to see if dad could get a spirit message through. I don't know what actually happened, but Cam was never the same after that. He began to study the Spiritualist church philosophy and take classes on becoming a medium.

I figured, screw it, if he wanted to spend his time pursuing mediumship and dead spirits, and if it made him feel better, then what the heck. It was his business.

We never talk much about it, because he knows how I feel. It just isn't my bag of tricks.

"Mr. Thomas?"

I turned towards the voice. Standing in the doorway was Cam's nurse. She was young, good looking, and energetic.

"Yes, ma'am" I said. "There's a message for you at the nurse's station to call an Angie Thomas when you arrive. I'll get the number for you."

"Thanks"

She smiled, turned, and went down the short hall to get the message. While she was gone, another nurse came in and needled a vial of medicine into one of the I.V. units in Cam's arm.

One of the major concerns the doctors had, was the fact that Cam had never regained consciousness. They believed that if he were to wake up, he'd have a better chance to survive. I guess they figured his natural desire to survive would kick in and give his chances a boost.

Mom sat quietly, solemnly watching the soft rise and fall of Cam's chest. The gentle hiss of the respirator and the soft click of the in-room monitors, playing a symphony of gloom in the shadowy light.

Cam's nurse, "Bubbles" was back with the message. I couldn't help but notice that she was married. I'd made her for twenty or twenty-one. I thought to myself, some dumb bastard is getting that every night and he probably hasn't any clue what he's got.

Life is indeed a bitch. In most cases, we gain the knowledge and wisdom we need to be happy or successful in life, only after it's too late in life to do us any good. I thought to myself, I would love to be twenty-one or twenty-two again and know what I know now. I felt stupid for even thinking it.

I looked at the number on the pink slip. It was Sandy's. "I'll be right back, ma. I've gotta call Angie."

Mom nodded weakly, not looking in my direction when I left. I walked out of the I.C.U. and down the hall to where the phones were. Finding one that was available, I picked up the receiver, dropped in two-bits, and dialed the number.

After two rings, Angie answered.

"Sean?" she said, anticipating that it was me.

"Yeah," I answered. "You called?"

"Sean, Sandy needs to use my car to come to the hospital later on. Will you come and pick me up?"

Angie knew that I would. I didn't understand exactly what the problem was. Jeff and Sandy had two cars. Why didn't Sandy drive her own car? At a time like this, why didn't Jeff take off of work.

As we spoke, I detected an unusual tone in Angie's voice. It wasn't like the grief or worry I had expected to hear. It was more like an air of inappropriate, casualness. There was also just a hint of excitement. It was contagious. I felt a chill run through my body.

I probably should have left my PI instincts back in Frisco, but these things become second nature after a while. Something about this whole situation was beginning to smell. Though, for the moment, I couldn't put my finger on exactly what it was, I made a mental note that I would get to the bottom of it.

I went back to the I.C.U. and told ma that I was gonna pick Angie up.

"Drive careful, Sean," mom said, more from reflex than thought.

I kissed her on the cheek, told her I would, and followed the yellow tape back to the main lobby.

As I stood outside the hospital, I sucked on a Red while waiting for my car. What was it that was out of kilter? I shook my head. Maybe nothing. Maybe I was just tired. After all, I was on, day two, without sleep. For now, I would just pass it off as jet lag, and my body finally running out of gas.

I got into the Escort and headed for Sandy's. The sun had begun to warm and some of the pristine mountains along the Edsel Ford freeway were melting, sending a flat stream of water across the roadway.

Sandy lived about twenty-minutes away from the hospital in a large four-bedroom, ranch, with tall cottonwood trees in the front yard, neatly manicured hedges in front of the house, and beautiful pansies lining the drive.

Now, the trees were bare, the hedges covered in white, and the pansies were deep in sleep beneath the winter blanket of snow.

I turned into the circular drive in front of the house, and shut off the Ford. Sandy met me at the door.

"Come on in, Sean," she said, opening the storm door and stepping back inside as I entered.

"Jeff will be home around six o'clock. He can come down to the hospital and pick me up and Angie can take ma home later on." Sandy turned towards the back of the house.

"I got the next door neighbor's daughter to baby-sit the kids while we're gone," she added, before finally leaving the room. Good ol' Sandy, I thought, She thinks of everything, as usual.

The house smelled of fresh paint and new carpet. Jeff made good bucks. He worked at some job where they filled animals with toxins to see how they would effect humans. Supposedly, the idea is, that it will ultimately lead to better medicine for humans.

In my mind, I could see Jeff trying to reason with a poor guinea pig before he injected him with some vile liquid. I felt a bit stupid for trying to rationalize everything. Yet, I figured that in some future life, Jeff would come back as a ground hog, and would end up in a "Road Kill" restaurant as a payback for his crimes against animals today. I shook out a Pall Mall and looked for an ash tray.

Where most civilized folks have ash trays, Jeff and Sandy had those obnoxious little "Thank You For Not Smoking" signs. I refiled the Red and made a mental note to tell Jeff to his face, that I thought he was an asshole.

Angie came into the room and gave me a hug.

"Where's your coat?" she asked. "Didn't you notice it was cold outside?"

"I didn't have time to pack," I lied.

Angie flashed her most sincere look of concern, and shook her head. "We can stop by the house and pick up one of Cam's, on the way to the hospital."

The kids had finally broken away from the television and came running into the room.

"Uncle Sean, Uncle Sean, did you bring us anything?" they asked excitedly. I sat down and hugged them.

I looked at Angie. She shook her head slowly from side to side. I looked back at the kids. "No kids, I didn't. They wouldn't let me bring anything on the plane," I said, lying my ass off again. I figured we could go shopping for a toy or something, tomorrow."

The kids squealed, jumping up and down.

Cam and Angie's kids were cute. Seven, six and two years old, they were a perfect linage of a good-looking couple. J.J. (named after Jerry) was a spitting image of Cam. Jessica, looked just like Angie. And, Mandy was a mix of the best parts of both parents.

I stood up and sighed.

"We should go," I said.

Angie and Sandy ushered the kids into the den to watch TV, and Angie went to get her coat.

I looked around the room. The kids had dragged Sandy into the kitchen and were screaming for a popsicle. J.J. came back into the room and stood quietly before me.

I'm sure he didn't fully understand what was happening, but at least he knew something was up.

"Uncle Sean, is my dad gonna be OK?" he asked.

I looked at his small face, seeing myself thirty-five or so years ago. I tried to be honest.

"I don't know son. Your dad is pretty sick. We sure hope he'll get better. You just keep him in your prayers, OK?"

J.J. nodded. He seemed satisfied with my answer, and headed back to the kitchen to get his iced treat.

Angie came into the room after putting on her coat. She was ready to go, so we edged toward the door. "I'll see you later," she said to Sandy.

"Nice to see you again," I echoed.

Sandy stuck her head around the corner. "Call me when you get there and let me know how he's doing."

"OK," Angie said, and closed the door behind us.

The cold air sent a chill through my body. Once we were in the car, the sun beating through the window took some of the chill out of the air, but it was still cold. Sunshine, or no sunshine, I was freezing my ass off. After we had driven a short way, the still warm engine finally began to heat the car and chase the goose bumps from my shivering body.

I looked over at Angie. She was quiet. Her attitude made me feel uneasy. Though I couldn't place it, I still got the feeling that something was off-center when she was around. She caught me looking at her, smiled wryly at me, and patted my hand as it lay on the gearshift console.

It took about fifteen minutes to get to Cam and Angie's from Sandy's. When finally we reached the house, Angie appeared nervous and frightened. I pulled in the drive, killed the engine and got out. Angie slowly followed and we walked through the snow to their door. Angie unlocked the door and hesitated. It appeared that she didn't really want to face the familiarity of the house, so I led the way in.

Walking into the foyer, it was easy to see that Cam and Angie lived a family life. Their house looked lived in and loved in.

The smell of last night's supper still lingered in the air and kids toys dotted the floor.

Angie stepped into the room behind me, placing her hand on the small of my back as she walked past me and headed for the hall closet where the coats were kept. She opened the closet door and paused,

"Do you want to take a shower or change before we leave?" she asked.

It had been almost two full days since I had washed my body, and nature was calling loud and clear.

"A shower sounds great," I said.

"You know where they are," she added. "I'll get you some clothes."

I nodded agreement and headed towards the back of the house where the bedrooms and showers were.

I can see your mind working. Yeah, Angie was a good looking, and occasionally hot chick. But, she was also my brother's wife. Besides, my brother was on his death bed. I really only wanted to shit, shower and shave.

After the normal preparation, I scraped the "Good News" across my face, removing a three-day growth. The shave made me feel clean. The warm water of the shower felt relaxing as it rained down on my body, chasing away the winter chill that I had so bravely denied. I soaped my body, shampooed my hair, and closed my eyes to the shower's solitude.

As I stood there in the steamy warmth, I thought to myself that I probably should have thought to lock the door. But, call it what you will, I didn't.

Deep in my subconscious, the memories of twenty years ago and the "West Side" flashed to the front of my thoughts.

Try as we might, old romances never seem to be totally forgotten, even when they amounted to nothing. For whatever reason, when they are unfulfilled, or incomplete, they seem to stay closer to our day-to-day memories.

Many times I had thought about that night. I don't know how I would have classified my encounter with Angie so long ago. Certainly I was enamored with her when I met her. However, because of the way Cam and I dealt with her, way back then, I never really got a chance to pursue it further.

All-in-all, I never really knew what to think of Angie. Certainly there was more to our relationship than just a sister-in-law, brother-in-law relationship. Maybe it seemed that way because Angie always said she thought there was unfinished business between us.

I laughed. I guess I secretly hoped Angie would sneak into the bathroom while I was in the shower. Of course, if she did, I would certainly have to protest.

I rinsed the soap off, shook my head and thought to myself. Sean Thomas, you are an asshole. How could I was even let those thoughts enter my mind. Cam was near death, Angie was his wife, and I had no business even thinking anything but the most solemn thoughts that the situation warranted.

I shut the water off and pushed the shower curtain back. As I wiped the water from my eyes and opened them, I saw her. Angie stood there, arm outstretched, holding a towel.

I took it. She looked at me and smiled, "Well, you're not exactly identical," then still laughing, she turned and walked out of the bathroom.

I thought back to my commitment to protest if she came in. Instead of protesting, I had said nothing. I dried off in silence, my thoughts in a scramble. This is sick, I thought. Here I was, thinking about popping Angie.

Don't get me wrong. I'm not perverted or anything like that, but Angie was right. I too, felt we had unfinished business. But now, was not the time. I made myself a mental note to book a room at the Holiday Inn at my first opportunity.

CHAPTER 5

Cam's clothes were a little loose on me. All the good home cooking and a settled life, had put a bit of a spread on him. But, at least the clothes were clean and comfortable.

I had been experiencing an unusual feeling since I first arrived in Detroit. The feeling was like deja' vu. I tried to rationalize it, but for me, the whole picture was wrong. Whether it was the house, the relationship, or me, I didn't know. All I knew was that it was wrong.

It's at moments like this that I get a little freaked out at being a twin. Cam's situation seemed almost too natural. It was as though I had been here before and was actually experiencing his tragedy and pain. His life seemed like it was my life. That thought unsettled me. I wanted to get out of this house just as fast as I could. I put my shoes back on and I was ready to go.

A private investigator learns to live by his instincts early in the game, and I didn't like the instincts that were now flashing warning signals in my mind.

I'm sure you'd think that a guy who's been a PI for the better part of his life, should be able to quickly put a finger on what was outta sync. Maybe, I should have been able to find the answer. But, I couldn't. This one was beyond even me.

Angie peeked in the door.

"Ready?" she asked.

"Sure thing," I answered compliantly. We headed for the car.

Outside, the sky looked grey. As the sun was beginning to set, it was also getting much colder. A harsh North wind blew, causing the temperature feel like it was below zero. I shivered all the way to my bones, and turned the collar of my coat up against the wind.

After a few minutes of warming the car engine, we were on our way back to the hospital. Angie looked at me, fixing her gaze in my direction.

"What?"

"You look just like Cam."

"Well, thank you Mrs. Thomas, for noticing. My brother and I are proud of our matching good looks. Please tell me you didn't just notice that we look alike?"

"No, I mean, dressed like you are, you look just like Cam."

I assured Angie that her perception of my appearance was the result of an over stressed imagination and the trauma of the situation at hand. But honestly, I knew she was right.

Driving through scenery that was only vaguely familiar, I fell into a light daze. I focused my thoughts on the situation at hand. For some reason, I felt that I had no control over what was happening here. As a rule, I make it a habit to avoid situations where I'm not in charge. I wanted to avoid this situation, but I couldn't. My instincts said to yell, stop. I wanted to jump on the next plane out, and fly back in Frisco. At least there, I could be doing my own thing. I was ready to go, brother or not.

The rest of the ride to the hospital was quiet, allowing me to think through some of the other events that had taken place since I arrived in Detroit.

Angie's brazenness frightened me. I didn't want to do anything to encourage any further inappropriate interactions with her. I tried to convince myself that I was probably reading a lot more into the situation than was really there. Yet, I wanted to be sure of my own mind and of my own intentions.

Riding the elevator to the hospital's second floor, Angie finally broke the silence.

"You're going to drive mom nuts dressed like that."

I guessed she was right. If I was going to be dressing in Cam's clothes, maybe today wasn't the best day to start.

* * * * * * * * * * * * *

The note in Cam's room, said that mom had gone down to the cafeteria for coffee. The room was quiet and empty.

Entering the room, I could sense that something was different. I felt a different kind of energy. It made my skin tingle. I walked around to the side of the bed and noticed that Cam's eyes were partially open.

"He's awake," I yelled to Angie.

Cam's eyes opened wider at the sound of my voice. He looked desperate. I hit the nurse's button and turned my attention back to Cam.

Looking down at his face, I noticed that his eyes didn't seem to be able to focus on me. After a moment, he took a deep breath and relaxed, closing his eyes. He made no other effort to see me, though his calmness indicated that he seemed to know that I was there.

The damn respirator had him scared. His B.P. was up to two-fifteen over one-twenty, and his heart rate was one-fifty. The I.C.U. nurse entered the room.

She took a quick look at the monitors, picked up the phone, and ordered a tranquilizer. Cam's eyes opened and searched for me. He struggled to speak, motioning ever so slightly with his hand by moving his fingers.

After about two minutes, the tranquilizer was coursing through his veins and his blood pressure and pulse were returning to a more normal level.

It seemed like a lifetime before the staff doctor finally arrived. While we waited, I had the nurse call down to the cafeteria to try and find my mother.

When Dr. Borin came into the room and looked at Cam's chart. He ran the normal heart checks, and tested Cam's pupils, making notes as he did. That complete, he spoke briefly with the nurse, then turned to face us.

"Could I ask you to wait in the lounge for a few minutes, please?"

Angie and I followed the doctor's suggestion without comment, and soon we were sitting in the lounge, waiting in anticipating silence. The silence was refreshing while it lasted.

After only a few moments, Angie looked around the room, and began talking. She started slowly and in a few moments, she was almost raving. Her words sounded crazy. She swore that it was my positive vibrations that brought Cam back from his death-like sleep. Her words became emphatic.

"You are probably a natural healer, Sean," she said.

I didn't say anything for a moment. I mean, what do you say to a statement like that? I didn't know how to respond to her, but I figured, I needed to say something to get through her insanity.

"Angie, thank you very much for your vote of confidence. But, please calm down. I didn't do anything. You were there, too. All I did was come to see my brother. Nothing more and nothing less. I know what kind of stress you're under here. But, I didn't do anything." I shook my head slowly. "I know this is a tough time, but right now, I think you could use some rest. I think everyone could use some rest."

To my surprise, Angie nodded agreement.

Actually, it was the only thing that seemed appropriate to say to her. I reinforced my mental note to get that room at the Holiday Inn just as soon as I got the chance to be away from her.

Angie sat quietly for a minute. Then as if possessed, turned to glare at me. She was obviously undeterred by my dismissal of her thoughts.

"Don't you try and do this to me, Sean Thomas. I'm not crazy. I know what I'm saying. You did this for Cam. I can feel it in your vibration. If Cam lives, it will be because of your healing energy. Don't look at this as a negative thing. It's a blessing. I wish I had your energy. Hell, I know a hundred people who would love to have your energy."

Angie fixed her gaze on my eyes for a moment, and then slowly glanced away. Her stare was fixed as she focused her eyes and her thoughts on another part of the room. She was facing an inner battle with her feelings. She was placing hope against hope, that somehow, some miracle, would allow Cam to recover.

I decided to say nothing, but thought to myself, and what if he dies. Will that be my fault too? I shook out a Red, torched it, and inhaled deeply.

Because of the excitement over the change in Cam's condition, we changed our conversation to the topic of taking him home, and his recovery period. Deep inside, we knew that we were lying to each other. Still, a glimmer of hope is better than no hope at all.

The discussion remained somewhat normal, until Angie took a deep breath and began again.

"It was your touch, Sean," Angie continued. "When you heal, you give your life energy. That's why he's better. You gave him your life energy. You must be a healing channel."

Enough was enough.

"Angie, knock it off," I said. "We covered this. You know I don't believe in that crap. The only channels I know of are the eighty-three on my TV set, and the English."

Annoyed, I snuffed out the butt, and lit another. I shook my head and reached for the two-year old Reader's Digest laying on the table. I mindlessly began to thumb through it. This is exactly what I felt when I thought about being out of control. The same thought flashed through my mind again. I had to get out of here as soon as I could.

Mom rushed into the lounge.

"What happened?" she asked.

I looked up at her. "Good news, mom. Cam's eyes—"

Angie cut me off short and started into the healing bit, again. To my surprise, mom didn't even blink. She listened, unfazed, appearing not the least bit confused or puzzled. Holding Angie's hand, she just nodded and smiled.

At seven-thirty, the nurse came and called us back into Cam's room. Cam was semi-conscious. Dr. Borin explained that while Cam's edging toward consciousness was a good sign, he still had no life support functions.

We stared at Cam in the shadowy light, while the respirator hissed softly.

"You can have about ten minutes," he said to us. Then turning to the nurse, he repeated, "I mean it, ten minutes."

We all moved closer to the bed. Cam's eyes were fixed and motionless. I gripped his hand.

"Cam," I whispered, "can you hear us?"

Cam slowly blinked his eyes. When they opened, they moved slowly toward the direction where I was standing. I felt a moment of relief.

It appeared that Cam was still trying to focus his eyes, but to no avail. I squeezed his hand softly, it was warm, not cold, like earlier in the day. It truly appeared as though new life was flowing through his veins. I began to get nervous.

Angie pressed her hand on top of mine, and pressed close to me. The look on her face was one of thanks. Thanks for what, I asked myself.

Cam squinted again trying to focus on my face. I leaned over the bed, asking again.

"Cam, can you hear me?"

Cam's thumb slowly moved to grip my hand and Angie's hand to his own. He slowly closed his eyes, and his grip relaxed. His breathing, though controlled by the respirator, seemed more calm and restful. He had obviously gone to sleep.

CHAPTER 6

As we were leaving, Dr. Borin approached us again.

"May I speak with you for a moment?" he asked. We looked at each other,

"Of course," I answered, speaking for all of us.

We followed Dr. Borin back into the lounge. He stopped, turned around and crossed his arms.

"Please sit down," he directed.

We all sat down, sitting on the edge of the cheap lounge furniture.

"I don't want to discourage you," he said. "It is a positive sign that he has shown signs of improvement, but. . . , " his voice trailed off.

As he paused, mom jumped in quickly.

"What you're trying tell us, is that he is still going to die, right?"

The doctor was very measured in his response.

"Mrs. Thomas, as difficult as this is for me to say, and as difficult as it may be for you to hear, the body has limits. Your son has seriously passed those limits. It is a miracle that he has lived this long."

"As it stands now, he could go at any moment. To answer your question more directly, I can't see anything, including this latest event, that would change my prognosis. As it stands, we are still moment-to-moment."

I held Angie's hand, and Angie held mom's. Why was this even happening, I wondered. The doctor was saying something about going home and, getting some rest, that they would call us if there were any changes.

Mom asked, "Can we go back in?"

Dr. Borin responded calmly. "Your son is in very critical condition, Mrs. Thomas. There is nothing you can do here, and you have already been here long enough to be exhausted. Please go home and rest. He's under the best care possible."

Mom suddenly looked very tired. Mom stared blankly at Dr. Borin for a silent moment before responding. "I guess you're right," she said. "Sean, take me home."

Sandy's great planning had evidently hit a snag. It seems as though Jeff had been delayed at work, and the baby-sitter had begged off at the last minute. As a result, they had missed all the excitement.

"I'll call Sandy before we go," Angie said, and went in search of a phone.

In minutes, when Angie returned, she said that Sandy had told her not to worry about the kids, that we could come and pick them up tomorrow. That fact would save at least a half an hour of driving time. I was still suffering jet lag, and my body was working in overdrive. Any time saved was fine with me.

"Ma, do you want to come and stay at Angie's, tonight?"

Mom looked sorrowfully at me, slowly shaking her head. "No. I just want to be alone." And then, adding to no one in particular, "I have said every prayer that I can think of. He's in God's hands now. I just want to go home."

Angie tried again to have mom stay at their house, but mom was a loner. She dealt with her grief in solitude. When dad died, she went into virtual isolation for a couple of days. I guess she wanted to deal with this one by herself too.

* * * * * * * * * * * * *

I put the Escort in reverse, and waited for mom to disappear into her house. When the door closed, I clicked the lighter, reached for my pack, and came up empty handed. The pack was empty.

"I gotta stop and get some smokes," I said, before heading to the "State Fair Market" at the end of the street. Angie nodded silently.

The Escort hummed softly as I stood outside and lit up a fresh Red. I inhaled deeply, the cold, fresh, air momentarily regenerating me and shaking off the extreme fatigue and drowsiness of a long couple of days.

I got back in the car and put it in gear. Angie appeared lost in thought, and sat looking out the window. As we drove, the flash of the passing street lights cast a strobe-like effect on her face.

You may remember that I made a mental note to check into the Holiday Inn. Right now, I was so tired that mental note or not, I just wanted to crash somewhere.

"Mind if I crash on your couch?" I asked.

Angie turned away from the window and looked in my direction.

"I thought you were going to stay at the Holiday," she mused.

I detected a note of sarcasm in her voice, but I was in no mood for it.

"Well, I can, if it's a problem. I'm just really tired," I answered.

Angie laughed, "Of course you can stay. You sleep in our bed, and I'll sleep in Jessie's."

As tired as I was, I would have slept on the floor. It had been a long couple of days. It was nice to look forward to sleeping in a bed.

I parked the Escort in the driveway and walked to the house. Somewhere it seemed, my little voice was saying, you'll be sorry, you'll be sorry. I was exhausted, so I ignored it. Often times when I do that, it comes back to haunt me.

Angie unlocked the door and stepped inside. I reassured myself that I was just gonna be there for the one night.

I said good-night to Angie, and closed the bedroom door. I undressed quickly, and lay my weary body down on the cool sheets of the California king size bed.

Cam always referred to the bed, as his, indoor playground. It certainly was big enough to play in, but there would be no playing tonight.

Even exhausted, my senses said that there was still something about this whole scenario that just didn't feel right. I had to book myself a room at the Holiday Inn on my way to the hospital in the morning.

I can recall getting undressed and getting in bed, but I was so tired, that I didn't really pay much attention to the time or to where Angie went after I went into the bedroom. All I knew was that I was beat. I fell fast asleep the minute my head hit the pillow.

* * * * * * * * * * * * *

My guess was, that it was around three-fifteen when I awoke. I was awakened not by the warmth of the smooth skin pressing against the back of my body, but by the same, strange, sensations, I had felt earlier, when I was here in the house.

The tingling, light-headed, sensation continued to grow stronger, until there was no mistaking it. I felt as though I was in an envelope of soothing warm air, relaxing.

There was also no mistaking the sensuous nakedness that gently caressed my body. I woke all the way up and peered over my shoulder at the figure laying naked behind me.

It was Angie. I jumped with a start, rolled over on my back, and covered myself up.

"Are you totally out of your friggin mind?" I yelled.

Angie giggled, threw her right leg over mine, and kissed me softly on the mouth.

I guess I should have gotten up or moved away or done something. But, at this point I was still in a state of semi-conscious shock. My mind struggled to wake up, searching for a plan of action.

As I had said earlier, there was always something different about Angie, so this shouldn't have surprised me. I tried to rationalize her advances and put blame on her. Yet, I couldn't deny that there was also a special feeling I had, when she and I were together.

For whatever reason, her presence mesmerized me. I didn't move away.

As much as I had attempted to deny it, Angie still had a lot of what I look for in a woman. Sure, she once had three kids, but her body was still tight and beautiful. Most of all, she was one of the most sensuous woman I had ever known.

In my book, sensuality is something that is not affected by age or kids. Cam always said that Angie had been born with a double dose of sensuality. Now, I believed it too.

As we lay in the semi-darkness, I could feel the heat of her animalism. I lost myself in her presence.

* * * * * * * * * * * * *

"Want breakfast?" Angie asked sticking her head in the door.

Her spritely vitality awoke me from a sound slumber. I tried to clear my head of the fog that follows a deep, restful, sleep. As I became more awake, I remembered our encounter.

I thought to myself, that maybe it had all been a dream. There had to be a rational explanation for it, I reasoned. The guilt I felt over my lack of good judgement gnawed at my gut. As hard as I tried to erase the feeling, my efforts were useless.

I nodded approval, "Yeah, mainly some coffee," I muttered, as I headed for the shower. I should have gone to the Holiday Inn. My little voice was now saying, I told you so, I told you so.

I dried off, and thought to my little voice, screw you, anyway. I was really disappointed in myself.

Angie had prepared a hearty breakfast, complete with, eggs, bacon, pancakes and coffee. I ate in silence. Angie was also quiet and didn't mention the night's activities. She seemed contented, and showed no signs of guilt or remorse.

"Do we need to talk?" I asked.

"No," she smiled and gently brushed the back of my neck with her hand as she went to pour me another cup of coffee.

Try as I might, I was unable to quell my feelings. I still felt guilty as hell. I thought for a moment that I should probably shoot myself or something, for what had happened. In truth, the guilt I was feeling, I was forcing upon myself. I really had no regrets.

It's not that I'm saying, so what, or trying to present an arrogant attitude. I had enjoyed the whole encounter. I just felt guilty because of Cam. If he had not been in the hospital, I could have more easily lived with myself.

Angie acted like it was the most natural thing in the world. As she puttered in the kitchen, straightening up before we left, I sat drinking my coffee and watching her. She did look nice.

She was wearing a pair of designer jeans, and a white blouse, with lace and small ruffles. She had on calf length boots, and looked like a million bucks in large bills.

I couldn't stand it any longer. "Angie, sit down a minute," I urged.

Angie kept on working and humming to the tune that played softly on the radio.

"I mean it," I repeated. "Please sit down."

Angie looked perturbed, but she finally put down the dish rag, walked to the table, and sat down. I lit up a Red.

"I want you to know that I'm not that kind of guy—," I began, my voice trailing off.

Angie laughed, almost sneering.

"Oh, really? Then, what you're telling me, is that I had a very interesting dream last night."

"That's not what I mean," I snapped.

"I know what you mean," she cooed, now trying to sooth my ruffled feathers.

"I know that basically, you are not the type of person that would go out of his way to put a move on his brother's wife. Just relax and let what comes natural, come. Anyway, how would you feel if the situations were reversed? Cam told me about Raven."

One of the biggest pains-in-the-ass that I know of, is a woman that is logical or can reason with you. You never know exactly what to expect, and they are tough to outsmart.

"I guess you're right," I countered. "If the situation was reversed, it would be no big deal," I said, trying to reverse roles.

Angie smiled, got up and walked around behind me. She leaned forward, and put her arms around my neck, kissing me lightly on the cheek.

"You're not going to try and tell me that you didn't enjoy it are you?" she asked.

I thought to myself, No, I was not going to try and tell her that.

At last Angie was ready to go. I had gone out and started the Escort to get it warm. On the way to the hospital, I turned into the Holiday, and you guessed it, I booked a room.

As I left the hotel, I lit up a Red and walked back to the car where Angie was waiting. She sat silently as I entered, and didn't say a word as we drove to Henry Ford.

I have many philosophies. One of them, is that I believe that each day, everyone has one thing happen to them, that really pisses them off. Evidently, my booking the room at the Holiday, was Angie's, one thing, for this day.

After a moment, she finally spoke

"You didn't have to do that," she said, half angry, half hurt.

"Didn't have to do what?," I asked innocently.

"You know, book a room. What's the matter, don't you trust yourself"?

I didn't say anything at first, but I didn't trust myself.

This doll looked like something out of a picture. I was truly having trouble keeping my thoughts in line, even now. It seemed to me that I was falling under the same spell that Cam had fallen under years before.

"No, I'm sorry to say," I began, "I don't trust myself. And, try as I might, I can't fully accept the fact that I want to sleep with my brother's wife."

A wry smile came across her face. "You mean, at least not after we were married, right?"

"Right," was the only thing I could think of to say. I rolled down the window, flicked the butt out, and hit the pack again. She had me there, and she knew it.

I shook my head. What the hell have I gotten myself into?

CHAPTER 7

With visiting hours beginning at noon, the hospital parking lot was nearly empty at nine-thirty a.m., when Angie and I got there. I needed some time alone to think, so I wheeled the Escort up to the "Visitor's Entrance" and stopped. Angie turned and looked at me.

"What're you doing?" she asked. "Aren't you coming in?"

"Yeah, I'll be right in. I'm just gonna grab a smoke. I'll be in right behind you."

We stared eye to eye for a moment, then Angie quickly turned, opened the door, and got out. When she shut the door, I was glad the Ford was a rental.

"Was it something I said?," I asked the glass, as Angie walked towards the door of the hospital.

Angie was definitely "PO'd". From the rock of the car when she slammed the door, I would rate her pissed level at about a, seven, on the "pissed scale", of ten. I made a mental note to check the door and see if it still worked. I clicked the Escort into drive.

In fairness to Angie, maybe she was right. Maybe it was no big deal. It was hard for me to accept that maybe I had gotten square over the years.

I parked the Ford, cracked the window and lit up a Red. It tasted stale. Figures, I thought. This habit is going to kill me one of these days. Right now, that thought didn't scare me. I inhaled deeply. Sitting in the Escort, I enjoyed the silence, and leisurely finished my smoke.

I had always detested chain smokers. That may seem ironic, for here I was finishing my tenth cigarette of the day before ten o'clock in the morning. It was time for a new habit.

I didn't really think of my interactions with Angie as being threatening, and she also hadn't really done anything special to make me think she had ulterior motives.

Over the years, we had enough cute conversations, to know that there was a mutual interest. True, we had never followed up on it before, but sometimes a traumatic experience such as Cam's accident, can be the trigger that places such events in motion.

I knew that this was something more than just Sean and Angie on a wild night on the "Playground," but I couldn't figure out why. I rolled the window all the way down, flicked the butt into the parking lot, and lit another.

Somehow all the pieces of this puzzle had to fit together. Why was Angie so bold? Didn't she care about Cam? Was there something in their lives that I didn't know about? Maybe she was paying him back for some past indiscretion. I didn't know.

I was sure of one thing however, I should have resisted her advances. I didn't know why I felt that way, I just knew that I did.

I made a mental note to keep my best instincts in high gear around Angie until I could figure it out. I also planned to put as much space as possible, between us.

At least now, I was being honest with myself. I didn't trust myself. When I was around her, I felt joyfully out of control. I was like a cat in a field of cat nip.

I wondered if perhaps this wasn't some aspect of my personal destiny, which was about to be fulfilled by some demonic mind, who somehow got his jollies by creating situations like the one I had become involved in.

I certainly didn't deserve to think of myself in a "holier than thou", perspective. I never really did anyway. But, my actions with Angie, were actions which were out of character, even for me.

I locked the Escort and walked around and checked the passenger door. Gladly, it still worked. I shook my head, smiled, and headed towards the hospital.

Walking toward the "Visitor's Entrance", the brisk morning air seemed to clear my head of some of the troubling thoughts of the day. The sun was still low behind the hospital building, and the crisp snow crunched beneath my feet. I did miss winter.

When I entered the "Visitor's Entrance", the bank of phones on my left caught my eye. I stopped, picked one up, dropped in two-bits, and dialed a long unused number.

After several rings there was click at the other end.

"Debbie Grant, may I help you?"

It was the same voice, but not the same name.

"Yes, I think you can help me," I said, anticipating the worst.

The pause on the other end of the phone was long and uncertain.

"No way, you bastard," she finally said, placing heavy emphasis on the "B" word. "You have no right coming back into my life. Why the hell didn't you leave well enough alone?"

Debbie was hissing her words. When she hissed, she was pissed. I thought to myself, this is not going to be my day. I wondered if maybe there was a full moon or something.

Let's be practical, here it was, not even ten o'clock in the morning, and I had already got two "PO" ratings of "seven" or more.

I waited until there was a noticeable pause.

"It's Cam, Debbie. He's been a terrible accident." Debbie and Cam had been close friends after the Navy, but there was never anything intimate between them.

Debbie and I were another case. Ours was a passion only relationship at first. I don't think I even realized what kind of a woman she was for the first six months that I knew her. When I did, I fell hopelessly in love.

Fortunately, or unfortunately, Jerry had invited me out to Frisco. I probably should have told Debbie that I was going, or better yet, told her that I wasn't coming back, but I didn't. At the time, I didn't figure I needed her. Now, times had changed. With all that was going on, I wondered if I was going to need her now.

"Is this another one of your God damn twin tricks"? she snapped, still hissing her words.

"No tricks," I answered. "Cam is in intensive care at Henry Ford, and I need to talk to you."

"Right, like I'm supposed to believe you."

"Deb, this is serious. No bullshit."

Debbie was never one to mince words. You knew exactly where you stood with her at all times.

"What room is he in?" she asked.

"He's in East I.C.U., room two-forty-three," I said, and before I could say another word, the line went dead. I looked at the phone, adding "See you later," to the now silent line, and placed the receiver back on the hook. I smiled, shook my head again, and followed the "yellow taped road" up to the second floor.

The doors to the East I.C.U. swung open, and I was once again transported back to reality. I had a flashing thought that I probably shouldn't have called Debbie, but what the hell. If Cam died, she would have been just as mad at me for not calling.

A number of people were standing outside Cam's room, and there seemed to be a good deal of conversation going on. Nearing the room, I could see Dr. Borin, and "Bubbles" standing over Cam. Dr. Borin had taken the respirator out, and at least for the moment, it appeared that Cam was breathing on his own.

Mom stood just outside the door.

"What's up?" I asked.

Mom was excited.

"He's breathing by himself," she whispered.

Dr. Borin looked intent as he checked through Cam's vitals.

I couldn't see Cam directly, but I could see the rise and fall of his chest. It didn't appear to be any different from anyone else.

"Is he conscious?"

Mom shook her head, "No, not yet. But, Dr. Borin says this is a good sign."

I was happy to see that he was coming around a bit, but I also had a fleeting thought that his recovery would put a crimp in my style, if you know what I mean. I cursed myself for my thoughts. I thought to myself, in addition to being an asshole, I must also be losing my mind."

Dr. Borin stood up, and turned to face the family.

"Well," he sighed, "He's basically on his own. I wouldn't get too excited, though. Please try and keep this in perspective. We will be monitoring him very closely for the next twenty-four hours, then we'll know more. Please keep your visit short."

Nature was beckoning strongly, so I turned to leave the room to go find a head. When I reached the I.C.U. doorway, Debbie was there. I was stunned. It was as though I had been transported back in time, back to way back when.

She was gorgeous. Still tall, still blonde, still beautiful, and from the look in her eyes, still in control. She brushed past me into the unit.

Angie and Sandy looked at Debbie, and gave her a look that was a cross between a, if looks could kill look, and a, what the hell are you doing here, look. Debbie simply smiled, and went over to sit on the edge of the bed. I went on to find the head.

When I got back from the rest room, Debbie was still on the side of the bed, gently holding Cam's hand. After a another moment, she said a silent prayer and then stood up, turning to face us.

"Hello, Debbie," mom said. "How have you been"?

Debbie smiled, and took mom's hand. "I'm fine, Mrs. Thomas, I'm so very sorry to hear about Cam, how is he?"

Mom explained Cam's condition to Debbie while we all listened in. Never once during their conversation did Debbie even glance in my direction.

The girls had stepped out of the room. There was no love lost between them. I guess it was because of Debbie's assertiveness. They resented her for being so mindful and headstrong.

They stood gossiping outside Cam's room. I overheard words like, "Bitch", and "Who called her". I knew there would be more conversation about it later. I made myself another mental note not to become involved in their petty bullshit.

Cam was resting peacefully, so we all started to the cafeteria where we could get a cup of coffee and I could have a smoke. I felt strangely out of place with this group. Perhaps, I had been in San Francisco, too long. There was no specific reason for me to feel out of touch. After all, this was my family. Yet, I really felt like I was an intruder here. I thought to myself again, maybe I have been away too long.

On the way to the cafeteria, I walked up beside Debbie.

"It is nice to see you again, even under these circumstances." Debbie turned and glared at me.

"You kiss my ass, Sean Thomas. You're not getting off that easy on this one.

"Hey, I just said—"

"Forget you, Sean Thomas. All your life you have skated through problems, using people, and then kissing up to them later on, to make up for it.

"Come on, Deb. Give me a break, will ya?"

"Give you a break? Bullshit. I know you too well," she continued, "and you are not gonna suck me in a second time."

I was done. "Well, excuse me for giving a shit, Deb. I shoulda saved my dime." We walked the rest of the way to the cafeteria in silence.

Like I said, with Debbie, there was never a doubt. You always knew exactly where you stood. I suddenly wished I had saved my quarter. I shook my head. She was right. My reason for calling her was not some chivalrous deed. I was interested in seeing her again, in seeing how she was doing, in seeing how she looked.

From the gist of what I had seen, she was doing just fine in all categories. I glanced over at her as we turned into the lunchroom.

She turned to look at me and said, "It's nice to see you again, too."

CHAPTER 8

I personally haven't spent a lot of time in hospitals in my life. However, when I have, I've always been intrigued by the people that you see there.

As I watched the other people in the cafeteria, I found myself wondering about the visitors. Who are they? Why are they here? What are their loved ones in for?

The cafeteria was also filled with hospital staff members. I looked around. What about the hospital staff? Do they really care about the people they treat? How do they turn off their emotions at the end the day?

I don't know if I would have the personality to work in a hospital. Sitting in a hospital always seems to reinforce the frailty of the human body. I'm not skittish, but I still like the false sense of invincibility that somehow I may miraculously live forever. It's easier than facing death honestly.

When you come to the hospital to visit someone you love, it challenges your emotions. It tests your love. It saps your strength. For what it's worth, it just all seems so unnecessary to me.

Debbie had gone to use the phone, preferring I guess, to not have to be faced with conversation with either myself or the girls. I sat, pretty much alone, my tush flattened into the molded plastic chair, hitting on a Red, and listening to mom and the girls talk.

They spoke at a volume, that with all the cafeteria noise, I was not able to hear. The few words, which were audible, were hard to understand. I sat and watched them. It was much like I was watching them from somewhere else, like on a remote television monitor, or through a glass window. I thought, maybe they didn't want me to hear what they were saying. I just sat there, in my own little world.

Sitting quietly, my thoughts drifted. After what seemed like only a few moments, I began experiencing a rush. The feeling was totally overwhelming. I was unable to catch my breath, or to speak. My hands tingled, and I felt faint. I felt a strong feeling of urgency and frustration. Then as quickly as it came, the feeling passed. I sat up, took a deep breath and sighed, looking around the room.

It took me a few seconds, but I slowly calmed down. Then after another minute, everything seemed to jog all the way back to normal.

I shook my head again. I had been doing a lot of that lately. Maybe, I was smoking too much. I had made a promise to myself to try and cut down. Unfortunately, the way things were going in Motown, I figured that was a promise that I would not be likely to keep.

The page echoing on the overhead speaker almost went unnoticed as we sat idly watching the visitors and the medical staff in the cafeteria. The page was calling us back to I.C.U.

"Will the Thomas family please return to I.C.U. Will the Thomas family please return to the I.C.U.."

I had a notion that this call would come, but don't ask me why. It was just another one of those strange feelings I have been having, since I got here.

In answer to the relentless call of the monotone voice, we walked back to the elevator for our ride back to the second floor. This time I didn't notice the yellow tape. I had learned the way back.

I looked over at my mother. She lifted her eyes and caught me looking at her and smiled sadly. She knew, as I did, what the page was for.

"What do you think it is?" she asked, squeezing my hand.

"I don't know ma," I lied. "Maybe he's conscious." I knew better and felt the worst was at hand.

* * * * * * * * * * * * *

The hiss of the I.C.U. automatic doors, brought us back to a point of reality that none of us were truly prepared to face.

Entering the unit, I had noticed several differences. The lights in the I.C.U. seemed unusually dim. The monitors were silent. The conversation of the staff was hushed.

Dr. Borin stood outside Cam's room, with a metal clipboard in his hand, writing notes. He looked up at the sound of the opening doors, flicked the aluminum cover closed, and put his arms down at his sides.

Before he even spoke, it was obvious why we had been called back. Dr. Borin approached us, took a deep breath and sighed.

"It was his heart. The rest of his body seemed to be recovering, but. . . ," his voice trailed off.

At a moment like this, a million questions fly through your mind, but no answers. Angie, mom and Sandy began crying softly.

"Why did you take him off the respirator if he wasn't ready to be on his own?" I asked.

Dr. Borin was a pro. He measured the situation, paused, and then answered calmly.

"Cam's heart was badly bruised. Sometimes the bruises cause no weaknesses. Other times, they act like a weak spot in a child's balloon. The longer time passes, the weaker they become, until the hearts stops functioning in that area and the patient suffers a cardiac arrest."

"In Cam's case, there was only a prayer of hope to begin with. The respirator was actually putting extra pressure on the heart by forcing it to beat with a strength, or a rhythm it wasn't capable of maintaining on its own."

"I thought he was doing better after you took the respirator out." I continued.

Dr. Borin nodded. "You're right. His heart was in normal sinus rhythm, with normal blood pressure and a normal pulse rate, for more than three hours, even without the support of the respirator. Generally this is a sign that everything is moving back towards normal. In Cam's case it wasn't meant to be. I am terribly sorry."

Mom looked up and spoke in a halting voice,

"Was there any suffering before he died?"

Dr. Borin slowly shook his head.

"No, Mrs. Thomas, Cam never really regained consciousness. From his vantage point, it was like being asleep. He never knew what happened."

Dr. Borin looked around the room at each of us and then added, "I am sorry, but there are some forms that you will need to sign now." He looked at all of us, pursed his mouth, nodded knowingly, and repeated, "I really am sorry."

Several of the nurses appeared and paired up with each of us to try and defuse the suffering somewhat. I wanted to see Cam one more time, so I excused myself and went into his room.

As I walked through the door to his room, I sensed a tremendous surge of energy. My skin tingled, and the hair stood up on my arms, and on the back of my neck.

The sensation I felt was like one of getting a slight jolt of electricity. But, like the rush I had felt earlier, this feeling also passed almost as quickly as it came.

I looked down at Cam. He looked peaceful at last. The tension was gone from his face, the pain gone from his mouth. He was finally at rest. I reached down and touched his hand. It was still warm. For the first time since I came back, I honestly felt the brotherly love of years gone by.

I cursed God for making me wait until Cam died to realize how I felt. That was the way things generally went in my life. When I reached the point where I could fix a problem, it was often too late to be fixed.

"I do love you, Cam." I kissed him softly on the cheek.

Standing up, I turned to leave. Everyone had moved into the room, and respectfully given me the final moment I needed. Angie went to Cam, bent over and hugged him, sobbing softly. I silently wondered about Cam's insurance, the kids, and how Angie would get by. There are just so many things to be concerned about at a time like this.

I left everyone in the room, and went to call Jerry and Raven. I realized I was late in calling them. But, things had been happening at a crazy pace. And well, now I had something, albeit negative, to tell them.

The door hissed open and Debbie walked in. She reached out her hands and I took them. She looked into my eyes softly,

"I'm so very sorry, Sean. I hoped and prayed he would recover. I guess it wasn't meant to be."

I nodded without saying anything and gave her a polite hug. I needed that more than I knew, but didn't tell her. We released and I went to search out the phones.

Debbie went into Cam's room and put her arms around mom and together they shared in the moment's grief.

CHAPTER 9

"Jerry's Emporium," came the response to the incessant ringing at the other end of the phone.

"Jerry?" I asked.

"This is," he said.

"Jerry, this is Sean."

"Hey, Sean," he answered. "How's Cam?"

I continued, "Jerry, Cam's dead. He died a few minutes ago."

There was a long pause before Jerry spoke again.

"Hang on a sec," he said, and laid the receiver down on the bar.

I could hear the music in the background go quiet, and the receiver in the kitchen click up.

"Sean?" The mellow voice cracked into my ear. I was very sorry that I was not in San Francisco at that moment.

Raven's voice seemed to calm the tension of the moment.

"Yeah doll, how are you doing? I answered.

"Jerry said that Cam had died?" she said, asking, but already knowing the answer.

"Yeah, they said he was just too badly hurt to recover. As badly as he was hurt, this is a blessing."

Jerry's voice came back on the line,

"Sean, I'm really sorry to hear about Cam. Is there anything we can do?"

I knew Jerry and Raven would want to help if they could.

"No, not really," I answered. "We're still in a daze, but thanks for asking."

Raven 's voice was solemn, "Do you know when the funeral is yet?"

I hadn't thought about that as yet, and said so. I told them that we were going to make the arrangements a little later. My mind figured ahead.

"I would assume it would be held on Friday, unless there's a glitch somewhere."

Jerry said "We'll be there, Sean. Call me back, at say, six o'clock our time and I'll give you our flight times."

Jerry's voice trailed off. I told them I would, and hung up the phone.

When I returned to the I.C.U., the nursing staff had everyone sitting in a room talking and drinking coffee. That seemed odd to me, but I guess they'll try anything to get your mind off the death.

Everyone sat and laughed about the past, reminiscing over times gone by. Mom wanted Cam to go to Spaulding Funeral Home, so I made the arrangements with the staff, and tried to encourage everyone to leave.

Everyone was moving in slow-motion. As the scene unfolded, it was like watching a sitcom on the tube, with other people portraying our lives. The eerie feeling I had, made me feel like I had gone into some kind of a time warp.

Debbie walked over to say that she had to leave for an appointment. I gave her my number at the Holiday, and told her to call me tonight for the funeral arrangements. She nodded without saying anything, and left the floor.

* * * * * * * * * * * * *

Leaving the hospital, Sandy drove Angie and mom, to mom's house. I followed close behind.

When we got there, I parked the Escort in front of the house and walked to the door. I closed the door behind me just as the grandfather clock was finishing the chimes for twelve noon.

Coming in from the cold, the house seemed stuffy and hot. Mom never seemed to open the windows anymore, and the house smelled of stale air.

Everyone shuffled into the living room, and sat down. I took the liberty of going to the kitchen where I knew the wine and the ashtrays would be kept. After a short search, I found ma's bottle of sherry and poured everyone a small glass of wine.

What I really needed, was a throw-the-cap-away session, with a bottle of tequila. For now, the wine would have to do.

That completed, I next looked for an ashtray. There was none to be found. After rummaging through the entire kitchen without success, I made a mental note that everyone was getting ashtrays for Christmas this year. That meant, no exceptions.

I finally settled on a saucer that appeared to be one of ma's least used dishes. I delivered the wine to the others, and I lit up a butt.

"Dad wouldn't like you smoking in this house, Sean," mom spouted, more from reflex, than real concern.

I waited a moment and exhaled.

"Dad wouldn't mind today, ma," I answered, being as nice as I could under the circumstances.

My real thoughts were, if he doesn't like me smoking in his house, let him come back from the grave and bite me in the ass, then I'll give up smoking all together.

Sandy glared at me as though she could read my mind. I just raised my eyebrows, raised my glass in the toast position, and shrugged.

Screw her. What did she know? For all I knew, Cam was probably running away, trying to avoid a family get-together with her, when he had his accident. I smiled at the stupidity of the thought, and crushed out the butt.

"I want the service at Flower Memorial" mom avowed, to no one in particular.

I was shocked. Flower Memorial was a Spiritualist church. To be exact, the one I had spoken about earlier.

I didn't say anything for a minute, then I answered.

"Mom, are you sure you want to do that? I mean, you bitch at me for smoking in dad's house, then you want Cam's funeral service held in one of *their* churches. Dad would turn over in his grave if he knew Cam was going to be eulogized in a church like that."

"Sean!"

Her firmness caught me off guard. Mom rarely raised her voice, yet she was now speaking to me like I was a child. I felt two feet tall.

After a moment, mom calmed down, and continued her answer.

"Sean, there have been some major changes in our lives since you left. Flower Memorial is also my church, and Cam and Angie's church. Cam would have wanted it this way."

I shook my head in disgust. But let's face it, it was more out of ignorance than disrespect. I was out-numbered. I made myself another mental note. I would find out what changes mom was talking about, just as soon as things settled down.

CHAPTER 10

I don't know if you have ever had the pleasure of making funeral arrangements. But, up until now, I hadn't. I personally classify it right down there with having a tooth pulled without pain-killer.

As we browsed through the room full of caskets, mom was stuck on the mahogany one. She looked at me.

"Sean, you know what Cam would want. Would he like this one?"

"Ma, Cam would not want you spending eight grand on a casket."

"Yes, but it looks awful nice."

"You're right, ma," I said. "But let's be practical."

Angie was over looking at a casket for around fifteen hundred dollars. She walked over, put her arm around mom and said, "Sean's right mom, Cam's gone now, there's no sense in wasting money on more material things.

"Yes, but he's still with us in spirit, he's—"

"No, mom," Angie insisted, "his spirit has already passed to the higher side. There's nothing here but his shell."

That struck me as funny, but I didn't know why. What Angie said didn't sink in at the time. That little voice of mine came back saying, "Pay attention, pay attention." Like before, I blew it off. But this time, I made a mental note to check it out later. I also made a mental note to pay more attention to my little voice.

I stood looking at the mahogany casket. Man, that casket was beautiful. As morbid as it sounds, I thought of putting a mannequin in one end, and a bar or stereo in the other.

When you lifted the cover to the bar or stereo, the mannequin in the other end would sit up. I made a mental note to tell mom and Angie my thoughts at a better time, though personally, I laughed at the thought now.

"Lurch" came back into the room to see if we had made a decision. It seems to me that in order to be a funeral director, you have to pass a test of bad looks. Unless you already looked dead, you couldn't qualify to take the undertaker test.

However, Mom and Angie seemed to feel comfortable with him, so who was I to say differently? I was glad that I hadn't shared my feelings about him.

I figured. Hey, if they're comfortable, then so be it. I really didn't have a right to have an opinion. Remember, I already said I felt ill at ease around people that dealt in death.

"Lurch" gave us the blue light special, telling us that the price he offered us, was a, today only, price. What the hell did he think we were going to do, shop around, or go home and decide, and then come back next week?

I decided that even being a PI had an advantage over being a coffin salesman. The thought of pedaling something so closely related to death gave me the willies.

Mom was not in the frame of mind to help make an intelligent choice. Angie and I looked at each other.

"We'll take the blue one," Angie said, and reached for her checkbook. Lurch nodded and wrote up the order. When he finished, he looked up at us with his sunken eyes and reminded us to bring a change of clothes for Cam's burial.

Angie wrote the check, signed the order, and we left to go home.

* * * * * * * * * * * * *

Going through Cam's clothes was no picnic. All the girls were in the closet digging through Cam's suits, and shirts and stuff. I sat back and watched.

Every so often, one of them would hold up a suit, and ask "What do you think, Sean?" Finally, Angie took out Cam's dark blue herring bone, with a pink shirt, and a solid blue tie. That was it. When she held it up, I nodded. She nodded back, took a deep breath, and lay the suit and accessories on the bed. I took the clothes and headed for Spaulding.

Cam and the casket were already at the funeral home when I arrived there. "Lurch" obviously served double duty. When I got to the funeral home with the clothes, it was he who was also the greeter.

"Is there going to be any problem fixing him up?" I asked sincerely.

"Lurch," was momentarily distracted, organizing the delivery of some of the flowers which had already begun to arrive for Cam.

"No problem at all, Mr. Thomas. Though your brother was seriously injured, our staff is accustomed to this type of restoration. Please rest easy."

I was upset about Cam's death, and I realized that my thinking may have been a little off base. I also realized that "Lurch" was only doing his job. Still, there was something about his manner that irritated the hell out of me.

"Do you mind if I see him again?" I asked.

"Lurch" frowned.

"Mr. Thomas, —"

"Just for a minute." I interrupted.

Lurch continued unfazed.

"Mr. Thomas, that would be inappropriate at this time. I believe the initial preparation has already begun. Why don't you come back this evening with the rest of the family?"

He was probably right, but damn it, I had this urge to see Cam.

"I think not," I said. "I would like to see him, now."

Lurch looked me straight in the eyes. We stared at each other for a few silent moments, then he answered.

"As you wish," then turning to lead the way, he added, "Please come with me."

We headed down the hall, and then into the back of the funeral home to what appeared to be a small operating room. I was amazed to see how clean it was. Cam's body lay naked, flat on his back, on a table that stood in he center of the room. There was a sheet over his loins.

The mortician was hard at work trying to make Cam appear as though he were going to his senior prom, instead of going to visit the grim reaper. Looking him over in the light, I could see that his body was badly bruised in many places.

To my surprise the mortician was a she.

"Margaret Wessels, this is Sean Thomas," Lurch said, introducing us.

I reached out my hand to shake her's. She ignored me. Margaret was deeply engrossed in what she was doing, and didn't even look up. She was leaning over Cam's face, working in his mouth. After what appeared to be a difficult time, she finally pressed his mouth closed, stood up and turned around.

She looked at me and gasped for air. You can imagine the look on her face when she saw me. She swivelled toward Lurch, shouting in anger.

"Marion, is this some kind of a sick joke?" she snapped.

"Lurch" turned red.

"No, Margaret. This is no not a joke. Mr. Sean Thomas, is Mr. Cam Thomas' twin brother. He wanted to see him again."

I stepped forward again to shake her hand. The lady undertaker still didn't smile, and ignored my hand.

"Family members are not allowed in here, Mr. Thomas. It's a company policy," she mouthed through tight lips. She then turned to glare at "Lurch," as though he had committed one of the original sins.

"I understand Mrs. . . . . Uh."

"Ms. Wessels," she interjected, adding special emphasis to the "Ms.".

"Ms. Wessels," I began, adding the same emphasis. "Marion tried to discourage me, but I insisted," I answered, before letting my hand return to my side. "I just had the need to see Cam again."

She didn't say anything, but just stared at me.

I continued, "We have been very close in the past, but we haven't been able to see each other for several years. This is a little difficult for me."

Her face softened, and a polite smile appeared at the corners of her mouth.

"I'm really am sorry," she said finally. "I'm a little frustrated at how the restoration is going, but seeing you will help."

She took off her rubber glove and extended her hand. I shook it.

"I'm sorry to have to meet you, under these circumstances Mr. Thomas."

Her eyes scanned my face, recording my features for later use.

"My, you are identical, aren't you?" she, said with some amazement. I nodded.

"I'm sorry about the hassle, but we really don't allow visitors in this area. It's a state law." Then smiling, she added, "I guess it won't hurt to make one exception though."

She reached up, and gently took my face in her hands, turning it from side to side, and nodding her head as she did so.

"I think I can fix it, now," she said.

I walked over to the table. Cam's face was bruised where the bandages had been, and there was a sunken area in his cheek. Margaret looked directly at me when I looked up.

"It must have been a terrible accident," she said, trying to make conversation, her voice trailing off.

I nodded.

"I really don't know," I said, "I haven't seen his car yet, but I'm sure you're right." I asked the inevitable question. "Are they going to have an open casket?"

Margaret nodded, "I know it doesn't seem possible now, but by tonight he'll be as good as new."

"Only dead," I added. Margaret said nothing, simply nodding agreement.

I turned to Marion. Suddenly he didn't look quite as much like "Lurch" as I had previously imagined. I reached out my hand and he shook it.

"Thanks for your help," I muttered and turned to leave.

I wanted to get out of there. I felt bad, almost sick. Now, I understood why they had the rules they did.

"Family viewing is at five o'clock tonight," Margaret offered. I just nodded, and left the home.

CHAPTER 11

The Escort struggled a bit, but finally came to life. I clicked the defroster on high, and sat shivering, waiting for the car to warm. The temperature outside was about five degrees, but the sun was extremely bright. I wished that I had remembered to bring my sun glasses. That's what you get when you leave town without packing. I made a mental note to pick up a pair later if I got the chance. For now, I would just have to squint against the bright sun.

Going back to mom's house seemed like a sure way to get drawn into the depression of the occasion. A beer and a shot sounded like a much better idea, so I tooled the Ford to the "East Side Bar and Grill".

This joint is a classic. It's a little neighborhood bar, that was wedged between two restaurants, on the main street front, in Ferndale. Cam and I used to go there with our dad when we were kids.

I know, dad was a minister, right? Pentecostal ministers aren't supposed to drink. Dad was an exception to that rule. He used to say, "As long as you only do it in moderation".

Moderation my ass. Dad didn't know the meaning of the word. Booze was his cross to bear in this life. He was frustrated that he couldn't break the habit, even with God's help. Maybe that's why he checked out so early.

Anyway, Cam and I also used stop at the "East Side" once in a while, after we got mustered out of the Navy. We'd stop in for a burger and a brew. I think that's why I originally identified so much with "Jerry's" place when I went to San Francisco. It reminded me of home.

I needed a smoke and reached for my pack. It was empty. Screw it, I thought, this will be a great time to cut down. Besides, I don't need it anyway. Yeah, right!

The Escort cruised into a parking space right in front of the bar. I got out, walked to the door, and opened it. When I stepped out of the bright sunshine into the darkness of the "East Side", I was blinded by the change in light.

The sound of "Free Bird" cascaded from the juke box, and the smell of beer was heavy in the air.

As my eyes adjusted to the difference in light, I saw the bartender walk to my end of the bar.

"Brighter than shit out there, ain't it?" he asked.

"You ain't lyin'," I said. "I still can't see."

"What'll it be, Mac?" he asked. "Give me a burger with the works, a fries, a double shot of Cutty, and a draft."

"Gotcha," he said, and left to get my order.

I listened to the last of "Free Bird" and thought back to when the song first came out. Man, those were partyin' times. The song ended and the bar keep was back with my drinks, placing them in front of me.

"Food will be up in a minute," he said, then turned back toward the kitchen. He took a couple of steps, and then turned back around, looking at me.

"I haven't seen you in here for a while. How have you been?

At first, I thought I didn't understand him. I looked up from my draft.

"Excuse me?" I asked, "What'd you say?"

He answered again, speaking more slowly.

"I said, I haven't seen you around here for a while, how have you been?"

"Uh, fine," I said trying to place him. The truth is, I hadn't been in this place in many, many years. There was no way he could have known me.

Also, I make it my business to remember faces, and I didn't remember his.

"Do I know you?" I asked.

"Sure," he said, "You used to come in here last year with that brunette. What was her name, Susan?"

He was obviously mixing me up with someone else.

"Sorry," I said "I think you have me confused with somebody else."

The bartender looked at me long and hard, and then laughed a knowing laugh.

"You may be right," he added, "But I don't think so."

I smiled back. "I don't live around here. I'm from San Francisco. I'm just here visiting family."

He shook his head in disbelief, and added, "Well then, welcome to Detroit."

Danny smiled again, shook his head and turned towards the kitchen to get my food.

I thought it was odd that he felt he knew me. Could it be a simple case of mistaken identity?

After a few moments he was back with the eats. He sat the burger within reach, and set me up with another round of drinks, and then started the conversation where we had left off.

"It's a funny world," he said. "Maybe I got you mixed up with another guy, but man, this guy looked just like you. Last year, this guy comes in here with this dame, maybe oh, two, three times a week. This broad is gorgeous. What a dish. Her name is Susan. I woulda give my eye teeth for twenty minutes alone with her, if you know what I mean."

I knew what he meant, and just nodded.

"Anyway, they come in here, like I said, maybe two, three nights a week, always about the same time. They sit in the same booth, play the same music, play a little kissy face, have a couple of brewskies, and leave at the same time."

I didn't say anything, but Danny, the bartender, may have given me a piece of the puzzle I had been trying to solve since I got here.

You're probably thinking. It doesn't take Sherlock Holmes to figure out that it looked like Cam was screwing around on Angie. But, why? I didn't know. One thing I've learned in this business is that everyone has their own little secrets. Cam being family, made it no different.

My mind began working in PI. I wondered if Angie knew about Cam and Susan. I wondered if Angie's need to be close to me was prompted by an effort to pay Cam back. I needed to find out. I also faintly entertained the idea that maybe Cam's accident, was no accident. I suddenly had an empty feeling in the pit of my stomach.

"How do you know her?" I asked, wondering how he could know Susan and not know Cam.

"Who?"

"Susan. How did you know it was Susan?"

"Hey, listen pal, a guy in my business, you see stuff like that, you remember it. Besides, a guy like me, remembers a dame like that. I make it my business to know my regulars."

I thought for a moment. The word regulars struck me as odd.

"Oh, she comes in here regularly?" I offered innocently.

"Oh, yeah," he answered, dragging out the yeah. "If things go right, she should be here in about half an hour."

"No kidding?"

"See for yourself."

I thought for a minute.

"Maybe I'll wait and meet her," I said.

I slid a fin across the bar.

"Gimme a pack of Pall Mall Reds, will ya, and while you're at it, give me some change for the juke box."

Danny took my bill and went to the register. He came back with the change.

"Smokes are in the machine," he said, pointing to the machine near the wall. I walked over, dropped in the quarters, pulled the lever and picked up my pack. My mind was mulling over a dozen possibilities. I opened the pack, tamped down a Red, and fired it up.

"How 'bout a refill," I asked Danny, pointing to my empty glasses.

"You got it," he answered and left me to my thoughts.

I felt nervous at the thought of seeing Susan. However, at this point, the only direction I could go, was straight ahead. I had to talk to her and get some answers. Danny was back as soon as I returned to the bar.

"I realize it's none of my business," he started, "But I don't want no trouble in my place. You know what I mean?"

"Trouble," I answered. "Why would there be any trouble?"

"Well, the dames seein' another guy. He'll probably be here, too."

"So you think that will cause trouble?"

Danny shrugged. "Hey, I don't know you. I don't know this Susan dame, and I don't know the new guy. All I know is that I don't want no trouble in my place. Kapish?."

I looked at Danny. He really didn't want any trouble. He was from the mold of "Joe the Bartender" of Jackie Gleason fame.

Danny was a large, but gentle appearing, guy that needed a shave, a haircut, a clean shirt, and a clean apron. He didn't strike me as the kind of guy that would handle adversity too well. I figured he has misread my intentions.

"Don't worry," I comforted, "There won't be any trouble. All I have is a curious interest, that's all."

"I hope so, " he added. "This is a peaceful place. People come here to relax and be invisible. Know what I mean?"

I nodded. I knew what he meant.

I walked to the juke box and dropped in eight bits. Why the secrecy? What was the big deal. If Susan was as good looking as Danny said, then maybe it was a sexual thing. Brother, or not, Cam was not a guy that didn't appreciate a good-looking woman. I'd just have to wait and see for myself.

* * * * * * * * * * * * *

One of the nice things about neighborhood bars is that they rarely change the records in their juke boxes. I picked "Free Bird" again, Willie Nelson's "City of New Orleans", a couple by the "Temps" and a couple by Stevie Wonder.

I picked up my drinks, and went to sit in one of the booths along the wall. It seemed colder there, as though the heat wasn't circulating very well. I slid in, and the cold plastic was noticeable on my ass, as I sat down.

After a couple of minutes, Danny brought another setup. I was starting to feel the effects of the alcohol, and shook him off.

"On the house," he said, sliding into the booth across from me. Danny sat quietly for a minute, then spoke. "Look, Mac, like I said, I don't know you from Adam, but I got a feeling something is wrong here, know what I mean?"

I looked him right in the eye. This would be an ideal time for me to get some preliminary info, so I lied and said,

"No, I don't know what you mean."

He shook out a Salem, and lit it up.

"See, I know you and this guy got something going. Maybe you're like, brothers or something. I know from the git-go, that this guy is married. I also know that Susan is not—, well, let's just say, she's not the kind of girl you'd want to take home to your mother."

"You mean she's a hooker?" I asked, feigning surprise.

"No, not exactly."

I found it hard to believe that Cam would ever pay for a piece of ass. But then, what the hell did I know? Things had changed, remember?

Danny continued, searching for the proper words.

"No, not a hooker. She's a sex therapist. She does it like a doctor does. Usually, she brings her patients here to let them get comfortable, and have quiet conversation, then she takes them to her office, and gives them therapy or whatever she does. She's a friggin Phd, or something."

"I've never seen her with a guy more than a month or two, but this guy—,."

"My, uh, brother?"

"Yeah, your brother, he was with her almost three months. Then one day she comes in with another guy, and I don't see him no more."

I was really getting soused. I wondered if Cam had some kind of sexual problem, or something. Certainly, as bad as that sounded, it was still a better idea, than the idea that he was screwing around on Angie.

I looked at my watch. It was three-fifty. It was also time to go. I wanted to stick around, but I was too buzzed to be logical, or coherent. Besides, the

"East Side", and Susan weren't going anywhere. I would have another day.

I paid my tab, slipped Danny a ten for the info, and walked into the cold. The wind had picked up, and the sun was setting. It was really getting cold. Damn Michigan winters.

I sat shivering, waiting for the car to warm up a little. My shaking from the cold helped me to sober up some. I didn't want to go home blasted, so I rolled the window down and drove the five minutes to ma's house, freezing my ass off.

A picture was forming in my mind. Angie, or Susan held the missing pieces. I figured I'd try Angie first.

CHAPTER 12

"You're drunk," Mom said, when I walked in the house. "How could you get drunk on a day like this?"

I looked at mom. She was right, but so was I.

"Ma, how can you not get drunk on a day like this?"

Mom thought for a moment, and then just nodded. Angie came over and hugged me.

"Maybe I'd feel better if I were drunk too," mom finally added.

When we were younger, Cam and I used to kid mom about getting drunk. We used to say she would get drunk carrying the communion wine to the altar for dad.

The truth is, we used to drink wine with our meals from time to time. Dad always said it wasn't a sin, because they did it in the Bible.

One Mother's Day, Cam bought mom a bottle of wine and a kite. When she questioned it, he told her he wanted her to get "high as a kite". Man, we laughed about that for months.

Everyone was pretty much ready to leave for the family viewing hour. I popped a couple of Excedrine, and washed my face. I had already seen Cam, and in all honesty, I wished I didn't have to go back through it a second time. I resigned myself to the thought that I was going, more to support mom and the ladies, than for my own edification.

I also debated about calling Debbie before family hour. I didn't know what everyone's reaction was going to be at the funeral home, and I didn't want to have to deal with an unhappy woman at the same time I was dealing with my brother's viewing. I decided I'd call her later.

"Time to go," I announced in the direction of the ladies. They all turned to look at me, said nothing and headed for their coats.

I went outside and started the Escort. Man it was cold. As I sat in the silence of the evening, I thought about Susan. How would I approach Angie? Should I confront her, or try and find out if she even knew about Cam and

Susan? Certainly this was not the best time to be concerned about such things, but hell, I really was curious.

Also, deep inside, I wanted to get an answer. Over the years, I've found it too hard to keep fighting with my thoughts, when I don't know what's going on. I get freaked out thinking that what I don't know will sneak up and bite me in the ass.

The door opened, and mom got in next to me. As we headed toward the funeral home, mom turned to face me.

"Sean?"

"Yeah?"

"I really am glad you're here to help me." She reached over and grasped my hand. I felt a tingling of warmth around my neck. I'm sure I was blushing. Moments like these always bring back the kid in me. I remembered the times when I would want a hug from mom or dad, just to be sure that I was okay.

"I know what you mean," I said. "I'm just glad I could be here."

I turned the Escort onto Nine Mile Road in the direction of the funeral home, with Angie and Sandy following in Sandy's car. Mom and I rode the rest of the way to Spaulding's in silence. When we got there, I parked the car, got out and all of us walked inside together.

The lighting seemed unusually bright inside the funeral home. No one was there to greet us when we arrived, so we all took off our coats and hung them up. After a few moments, "Lurch" came out of the back of the home to greet us. His tall, rough stature, caught my attention once again.

"Good evening, Mrs. Thomas. Good evening, Mr. Thomas," he repeated, matter-of-factly. "I'll be with you in just a moment. Please wait here."

I stood outside the room where Cam's casket was laid, waiting for "Lurch" to come and lead us in for the initial viewing. In only a few moments, he was back. Because of the situation, it had seemed like an eternity, no pun intended.

Looking into the room, I could see the open casket, and the outline of Cam's facial features. The casket was already flanked by many floral arrangements sent by well wishers.

Marion appeared and stood by mom's right arm. She looked at me pleadingly.

"Sean, I don't want to do this. I'm not ready for this."

I had nothing to say, so I simply squeezed her hand.

I guess it was at this point, that I really realized what was going on here. When dad passed away, he had lived a full life, so to speak, and there is always the expectation that when someone passes middle age, they can check-out at any time.

This was different. This was too close. This was not planned. I now felt a real sense of sympathy for mom, Angie and the kids. For me, well, for me, nothing would change much. I had lost buddies in Viet Namm that were as close to me as Cam was, but for mom and Angie, well their whole lives were now topsy-turvy. I wished I could have changed that.

Marion nodded, and I took mom's left arm, Angie on my left, and Sandy next to Marion. We walked towards the casket.

As we neared the casket, the sounds of "The Old Rugged Cross", played softly in the background. When we reached the casket, I had an experience that only an identical twin can have. That is, the experience of seeing exactly how I would have looked, if I were the one to have died. As skittish as I was about death, it was a chilling moment.

Margaret had done an outstanding job. Cam actually looked better than I remembered him looking the last time I saw him alive, a couple of years ago.

"He looks more like you than he does himself."

I didn't tell mom, that I had stopped down to see Cam earlier in the day, or that Margaret had used me as a model for Cam's restoration. This was my mother's last chance to see her son, so I kept it to myself.

"I think you're right ma."

"They did a real good job, mom," Angie said.

Sandy nodded, throwing her two-cents worth in and adding the stock phrase, "It's amazing what they can do."

Marion stepped back and turned, leaving the room.

Mom reached up, and gently touched Cam's face and then bent over to kiss him softly on his cheek.

I had a fleeting desire to take his place, just to ease the pain that everyone was feeling. It's that vicarious part in me. I tend to feel too much for people at times. Who knows, maybe that's why my feelings about people are always right on.

"I don't know why God takes the young ones," mom said, to no one in particular. Then turning to look at me, her face glazed.

"Why couldn't he have taken me?" she asked, tears welling in her eyes.

Sandy came around and hugged mom.

"Come on mom, let's go sit down."

Mom nodded slightly and three of them went to the side of the room and sat down.

I looked down at Cam. He did look good. I took a deep breath, and turned around. Margaret was standing in the doorway. I walked over to her and extended my hand. Margaret took it and placed her other hand on top of it. Her hands were warm, and soft.

"Thank you so very much for your efforts," I said. "You really outdid yourself."

She smiled softly, "I do appreciate your noticing. I try very hard to do my best, Mr. Thomas—."

"—Sean," I said.

"OK, Sean," she said, smiling again slightly.

"I've got to run." she said. "If I can be of any help, please call."

"I will." I didn't know what she meant by that, but I figured it was the right thing to say. Margaret turned and went down the stairs, and out into the cold.

CHAPTER 13

We left the funeral home a little after eight o'clock. A light snow had begun falling and it was extremely cold. I went out earlier and started Sandy's car, and the Escort, so at least they would be warm for the ride home.

Mom and Sandy, went in Sandy's car. Angie rode with me. I opened her door and waited patiently for her to get in. I closed her door and walked around the back of the Escort. Maybe now I could get a few answers, I thought. Angie had other ideas. I knew that as soon as I got in the car.

"Are you staying at the Holiday?" she began.

I clicked in the lighter and shook out a Red.

"Yeah, I think so. I need some time to be alone. It's been a long couple of days—"

"Yeah, I know"

"And, I'm beat."

Angie didn't say anything for a minute, figuring I guess, that she couldn't change my mind anyway, and then added,

"Just so you know that you're welcome."

I nodded affirmatively.

"I do."

We drove in silence. I glanced in her direction. Looking at her, I almost broke my resolve. Angie leaned over, and put her head on my shoulder.

"What am I going to do, Sean? What will the kids do?"

"That's a good question, Ang," I answered. "This happens to people all the time. Most of them are a lot less capable of taking care of themselves than you are. If they can make it, certainly, you can make it too."

"I hope you're right," she said thoughtfully. "I sure hope you're right."

The small talk was touching, but it was also killing me. I had to get some answers to exactly what was going on.

"Angie," I started, "Can I ask you a question?"

She looked up innocently.

"Does this mean that you're going to ask me anyway?"

I shrugged, "Well, yes, I guess it does."

Angie smiled, and leaned over closer to me.

"Okay, what is it?"

"See," I continued, "a lot of weird things have happened to me since I've been here. Most of them don't compute a hundred percent."

"Like what?" she asked.

"Like us, for one thing," I said.

"Oh that." She laughed nervously.

"Yeah, that," I pressed. "You've got to admit that our making love, while your husband lay on his death bed in the hospital, is a just a bit unusual for most people, don't you think."

"Well, maybe."

"Maybe?" I asked, the emotions showing in my voice. "He was my brother for Christ's sake."

To my surprise, Angie sat up and smiled again, looking straight at me. There was an unusual softness or tenderness in her gaze.

"Sean, why are you so hung up on that. It wasn't a fluke. It was something I have wanted to do for a long time. Maybe the timing wasn't perfect, but if I had waited, or thought it out, it may never have happened."

I looked at her. Her directness had caught me a bit off guard, and I didn't have a clue of what I should say next.

"Well, maybe it never should have happened."

Angie nodded, now looking serious.

"Sean, you are not the first guy that I have slept with since Cam and I got married. We kinda had this thing."

I almost ran a red light.

"Thing?" I glared at her. "What kind of thing?"

Angie saw a Big Boy's Restaurant, and pointed to it.

"Let's get some coffee," she directed.

I turned into the parking lot, got out, went in and got two double-doubles.

When I returned to the car, I set the cups on the top of the car and opened the door. Soft music was coming from the radio. Angie had kicked the back of the seat back, and had closed her eyes.

"Wake up sleeping beauty."

Angie stirred softly, and sat up. I handed her a cup.

We took the lids off, sat in the darkness, and sipped the hot liquid. I was dead earnest.

"Now, tell me about this thing.

Angie took a deep breath, and sighed. After a moment or two, she chuckled nervously, and shook her head.

"I guess I really don't know where to start."

The way Angie spoke, I detected a stall. I said what I usually say to my clients.

"Maybe the beginning, is the best place." I suggested.

Angie nodded, and took a deep breath, exhaling slowly.

"Well, when Cam and I got married, I was marrying you by proxy. I figured you would always be around. Then you got hooked up with Debbie, and then to top it off, you left town for good. What was I to do? I just kinda figured if I closed my eyes real tight, I mean you were identical twins. How bad could it be. I just figured, somehow it would be you."

As I listened to Angie talk, I felt a strong desire to tell her that I had wanted to be with her all these years, too. Fortunately, my PI instincts kicked in full blast, and I realized that my feelings were emotional, and not logical. Angie continued.

"Then after we got married, Cam figured it out. He was so pissed. He didn't talk to me for a month.

"J.J. was the glue that kept our marriage going. He was our life. Then when I got pregnant with Jessica, things got better for a while. One day when Jessie was about a year old, Cam comes home, and says he wants to swap with some guy and his wife at work. I freaked out.

"Well, it took him a month of convincing, but I finally gave in, sight unseen. I guess I gave in because I felt so guilty about secretly wanting you."

"Well, we go over to these guy's house, and this guy is a god. I mean, he is tall, and muscular, and he wants to screw my brains out."

"Well, Cam wanted to watch, you know, me and Kyle, and his wife was into it too, so I said "What the heck". Well, we did it, and they watched. I tried not to get into it, you know, be cool, like it was no big deal. Shit, after about five minutes, I was thrashing about, orgasm city. I never had it so good. I never even saw Cam and Gale leave."

Angie took a sip of coffee, and a deep breath, turning to look out the window, tears gently creeping down her cheeks. There was a few moments of absolute silence, and then Angie continued.

"We did it with them a few more times over the next year. Then one day, I made the mistake of asking Cam if we were going to their house, and that was it. I was pregnant with Mandy at the time, and Cam was sure she was Kyle's. He even went so far as to have her blood tested."

"After that we were never the same. Cam couldn't even get it up, no matter what I did. It had a tremendous effect on him. We started seeing a sex therapist, and it helped a little. I used to go and watch them screw, supposedly to make our life better. That was a laugh. Cam would screw his brains out with this lady, and then cry for two days. I realized then, that I loved him and had loved him for all of those years. It wasn't exactly like loving you, but I did love him with all my heart."

"Well, that explains Susan," I thought to myself. Sure enough Danny the bartender knew what the hell he was talking about. My thoughts of Cam secretly meeting this therapist distracted me for the moment. But not for long. I needed to keep my wits about me. Angie was in the confession cycle, and I didn't want to miss a word.

"It got so bad, that we wouldn't even try after a while. I used to beg him, and he tried so hard. He just couldn't do it. He said that he had ruined our lives. Basically, he was unreconcilable. We made some progress after he stopped seeing the therapist, and things were getting better, then this happened. I just wish I could have one more chance to make it with him. I know now, I could make it right."

She was finally finished. I wanted to jump right in with questions, but I didn't. I let her story soak in, and didn't say a word for several minutes. I had smoked three Reds listening to her. My mouth was dry, and my coffee was about gone. I wet my lips with my tongue, stroked my five-o'clock shadow, and then asked the most logical question.

"Then, why us?"

"That's the easiest part," she answered quickly. "I had to find out if it was me. I needed to know if I could live in this world without him."

"And? What was the verdict?" I asked.

Angie thought for a minute.

"I don't know Sean. I know now that I'm not just a screwing machine for Kyle, and I know I'm still alluring to some degree. I guess I'm mixed up a lot. I'll have to let things settle in. You know, find the feelings in my heart"

Angie was definitely confused, all right. I felt badly, that my presence may have added to her confusion. I messed with her mind, at a time when she needed clear thinking. But, Angie was on a roll, so I kept operating in PI.

"Are you still seeing Kyle?"

Angie looked away.

"No," she said softly.

For some reason, I didn't believe her, but at least we were making progress. I drank the last of my coffee, and sat silently for a few minutes. Angie stared into her cup. It seemed to me that we had a real mess here. My guess was, the payback that Cam had anticipated to give Angie, had backfired in his face.

"Is Mandy Kyle's?" I asked.

"No, she's not," Angie snapped, glaring in my direction. "What is it with you guys? Don't you think we know who we get pregnant by?"

"Well, hey, I just thought—"

"You men are such assholes."

"Angie, chill out," I said. "It was a fair question."

Angie stared right through me, intense anger in her eyes. I must have hit a nerve somewhere. After a moment, she looked away, staring into the night, and apologized softly.

"I'm sorry. I guess you're right. Basically, I was mostly true to Cam until this, and it kills me to think that maybe in some way, I caused him to be unhappy. I was only screwing Kyle because I thought Cam wanted me to."

Now, that struck me as funny. I chuckled. "Is that right?"

To my surprise, Angie smiled slightly. "I guess it did get out of hand at the end there. I mean, it was so crazy that I couldn't keep up with Cam's moods, and the lack of sex just about drove me nuts."

"So when did you start seeing Kyle on the side?"

Angie's head snapped in my direction, and she started to say something, then thought better of it. I guess she figured we were beyond further bullshitting at this point.

She slowly looked away again.

"I never really stopped." Her pause seemed to last forever. "Cam came home from work last week, and Kyle was there. He didn't actually catch us doing anything, but that was it. He didn't say a word, he just turned around and walked out of the house."

I sighed. After being in the PI business for a great many years, I've have heard all the stories. Most of them have a humorous side to them, and since they don't really touch your life, you can do your job objectively and move on.

This time it was too weird, and too close to home.

"Do you think Cam killed himself?" I asked.

Angie shrugged and then nodded slightly.

"I've thought a lot about that. I think it certainly is possible. If he did kill himself, it was my fault. By screwing around, I killed him, just the same as if I put a gun to his head."

Angie sighed deeply. I don't think I could live with myself if I knew he had killed himself.

At least the picture was a little clearer now. I didn't know where I went from here. Anything I would do at this point would be reactionary. I wanted some time to think.

Angie finished her coffee, and reached over to put her arms around my neck, not romantically, but for reassurance. At this point she needed it badly. I knew how she felt. When my clients finally get their personal problems off their chest, they feel naked, vulnerable, and scared. I think she felt as though she were going to be cast out or something. I couldn't let her feel that way. I cared, and I wanted her to know it.

I drew her closer to me, and kissed her forehead. I could feel her warm brow and wet eyes against my cheek. Somehow I would make Angie know that it was going to be okay.

I wanted to meet Kyle and be sure that he was out of Angie's life, if for no other reason, than to try and give her a little space to think her life through.

* * * * * * * * * * * * *

We drove the rest of the way to Angie's house in silence. I needed some more clothes.

"Mind if I get a change of clothes," I asked.

"No problem, help yourself," Angie answered.

I got a couple of sets of clothes, told Angie good night, and headed to the car. I tossed the clothes in the back of the car, and watched the porch light go out. The soft green glow of the instrument panel cast a soothing light on the inside of Escort. I clicked her into gear.

I needed a shower, and a bed. Preferably alone. I was beat, confused, and frustrated. I had wanted answers, but didn't like the answers that I had gotten. Welcome back to Motown, I thought.

The ride to the Holiday was quiet, and uneventful. I thought about Kyle, and his effect on Cam and Angie's relationship. It's funny how people can get themselves into a hole that is so deep, and filled with such drastic repercussions, that they never feel like they can get out.

I've had handled cases where people started out swapping, and ended up divorcing, but I had never had one which resulted in one of the spouses actually killing themselves.

That seems to be the story of my life. It just follows the normal pattern of my life, that my first case involving these circumstances, would have to be one that involved my family. Wouldn't you know it. Life is sure crazy that way.

I give Cam an "A+" in the shit-for-brains category. We all have our fantasies. But, when we finally live them out, and the dust settles, reality is a much better place to be. Still, when I consider the mentality of the inhabitants of this planet as a whole, nothing surprises me.

Tomorrow was another day. I would get an early start, and try and get some answers. I would start with Susan.

CHAPTER 14

I smelled it even before I got to my room. The smell of Debbie's perfume was so unique, that even with smoker's nostrils, I could smell it halfway down the hall.

The perfume was called Red. It was made by some foreign company, whose name I couldn't pronounce, and it cost a small king's ransom. From my vantage point it was worth every penny. Man, the things it did to my libido. Let's just say, suddenly, I was feeling less tired.

I slipped the key into the lock, and pushed the door open. The lights were soft, candles were strategically placed around the room, "Lionell" sang softly on the ghetto blaster, and in the center of my king-size bed, lay one very beautiful woman.

"I thought I'd save myself a quarter," she said.

Debbie looked delicious. I really didn't care why she was here but was curious as to how she got in.

"How did you get in?" I asked.

Debbie laughed. "You're not the only person in the world that can slip into a room unnoticed, Sean Thomas. I have my ways."

I smiled, "I'll bet."

"If you would rather I not be here, I could leave—," she said, without completing her thought.

"No," I said, feasting my eyes on her beauty. "No, I don't want you to leave."

I thought to myself, Leave? Why in the world would any man, in his right mind, want you to leave? I waited for my small voice to tell me that I was in deep doo-doo, or that I should not have booked a room at the Holiday, but for once, my voice of reason was keeping its mouth shut.

Debbie was as gorgeous as ever. She lay back against the head board, my favorite colored robe wrapped appropriately around her body, causing an enticing contrast between the silky black material and her smooth white skin.

"How did it go?" she asked.

I didn't answer for a moment. I was mesmerized by her beauty.

I sat down on the edge of the bed.

"How did what go?"

"The viewing."

"Oh, about as well as expected. Cam's death is only the tip of the iceberg. These people are nuts. Mom is standing tall, and Angie is in shock, but not any different than anyone else under the circumstances. There is some weird stuff going on though."

"Weird. Now that sounds interesting. Like what's weird."

"Like Cam's death for instance. There are people involved and things going on, that are too involved to explain. I'll tell you more when I get it figured out."

I stopped there. It had been a long time since I had seen Debbie, and even though we were real close at one time, I didn't know her now, and I didn't want to spill the beans on the whole scenario until I found out who she was or who she knew.

"When's the funeral?" Debbie asked.

"Friday morning. They've got a memorial service Thursday night at their church, and then the funeral is Friday. I think they're having a eulogy at the funeral home. Are you going?"

"Well, I would like to," she said. "But I don't want to get in the middle of family feelings at a time like this."

"Honey, I can't imagine anyone would really give a shit one way or the other these days. I mean everyone is walking around like a zombie. Even I'm walking around like a friggin' zombie."

"Sean, Angie and Sandy will care. They always had this problem about me and Cam. Angie thought because Cam and I talked from time to time, that he had some interest in me."

"Well, did he?"

"I guess in a way, he did. Cam was one screwed up cowboy, for a long time. Do you know that most of us that were close to him, figured he killed himself?"

I kept my composure, and continued to look directly into her eyes, searching for a give-away. I knew there was more to this, and I had to get to the bottom of it. If Debbie knew something, I needed to find out what.

My PI instincts were beginning to whistle a familiar tune. I wondered what it was that Debbie knew. I also wondered if she knew Kyle, and/or Susan. I also sensed she wanted to tell me all that she knew. If that were true, then this was the Debbie I remembered.

I laughed to myself. If this were a cash money case of mine, I would be sitting back on easy street. Everyone was just dumping information on me like I was a confessional or something. In all my years of work, I had never had a case where leads came to me this easy.

"No, I didn't know that," I lied. "Why would he want to kill himself?"

Debbie leaned over to me, and kissed me softly on the lips.

"Why don't you take a hot shower, let me fix you a drink, and then we can talk."

She put her arms around me and kissing me more deeply, the scent of the Red doing its best thing.

"Yeah, shower," I mumbled. "Cold, shower."

Debbie laughed, "Still take your Cutty straight up?"

"Yeah, go easy on the ice, I'm freezing."

Debbie's easy laugh came again.

"I'll fix that problem soon enough."

I headed to the shower.

The warmth of the water cascading down my back, had slowly begun to erase the chill that had worked its way deep into my body. After a moment of languishing in the spray, I turned and reached for the soap.

The soft click, and the rush of steamy air being sucked out of the bathroom, indicated that the door had been opened and then quickly closed. The back of the shower curtain was pushed aside and Debbie was there, drink in hand. She stared at me, smiling. After a moment, her stare made me uncomfortable.

"May I help you," I asked.

"Uh, no thanks," she answered, demurely. "I'll help myself."

I reached for the drink, she pulled it back. She was teasing me, and I loved it. I reached again, and this time I grabbed her wrist.

"Come on in, the water's fine."

Deb just laughed, and switched the drink to her other hand.

"My, my, aren't we a little aggressive tonight?"

I took the drink, and drank a heavy pull, while still trying to pull her into the shower with me. The Cutty tasted great, warming my innards as it coursed to my stomach. I set the plastic cup on the soap holder. Debbie untied the belt to her robe, and pulled away, tossing the robe to the floor.

When I turned back around, Debbie was there in the shower with me.

"Want to wash my back?" she asked.

Who wouldn't? I picked up the soap, and the rest, as I always say, is history.

* * * * * * * * * * * * *

The morning light peeked brightly through a small opening in the heavy motel curtain. It appeared as though it was going to be a beautiful day.

I looked around the room at the standard Holiday Inn fare. Red carpet, red bedspread, red curtains. I was o.d.ing on red.

Here I was staying in a red room, being intrigued by a beautiful woman wearing Red perfume, and smoking a Pall Mall Red.

I looked down at Debbie. She lay quietly beside me, sleeping softly. My watch said it was almost nine in the morning. Time for some corned beef hash and eggs. I knew Debbie was tired. Shit, we were up half the night. And the Cutty, well, let's just say the Cutty was a memory. My head ached.

I made a mental note to only stay in hotels with room service in the future. Right now, I needed a cup of coffee, bad.

The water from the shower stayed on the cool side this time, and I slowly shook my head from side to side to try and remove the fog from between my ears.

I knew the D.W.I. level in Michigan, was point one-oh. I figured my alcohol level to be closer to point two-oh. Ah, but life goes on. The shower had helped a little, but I was still stumbling around as I attempted to get dressed. Debbie stirred.

"What time is it?" she asked.

"My time, or your time," I answered playfully.

"My time, Mr. Smart Ass," she said, hissing her words. "Why would I want to know what time it is in San Francisco?"

"Curiosity maybe?" I mused.

Debbie rolled back over.

"OK, good night." She said.

I gave in, "It's nineish," I said. "Let's go get a cup and some eats."

Debbie smirked, "Just like a man," she said, "always thinking of his stomach first."

I looked at her in the dim light. Her hair was tousled, and her face clean of make-up, her body soft and aromatic. I was going to need another shower.

* * * * * * * * * * * * * * *

Jerry, and Raven were coming in to Detroit on Northwest, at five-fifteen. Before we went in for breakfast, I stopped at the front desk and booked them a room. That done, Debbie and I headed into the restaurant. I ordered the Farmer's breakfast for both of us. It was going to take a feast to rejuvenate our energy.

Mom and Angie planned to meet us at the funeral home at eight o'clock tonight. Sandy was taking care of the kids during the afternoon session, and we would all be there for the evening viewing.

Debbie sat across from me, both of us sitting quietly, anticipating the food that would erase the gnawing appetites we had worked up. The waitress sat the steaming cups of brew before us.

"Tell me about you and Cam," I started.

Debbie set her cup down.

"Now?"

"Yeah, now."

Debbie looked at me with a smirk on her face. Then she shifted her posture in the chair, and sighed.

I don't know what I really expected her to say. Were they sexually involved? Was it a love thing, or were they just friends. I thought to myself that I may have been rude for asking, but when your brother has just died, sometimes manners are in short supply.

The waitress was back, delivering our food. The issue of the moment was set aside while we began eating in silence. After a few bites, I set my knife and fork down, and looked up at Debbie.

"Well?"

Debbie took a bite of toast, looked down into her plate, shrugged her shoulders, and answered.

"Really, there's nothing to tell. When Angie started seeing this Kyle guy, Cam freaked out. I guess it was like Kyle had some kind of spell on her or something.

"Spell? What kind of a spell?"

"I don't know, really. She just didn't seem to be able to get enough of him. You know Angie, she always gave us girls the impression that she would screw just about anything. Then she would try and present a "Goody-two-shoes" image to the rest of the world."

"Okay, so?"

"So, the truth is, that for a while there, she really would screw anyone if the timing was right. Personally, I felt like she was growing out of it near the end there, but then she met Kyle."

"What made Kyle so special?"

"I don't know, but Angie was usually in control when she was playing around. This time she really gets hooked up. She met Kyle at a party somewhere. After a couple of months of screwing around, Kyle convinced Angie that they should try and swap with their spouses."

"And Angie went for that?"

"Oh, not at first. Kyle had to really work on her. I guessed Kyle's old lady was giving him a ton of shit about Angie. Then after Kyle convinced Angie, Angie went into a full court press, and tried to convince Cam."

"Eventually, Cam gave in. Even though he finally gave in and became a willing participant, he couldn't deal with the magnitude of it all."

"Then what you're telling me is that he did it, but wasn't into it."

Debbie nodded, still chewing and talking with her mouth partially full.

"I guess at first he was into it. I mean, Kyle's wife is a real beautiful girl. When Cam started to show he was interested in the program, Angie got jealous and popped his bubble."

That sounded like Angie. Even though she had her soft and sensitive moments, she wanted to be the center of attention, and if she couldn't be the "Queen", there would be hell to pay. I decided to let Debbie keep talking.

"So, then what?"

"Well, Angie was the epitome of the double standard. She kept seeing Kyle for quite a while after that. She wouldn't let Cam see Gale, but she had no restraint."

"And?"

"And, it gets worse. Cam said he caught them screwing around several times, but Angie just said, Hey, you've seen it before, it shouldn't be any big deal. Cam put up with it for a while, then he finally went off the deep end."

"Is that it?"

"Not, hardly. I don't know what the big attraction was, but Angie couldn't seem to break it off. Last week, Cam came home and they were in the thick of it. He just turned around and walked out."

Debbie was describing the pieces of a puzzle. As I listened, a picture was beginning to form. Maybe the pieces fit too well. But, from where I sat, there were still a lot of pieces missing.

"So how do you fit into this mess?"

"The reason Angie doesn't want me around, is that she's afraid I will blow the whistle on her "goodie-two-shoes" image, to the rest of the family. Cam was the only person except me, that knew about Angie. Now, Angie has Sandy thinking I'm the bad guy, here."

You can imagine what was going through my mind. I had heard two different stories and I didn't know which one to believe. I thought for a minute.

"Are you saying that Angie initiated the relationship?"

Deb was slow to answer. She took a slow drink of brew, and set the cup back on the table.

"Maybe not initiated, but once it got rolling, when things got slow, she was there to push it along. I told her I thought it was cheap, but she told me in no uncertain terms, to "F" off. It's sad, but up until then, Angie and I were real close."

"So what about this party you mentioned?"

Debbie nodded, and continued. "The party was the key. After Angie went to the party with Kyle, she and Cam went downhill fast. When she first started messing around, she hid it. After a while Cam found out, and begged her to knock it off, but she wouldn't."

"When she told Kyle about Cam knowing what was going on, Kyle planned the swapping thing to settle Cam down. After that, all he had to do was convince Angie."

"Kyle convinced Angie they should swap, and Angie convinced Cam. Right?"

"Bullseye. Like I said, Cam finally did it a couple of times with Kyle's wife, Gale. From what Angie told me, it didn't seem like she was really into it either."

"Cam wanted to be in love with someone, so he thought maybe it would be Gale. But, when his feelings were known, Angie went nuts, and threatened to take the kids and leave. Cam didn't know what to do, so he just took it, until last week. He was a wreck."

"Until last week?"

"Yeah. That's when Cam walked out."

"Did Angie know that you and Cam were just friends?"

Debbie sat her fork down, wiped her mouth, took a drink, and answered. "Cam and I were friends. Only friends, OK. I ain't sayin' I didn't side with him a little, but the last thing he needed was to have another woman screwing up his life. I was a good listener, a drinking companion, and that's it. I don't know what Angie believed. All I know, is what the truth was."

"So you're telling me that you and Cam were not sexually involved?"

"Screw you, Sean. Don't you understand the concept of friendship."

I shrugged. Debbie was getting pissed. Maybe it was because I had hit a nerve.

"Don't take it personal. I was just asking."

I wondered to myself, how Cam could have allowed himself to get involved in this whole mess, and how no one was able to see what was going on.

"So how come he told you and nobody else?"

"I guess, he just figured no one else would listen, or care. It isn't like we had intimate moments or anything. Cam trusted me. We would just get together, have a couple of drinks, and talk. Nothing more."

"So what did you talk about?"

"A lot of stuff. Some about his work and the like, and some about his problems with Angie."

"Did he ask for your advice?"

"Of course. Why do you think we talked?"

"What did you suggest that he do about Angie?"

"What could I suggest? Relationships are personal things. I told him to follow his heart, but I also told him that he should get some professional help, that I wasn't qualified to run his life."

"Did he?"

"Yeah, he did. He called a group called "Intimate Assistants", or something like that, and met a sex therapist named Susan. After he met her he took on a totally different attitude. I know he was getting love and affection there, if you know what I mean. Once again, when Angie found out, that was the end of that, too."

"Did the sex therapist thing bother you."

"No, not at all."

"Why don't I believe you?"

"I don't know. Maybe you have a problem?"

I didn't think I did, but this did put a new perspective into the picture. Debbie finished her last bite and sat her fork down before continuing.

"Honestly Sean, you know I've known you guys for a long time. I never did have sexual feelings for Cam. He was a nice guy, but for some reason, those feelings all went to you. I can't do anything to make you think differently, but it's the truth, none the less."

I believed her, and I decided for the second time that only Susan could help. I also decided that after I got a chance to talk to Susan alone, Angie and I would go for a ride, to Susan's office. I wanted to see her reaction, to see if she knew where it was, to see if she would be honest with me about knowing about Cam and Susan.

I sopped up the last bit of syrup, crunched the last piece of bacon, and washed them down with coffee. I pushed away from the table. Debbie looked at me.

"What's up?" she asked.

"I gotta split," I said, and stood up.

I kissed Debbie on the cheek, and asked her to meet Jerry, Raven and I for supper at the Rialto at six-thirty.

"If you need help with anything, I'll be in the office all day," Debbie said.

"Thanks, I'll call you later," I answered. "I've got work to do."

CHAPTER 15

Angie met me at the door in her night gown.

"What do you want," she asked, not opening he door.

"I want to get my freezing ass out of the cold, if it's all the same to you."

Angie glanced tentatively over her shoulder, towards the back of the house.

"Uh—, well—, come on in. I'll be with you in a minute," she said, and turned to walk towards the back bedroom.

I guess I should have made myself comfortable in the living room, but remember, I had shared the same bed with her, not more than forty-eight hours earlier. Besides, my instincts said to check it out.

I heard Angie's muffled voice trying to calm someone down.

"Just be quiet for a minute, and I'll get him out of here. If you keep talking, he'll hear you."

My curiosity was killing me. I walked over and pushed the bedroom door open. Kyle sat naked on the edge of the bed. He glared at me.

"My, my, haven't we been busy?" I said, looking at Angie.

"It's not what you think, Sean," Angie defended.

"Oh really?" I said, motioning at Kyle with my hand. "Then, this is some new kind of nude aerobics, right?"

Kyle started to speak. I turned and glared at him, "Shut the hell up, creep."

Kyle glared back at me. We stared eye to eye for a moment, then he stood up and stepped toward me. I made him for just a bit over 6 feet tall. His body was well muscled, and now his attitude was aggressive.

I guess he thought his size, or his physique frightened me. That was his first mistake. He also fashioned himself to be a fighter. That was mistake number two. Next, came mistake number three. In my book, it's three strikes, and you're out.

Kyle took a wild swing at me and missed. Struggling to recover, he again swung wildly, missing me by a mile. I thought to myself, enough of this bullshit, and reaching over, I picked up the heavy bedroom lamp, sitting on the table next to the bed. When Kyle's last swing also flew harmlessly over my head, I swung the lamp.

The heavy ceramic crashed into the side of his head, breaking into a million pieces. Kyle slumped to the floor unconscious.

To my surprise, Angie didn't go to his aid.

"Aren't you going to help him up?" I asked.

Angie was quiet, and appeared stunned.

"I know you won't believe me, but he won't leave me alone."

"Right," I muttered.

Angie continued. "I feel like he's got some kind of a spell over me. I just can't say no, when he's around."

Angie was right, I didn't believe her. At this point I was confused. For the moment, I didn't know what Angie's problem was. But, Kyle had a real problem. He was bleeding pretty good.

Mom had always taught us, that the best way to stop a bleeding cut, was to put ice on it. So, I picked up his car keys, dragged his naked ass to the back door, opened it, and threw both of them out into the snow.

I shut the door, and walked back into the bedroom. Angie looked at me, then looked away. I wasn't bashful.

"OK lady, I want some straight answers."

I shook out a Red and continued. "And, no more bullshit, got it?"

Angie sat down on the side of the bed, and began sobbing softly. She shook her head, staring down at the floor.

"I don't know when it all began," she started, again shaking her head in disbelief. "It all seems like a blur now. I went to this party with Sandy and Debbie, and Kyle was there. He bought me a drink, and the next thing I know, we were in his car, you know, doing it. I wanted to stop him, but it seemed so right."

At last, I felt I was finally hearing the truth. I had hoped that Angie would open up and clean the slate, but I honestly didn't think it would be this easy.

"The next day when he called, I didn't even think to say no, when he asked to see me. I just went." Angie raised her eyes from the floor, and stared into space as though reliving the moment. Then she turned to me.

"It was crazy. We were in his house, in his bed, with his wife watching us screw, and I thought it was the most natural thing in the world. I felt so comfortable. When I got home, I even told Cam about it."

"Well, Cam went nuts. He goes over there to kill this guy, and Kyle was as smooth as silk. He shakes Cam's hand, and says, hey, no big deal. You can screw my wife."

"You mean, Gale?"

"Yeah, Gale. Gale is really beautiful, and Cam figured, he'd do Gale to get back at me and then Kyle would be paid back too. Instead, Kyle is there encouraging them, and stuff. I guess the fantasy of the moment got to Cam, and it was OK for a while, but then when he found out that I was seeing Kyle on my own, he really flipped out."

The PI light went off in my skull somewhere. I had a hunch Angie may have been trying to manipulate me, so I had to check it out.

"What do you mean, on your own?" I asked, not sure where the next step would take me.

Angie stared back at the floor.

"Well for a while, we use to swap, you know, do each other together. Kyle said it was an easy way to keep Cam and Gale occupied, and he liked to see me do Cam, and Cam do Gale. I know it all sounds sick now, but it seemed OK then. Cam seemed to get frustrated with it all, and wanted to stop getting together. I told Kyle it was over, but he ignored me. He just kept coming around, and I couldn't seem to stop him, I don't know why, I just couldn't."

"So Cam thought it was over, right?"

Angie nodded. "Cam thought we had stopped, but in truth, the only thing that stopped was Cam screwing Gale. Then Cam found out about me and Kyle. For all I know, I may have just told him. I don't even remember. I do know that it ultimately killed Cam, and do you know what? I don't even feel any real remorse about it."

My first thought was "You bitch. My brother is about to be planted six feet under, and you could care less." I quickly realized that there was more to this picture than what appeared on the surface. I also realized that my thinking was more from emotion than logic. I needed to hear the rest of Angie's confession. Showing any emotions now, would ruin the moment. I let my PI instincts rule.

"Did you ever stop loving Cam"? I asked.

"No," Angie snapped quickly, looking up and glaring at me. "I told you. I've always loved Cam. Always." Angie paused a minute, "As a matter of fact, I still do, even though now it's too late."

Angie looked numb, like a zombie. A sense of grief and relief showed on her face, changing her expression. It sounded to me like she might have been trying to convince herself how much she really loved Cam.

I wasn't sure what Angie's true feelings were at the moment. If she didn't still love Cam, she was a damn good actor. I should know, in my business, I've seen them all. What I was sure of, was the fact that Susan played an important role in the whole picture. I needed to find out why.

"Why was Cam seeing a sex therapist?" I asked.

Angie thought quietly, and then answered softly.

"He felt like I let him down. I guess he was right. Cam needed to be loved exclusively. He wanted someone who could give him sex, and affection too. I tried, and since I got involved with Kyle, I couldn't do it anymore."

Angie was quiet for a moment before continuing.

"Gale tried, but she just couldn't do it either. It seems like Kyle has the same spell over her. Cam thought that I didn't want to love him like that anymore, so he felt left alone."

I could see why Cam would feel that way. How else would you feel if you were screwed over by the people you loved and trusted?

"I really did, truly, love him. You have got to believe me."

Angie was pleading with me to believe her.

"I tried to tell him that I loved him, and I tried to change, but I couldn't get away from Kyle. I think Gale felt the same way."

"Where do you think you and Kyle stand now?" I asked.

"I honestly don't know, Sean," she said with a slight chuckle, "I hope it's over, but I'm so confused. Kyle seems so right, even now when I know it's wrong."

There was no doubt that Angie was confused. She reminded me of a fly with only one wing. From where she sat, she didn't know which way was up. And, I'm not sure she knew what was right, from that was wrong.

I needed to get down to specifics if I hoped to figure this out.

"How did you get into the swapping?"

Angie's stare was back on the floor.

"Well, it was like I said. It was kinda by accident. I think Cam felt it was the only way he could keep track of me. As dumb as I sounds, it bugged me to see Cam doing Gale, but I wanted to keep seeing Kyle, so I put up with it."

She paused thoughtfully.

"Then, Cam fell in love with Gale. That was too much for me. I know it seems sexist, but I didn't love Kyle. One thing for certain, I didn't want Cam loving Gale. Besides, she made me jealous."

"So you had to do something dramatic, right?"

Gale nodded. "I guess so. I told Cam I wasn't gonna see Kyle anymore, but like I said, I did anyway. When I asked Cam to stop seeing Gale, he got really frustrated and confused. Angie paused again.

"Then, he found out I was still seeing Kyle, and he freaked out totally."

I knew now, how the friendly foursome got together. That seemed logical. What I still didn't know, and Angie seemed to be avoiding the issue, was how the sex therapist came into the picture.

"You still didn't tell me why Cam started seeing the therapist?"

This time Angie nodded affirmedly.

"Susan, was my idea."

"Your idea?"

"Yeah, I figured maybe she could fix our situation. I got her number out of the phone book."

"So, what'd she do, put on a couple of bandages?"

Angie almost laughed.

"No, she did more than that. A lot more than that. At first I thought it was a great idea. But once again, Cam's magnetism screwed things up. They weren't supposed to really have sex. I mean, it turned out to be Cam's secret love. It was supposed to be therapeutic. I don't know when it actually started, but I do know at first, Susan tried to keep it business, but Cam insisted."

Angie stood up, crossed her arms over her chest, and began pacing the bedroom, as though deep in thought.

"After a while, Susan seemed to get a grip on herself and then she broke it off. Cam went back to Gale, and then back to me. I kept seeing Kyle until Cam caught us last week."

I took a deep breath. There were still a lot of unanswered questions, but I had a much better idea of how things got started. I wasn't sure how all the pieces fit together yet, but, I did have a better picture.

It was time for me to leave. I had a lot of things to do. I walked into the living room and turned around. Angie was right behind me. I looked her straight in the eyes.

"Do me a favor, I'm gonna go talk to Gale. Don't see Kyle again under any circumstances until you hear from me again. I'll call you later."

Angie said nothing, simply nodding agreement. Without saying a word, I left her standing in the living room, and headed for the cold.

I had taken Kyle's wallet from his pants on the floor. I knew that he was OK, because I heard his car leave the garage. I laughed, thinking of how he would get his naked ass into the house in broad daylight. The wallet would give me an address, and an excuse, to be at his house. Little did I know that the joke was on me.

CHAPTER 16

Kyle had one of those ding-dong, ding-dong, door bells. I waited patiently in the cold shadows until the inner door opened. The person who finally stood behind the door was a knock-out. I mean rated 10+ on a 9 point scale of beauty.

Gale was everything I had heard about her. Tow blonde hair, meticulously groomed, stacked, and good looking too. She certainly was a beauty. I couldn't figure myself ever letting anybody get within ten feet of her if she was my wife, but then what the hell did I know.

The blonde looked at me questioningly.

"My name is Sean Thomas," I said to the glass. "I have Kyle's wallet."

Gale looked at the wallet I held up for inspection. She then slowly opened the door, looking me up and down. She seemed shocked, and didn't seem to believe her eyes.

"Who are you?"

"Sean Thomas. Cam's brother."

"How come you have Kyle's wallet?" she asked.

Then, as if answering her own question, she continued.

"He must have left it at Angie's last night."

I nodded.

Gale's matter-of-fact attitude left me speechless. Seeing her in person also confused the issue. She was even better looking than I had imagined.

"Do you have a moment to talk?" I asked.

"Sure, come on in," she said opening the door the rest of the way for me. I stepped inside. As I did, Gale looked me up and down.

It's nice to be noticed, I thought.

Gale continued. "I had heard you were in town. I'm really sorry to hear about your brother."

I nodded, Thanks. Do you know where Kyle is?" I asked, watching her eyes for a give-away.

Gale nodded. "Yes I do. He's at the hospital getting stitches. He got mugged on the way home from Angie's last night. They took all of his clothes and everything."

"Gale—"

"I'm sure he'll be alright. Kyle gets in scuffles all the time."

"Gale!" I interrupted.

"Not this time," I started, "Kyle didn't get mugged. I hit him in the head with a lamp because he tried to punch me. His clothes are still at Angie's house."

Gale didn't say anything for a long moment. The silence was almost deafening. After another moment, she burst out laughing.

"Well, it's about time," she said, finally. "No one ever kicked Kyle's ass before."

"No? Why not?"

"I don't know. People don't really take their anger out on Kyle. He has a way of making people do exactly what he wants them to do. Most people find his personality to be addictive."

"Like cocaine?"

Gale laughed again. "That's not a bad analogy. I know I've been trying to get away from him for a long time. Just when I think I can do it, leaving stops seeming like such a good idea."

"Gale," I began, "Tell me what you know about Cam and Angie." Gale turned and went into the kitchen.

"Coffee?" she asked.

"Yeah, black," I answered, shaking out a Red. "You got an ash tray?"

Gale poured the cup, and went to the kitchen counter, returning with an ash tray. I fired up the *Red.*

"Sean, Cam and Angie is a broad subject, no pun intended. I know Kyle has this thing for Angie.

"Yeah, tell me about it."

"I wish I could. I don't know why he's so stuck on her. I try and keep him happy at home. I mean, it's not like he's missing out on anything here."

Looking at her standing there, I knew that was a statement that was absolutely true.

"Maybe she's just a challenge." Gale added. "I know she wants to stop seeing him too, so I figure he's just obsessed.

"Obsessed? What do you mean obsessed?"

"Like a quest. You know. He wants to say that he can screw her anytime he wants, anywhere, and she won't say no. Like a macho thing. He uses her as some kind measurement for his masculinity, or something."

"What about you and Cam?"

Gale took a slow deep breath, and let it out just as slowly."

"You see, I got a past. I can't just go anywhere I want and get a job. I got no money, and no skills. All I got, is looks."

I looked at Gale. She had beauty by the bushels. Yet listening to her talk, I think she was selling herself short. In the few short moments since we had met, I sensed a deepness, a sincerity, that is rare in people these days. For a person in her situation, it was almost unbelievable.

Gale continued to talk. "Because of my looks, and my body, I got Kyle. Now it looks like I don't have much of him. So, I pretty much do as he says. He tells me all the time that if I don't do what he wants, he'll throw me out."

She looked around.

"I couldn't do this well on my own."

"Go on," I said.

Gale sighed, lit up a "More" and stared into space, dazed in memory.

"One day Kyle comes home with Angie. I mean, I think she's gorgeous. Just a natural beauty. Well, he wants to have sex with her and have me watch him and her do it. So they do it right on the floor in the living room.

"With you watching?"

"Yeah, with me watching. When he's done he just laughs, gets dressed and goes out. Angie cried for a long time, then she gets dressed and leaves too. I tried to console her and tell her what a jerk Kyle is, but I ain't no shrink. She was still pretty unhappy when she left."

"And?"

"After an hour or so, Cam shows up looking for Angie. Kyle comes home while we're talking and he and Cam exchange words, but Kyle is so smooth. He says hey, you can screw my wife if you want. The truth is we ain't never really been married. I just live here because I ain't got no place else to go."

"So why didn't you say something?"

"What was I gonna say? I have no place to go, remember. I'm trapped here. So, I looked at Cam, and he looks okay to me, so he and I have sex, and Kyle watches. Well, me and Cam hit it off real good. I mean, I got feelings for the guy. I mean, real feelings. Cam, he likes me too, but he's so much in love with Angie, he can't really get into it."

"What happened next?"

"Well, I really liked Cam, but I wasn't about to force my way into his life. Shit, he and Angie had enough problems with Kyle being in their lives. They didn't need me messing things up too. But, we did have time to be together as long as Kyle and Angie were swapping."

"So much for romance."

"Sean, it wasn't like that. I really liked Cam. I wouldn't say I loved him, but the moments were special. I needed those moments. Does that make me a criminal?"

No, it didn't make her a criminal. I guess if my mate was screwing around on me and I knew it, I would need someone, too.

"It hurt real deep when Cam got killed. I mean, I couldn't take the news."

"Of his death?"

"Yeah. When Cam got killed, Kyle laughed. He says, now she's totally mine. He scared me when he said that, but what could I do. I just try and do what he says, then he leaves me alone."

I had run into some pretty serious slime balls in my time, but Kyle Washington just about took the cake.

Most of my clients were involved with the sneaky, behind the scenes, screwing around on their mates. I have never able to condone adulterous behavior, even on the small scale. This scenario was more than I had ever run into, and I was having major difficulties keeping my thinking in the proper perspective. I knew that Kyle and I would meet again. That was a promise I had made to myself. We would surely meet again.

"What will he do if he sees us together," I asked.

"Absolutely nothing." she answered. "If he comes home when you're here, he'll act like nothing has happened. That's just the way he is."

Almost at the moment she finished, the side door pushed open with a rush. I set down my cup, and lit up another *Red.* Kyle strolled into the kitchen.

* * * * * * * * * * * * *

"Hi, Sean, how's it going?" he asked, leaning over to kiss Gale on the cheek.

"Did you happen to see my wallet at Angie's?"

I reached into my pocket, and tossed it onto the counter. Kyle had a four-by-four taped to the side of his head. I thought to myself, this guy is not carrying a full load.

Just as Gale had said, Kyle seemed totally unfettered at my being there. He was totally oblivious to it all. I thought to myself, either he's brain dead, or so aloof he wouldn't know the house was on fire, if he were in it.

Kyle picked up the wallet and put it in his pocket.

"I really appreciate your returning it," he said. "I must have dropped it last night."

My first instinct was to eliminate his species from the face of the earth, but I needed some answers.

"Why don't you just cut the bullshit, and leave Angie alone?"

Kyle laughed, almost sneering. "Sean, it's simple. Angie doesn't want me to leave her alone." Kyle paused. "Now, with Cam gone and all, she needs someone. That someone is me."

"Who made you judge and jury on what Angie needs?" I said, moving off the kitchen stool. Kyle took a step back.

"Hey, cool down man," he said. "Angie did. She asked me to come back."

"No way."

Kyle smiled again, "No? Then, man you don't know nothing. I was there again just before I came here." He picked up the receiver of the phone, and held it up to me. "Here, call her and ask her yourself.

I reached for the phone.

"And what about Gale?" I asked.

Kyle laughed, "Gale? Gale, doesn't mind." Then looking at Gale intently, he continued, "You don't mind, do you baby?"

Gale slowly shook her head.

His arrogance told me that a phone call to Angie was not necessary. I knew he was telling the truth, so I slid the phone back to him, got up and turned to Gale.

"I've got some friends coming in from the coast. They can help you. Call me at the Holiday around ten tonight."

Gale took the number I wrote down, looked at it, folded it, and put it in the pocket of her pants.

I looked at Kyle, "I'll talk to you, later."

Kyle's forced grin was one of total arrogance.

"Hey, I'll look forward to it," he said, extending his hand for me to shake. I ignored it, turned and headed to the door.

"Call me later, Gale," I said, before leaving.

I stepped back into the cold, the chill of the air momentarily chasing away the tension of the past few moments.

Shake his hand? What gall he had, the son-of-a-bitch. All I really wanted to do was kick his ass. All in due time, I assured myself, all in due time.

I didn't like this guy. Not one bit. Sooner or later, someone would have to stop him. I made myself a personal promise. Somehow I would pay him back.

One thing, that was obvious to me, was that I had allowed myself to become personally involved in my brother's death. I know how stupid it sounds, but you cannot conduct an objective investigation when you are personally involved, or when the case involves family members. That was the first rule of the trade, and I had broken it.

Lawyers can't defend themselves, shrinks can't shrink themselves, doctors can't doctor themselves, and PI's, can't PI, themselves.

I was a sucker like everyone else, I guess. I wanted to believe the best about those that I loved. Angie had taken me in. At least, I think she took me in. Maybe Debbie took me in. Maybe it was Gale. Shit, I didn't know. One thing was for certain, I had a lot of loose ends to tie up. It was time to call Susan. I reached for the phone and keyed in the number. After a moment or two, it began ringing. Once, twice, three times. The answering machine kicked in, and I prepared myself to leave a message.

"Hello, and thank you for calling "Intimate Assistants". We are temporarily unable to answer your call. Please leave your name and number after the tone, and we'll return your call as soon as we can."

I waited for the beep. "Susan, this is Sean Thomas. I would—," the phone clicked up.

"Sean?"

"Yes," I answered. "Is this Susan?"

Susan was a little breathless. "Yes, it is. I've been waiting for your call. I'm so sorry to hear about Cam."

"Thanks. Susan, I have some questions I would like to ask you about Cam. Can we get together for a few minutes?"

Susan was quiet for a moment as she checked her calendar.

"We could have lunch today, say eleven-thirty."

I needed to get some facts soon, so we agreed to meet at the "China Star" for lunch.

I checked my watch. I had about forty minutes. I decided to get some smokes, and fill up the Escort.

* * * * * * * * * * * * *

Chinese restaurants all have a unique smell. After answering "Two", and "Smoking", I was ushered to a booth along the wall. Fortunately, it was clean.

I sat in the booth sipping tea and waiting for Susan. I felt a little strange about meeting her. I mean, this lady was my brother's lover, confidant and doctor, and I believed that she had key answers to my questions regarding Cam, Angie, Kyle and Gale.

A flash of light indicated that the front door had opened, and closed. I looked up, and Susan stood in the archway.

My first thought was no way this lady screws for a living. Susan smiled, and walked over to the booth. I slid out and stood up.

"Sean?" she inquired.

"Hello, Susan," I answered, reaching out my hand. Susan took it and held it for a moment.

"I've heard so much about you."

Susan seemed to stare at me as we sat back down. She had the twin, catch. She couldn't believe that Cam and I looked so much alike.

The waiter brought us more tea, and took our order. I hit my pack, lit up a Red, and took a drag.

"We need to talk about Cam, Susan."

Susan frowned, a little.

"I can't."

"What do you mean, you can't?"

"I'm not supposed to talk about my clients. It's part of the code of ethics in my profession. Those ethics, are very critical," she said, emphasizing the word, very.

"Susan, we're talking about my brother here. I have some very serious questions about his cause of death. You hold the key to some vital information."

"I'm sorry, Sean. I really can't."

I caught my breath, and looked away. I didn't want to lose my temper.

Especially not with Susan. She was a very key player, and I needed her information. Besides, looking at her, it was hard to stay mad at her for long. I looked at her. She was a catch. Danny, had hit the nail right on the head. Long dark hair, large doe like eyes, high cheek bones and a full, shapely mouth. Cam was lucky to get in the sack with this one.

I regained my focus, and addressed the ethics-thing.

"Susan, I know about your ethics," I said. "I respect those, but I have a problem. My brother is dead, and I think he killed himself over some bizarre sexual problem. I have talked to his wife, his wife's friend, and his lover. Each of them gave me a different story. As near as I can tell, all of them are wrong. I need your help."

"I don't know how discussing our meetings can help."

"I'm looking for even the smallest bits of information. You spent a great deal of very personal time with him. I need to know what you know."

Susan looked totally frustrated. I had either hit a nerve, or crossed the lines of decency. I decided I'd try and smooth things out.

"Look, I just want to get some answers, so my brother can rest in peace."

Susan reached into her purse, and took out a pack of Virginia Slims and lit one up. I expected her to say something, but she just looked at me. I turned my hands palms up, in a gesture of desperation. Finally, Susan spoke. She looked me directly in the eye, sighed deeply, took sip of tea, and spoke.

"This is highly unusual," she began. "What do you know?"

"I know," I started, "that Cam and Angie were involved with Kyle and Gale, and that Cam ended up coming to see you. What I don't know, is who started it, and who was the victim."

Susan smiled, raising her eyebrows.

"Victim? That's a pretty harsh word, Sean."

"It's a pretty harsh case Susan."

"Yes, but just the same, I—."

"Let me put it to you simply. I've got a dead brother. I've got a sister-in-law that is totally screwed up. I've got a guy that thinks he owns my sister-in-law. And, I've got three conflicting stories. Victim is what I mean."

"I guess you may be right," she said pausing. "I'll tell you what I know."

Susan took a long drag on her Slim, crushed out the butt and spoke.

"Cam came to see me a while back. At the time, he was unable to have sex with Angie. They also had gotten involved with a couple named Kyle and Gale."

At last, I thought, leaning forward. Maybe now I would get the truth.

"Cam said that Angie and he had been having problems over her getting pregnant with their third child. Angie evidently had been having sex with Kyle and Cam thought the baby was his. Angie had told me that when she first started seeing Kyle, that she never slept with Kyle later than the second day after her period ended. Later, she went on the pill. She was sure the baby was Cam's.

Cam finally met Kyle, and they had a tremendous fight. As Angie tells it, Cam was drunk, and lost. Cam decided that he could get back at Kyle and Angie by shacking up with Kyle's girlfriend."

"Cam, was clever. After a while, he worked it out, and he and Gale were a hot number on the side until Angie found out and confronted him. I guess she wanted to have her cake and eat it too."

"Then what happened?," I asked.

Susan chuckled. "Believe it or not, things got worse."

"Like, how?"

"Like, Angie going ballistic. Angie bitched up a storm, and Cam stopped seeing Gale, but Angie kept seeing Kyle, whenever and wherever, she and he wanted."

"Cam, knew all along, but he never told Angie right out. Cam, said that he and Kyle worked out their animosities somehow and got along OK. I figure, Cam just gave in to Angie's need to be with Kyle.

"It's not like him to be a quitter."

"I'm not so sure he was."

"What to you, mean?"

"You have to remember," she added, he was also screwing Gale whenever they were all together. After a while, Cam got tired of swapping, and wanted to break it off. Like I said, he stopped with Gale, but Angie didn't stop seeing Kyle. Cam, thought that since Angie wouldn't stop seeing Kyle, that Kyle must have been poisoning her mind.

"Poisoning?" I asked.

Susan nodded.

"Yeah, Sandy even thought that Kyle may have been drugging Angie."

The word drugs caught my attention. I had never considered this angle.

"What kind of drugs?"

Susan shrugged her shoulders, and slowly shook her head. "I don't know. A hallucinogen, a tranquilizer, I don't honestly know."

The thought of Kyle giving drugs to my sister-in-law didn't take much effort to believe. I didn't see how Angie taking drugs would really effect Cam. It might cause concern, but not enough for him to kill himself. I took a deep drag on the Red, and thought out loud.

"What do you think about Cam's frame of mind?"

"Like what?"

"Do you think Cam killed himself?"

Susan shook her head negatively.

"No. I don't think so. From what I knew of him, I can't imagine it. I don't really know one way or the other, for sure. I mean, he was upset, but not, that upset."

"Most suicides have deep-seated problems. That wasn't Cam. His problems were temporary. He didn't have a real reason to take his own life."

Her words were comforting. I wanted very much to believe her. Susan continued.

"You know Sean, sex wasn't his problem. He was a tremendous lover. He could have had almost any woman he wanted, but he was also tremendously insecure."

"So I've heard."

I had asked for answers, and I had gotten answers. I shook out a Red, and torched it. My thoughts were drifting from Cam and were on Susan. I wondered who she really was.

"What about you?" I asked, sending up a billow of blue. "Were you emotionally involved with him?"

Susan lit a fresh cigarette, and took a long drag before answering. She thought for a moment, and then answered.

"You know, I'm a professional. I won't lie to you," she answered seriously. "I liked Cam a lot. He liked me, too. But, we finally had to break it off. He was reaching so hard, for what I'm not sure. Even with all my training, I wasn't able to help him. I wasn't able to deal with it all. I was just too close. That was my mistake. If I had it to do over, I wouldn't have let my emotions get involved."

"I know what you mean." I said, thinking back to my earlier thoughts on the matter. "So what finally happened?"

"Well, like I said, we broke it off. When we finally stopped seeing each other, he went back to Gale, and then, back to Angie. Cam, was frustrated. He really wanted Angie back, but Kyle did seem to have some hold, over her that Cam couldn't break."

"How did he take the news?"

"About as good as expected. We had talked about the absurdity of our relationship many times. When we finally reached the end, I think he was prepared, and in a way, agreed with my decision."

"What made you decide to end the relationship?"

"At one point, I thought Cam was going to kill Kyle. That's when I told him that he was too far along for me to help him professionally. His problem was not sexual. He just wanted to get his life back together."

I thought for a moment. Maybe Susan had done her homework.

"Did you ever talk to Angie about Kyle?"

Susan nodded again.

"Yes, as a matter of fact I did. Angie said that she didn't want to stay with Kyle, but he had this thing she couldn't resist. She said that she had tried to get him out of her life, but Kyle figured that since Cam wasn't a threat, he would just hang out. That was the last I heard."

I put out the butt. My mind was trying to process the information Susan had given me. She had convinced me that she was sincere, and I hoped, honest. I decided I would take a chance.

"Susan, would you be willing to help me with a project?"

"Like what?"

"Like getting everyone's life back in order."

"Sure, if I can. But, I don't know how I can help."

"Let me work on the details. If things go right, I may have a proposition for you in a day or so. There are a few things that I still have to figure out yet, but I'll be in touch."

Susan nodded, adding "Sure. Anything. Can you give me a clue?"

I nodded. "Somehow or other, I think Kyle is involved in Cam's death. I also think he is responsible for Angie and Gale's lack of self control. I've got to figure out how and why. When I do, I would like you to help me set a trap for him."

"A trap? What kind of a trap?"

"I'm not sure yet. That's one of the details I still have to work out. One thing I am sure about, is trying to find a way to catch Kyle at his own game."

"How are you going to figure a way to do that?" Susan asked, "More importantly, how are you going to prove it?"

I also didn't know that part of the plan yet either. But, I did know, that a good PI never tips his hand, and I didn't want to break that code now.

My mind was working, but unfortunately, I didn't have a clue at this point as to how I would pull this one off. I didn't want Susan to figure out that I was totally lost, so I smiled confidently,

"Let me work that part out. I'll let you know when I get ready to put the plan in action."

After we finished lunch, and bid our adieus, I cranked up the Escort and sat for a minute. Kyle Washington was a scumbag and a con man. But, his actions were beyond being normal activities, even for a scumbag, con man.

I could understand the screwing around part, but why would he want to kill Cam? Cam was no threat to him or to his actions. Screwing someone's wife is one thing, murder is an entirely different matter.

It just didn't fit. Maybe Cam was killed by accident. Susan had mentioned drugs. Maybe that was what was causing all the fuzziness in everyone's stories.

I did know several things for certain. For one, Kyle Washington was a sleeze. I also knew that Cam, Angie and Gale were all involved with him. I know what you're thinking. It doesn't take a rocket scientist PI to figure all of that out, right? Well, even I had to start somewhere.

I also knew Cam was not a druggie. From where I stood, unless I was totally wrong, Cam's death appeared to be an accident. Cam, could have been distracted or he may have not been concentrating because of the pressure, or confusion, but heavy drugs were just not his style.

I made myself a mental note to see if an autopsy, or toxology tests had been done. If not, I'd have to get them done. I drove to a pay phone, dropped in two bits, and called Dr. Borin. The doc told me—no autopsy—but they had run a thorough blood test. What they found was not surprising. A little booze, a little dope, but no toxins. That meant no hard drugs, and no poison. Kyle was off the hook on that one.

CHAPTER 17

Thursday night, after we left the funeral home, we all drove to the "Flower Memorial Spiritualist Church". Once there, we went to the basement for coffee before the service began.

Jerry and Raven were waiting at the church when we got there. It was great to see them again. I kissed Raven on the cheek, and shook Jerry's hand.

"Why didn't you call me?" I asked Jerry.

He laughed.

"We did, but you were incognito, or some shit. We just figured you were busy, and took the limo. It was free, and we got a chance to see a lot of the beautiful scenery coming in."

I apologized, "Sorry, if I let you guys down. I'll make it up to you." There had been so much on my mind in the past two days, that I didn't even think to see if mom or Angie would want them to stay at their house.

My feeling of stupidity grew a leap or so when mom said, "Sean, why did you make them stay at the Holiday Inn? I've got plenty of room right at the house."

What could I say? She was right. I looked at my friends, shrugged, and said again, "Sorry, I really wasn't thinking."

One of the things that happens to a lot of PI's, is that when they get into an investigation, they begin thinking in PI.

That means that we have to think of ourselves and our needs first. PI thinking is necessary for survival. When you get into that mode, personal details regarding family and friends, are sometimes overlooked.

Fortunately for me, both Jerry and Raven knew me well enough, to know what state I was in.

They both laughed.

"We had a great time. We told them we were married and freaked them out."

Mom was undeterred.

"Well, you kids get your things and come to my house. I'm feeling better now, and I could use your company."

Mom always liked Raven's spunk, and she thought the world of Jerry. With that settled, we all went upstairs to begin the service.

Having never been in a Spiritualist church before, I was surprised to see that the inside of the church looked like any other church. Even though it looked the same, I didn't feel the same here, as I did in other churches. I felt eerie. Maybe it was my nerves.

We all took our seats in the front rows of pews. As the service began, the minister, a small, older woman with white hair, named Lillian, and a tall young man named Jonathan, walked down the center aisle from the rear of the church, scaled the short steps to the side of the podium, and took their seats on the platform.

Almost on cue, the music began to play, and everyone began to sing through an introductory hymn. I sang along, mouthing the words, singing the song that sounded a lot like a song I knew from my Christian upbringing, except with a few different words in the verse. Finally, we concluded the song by singing the closing "Amen".

It became very quiet in the church, and we all sat in anticipation, waiting for the next part of the service.

Lillian pushed herself up off of her chair, and shuffled up to the podium. She stood for a moment, looking down, while she organized her notes. Finally, she took a deep breath, and raised her head, looking out at the congregation through steel blue eyes.

When our eyes met, I detected a fire that belied her age. She continued to stand in front of us for a moment and then spoke.

"My dear friends, we come here tonight, in the essence of spirit. We ask for the blessings and guidance of spirit."

Her voice was deep and coarse as she led the small group through several readings, and incantations. When she had finished, she raised a small, gnarled, finger, signaling to someone in the rear of the church to begin dimming the lights.

There was an unusual energy in this church. As the lights began to go out, I felt the hair stand up on the back of my neck, and a chill rushed up and down my spine.

I didn't have a clue as to what to expect, but I was afraid there might be ghosts involved in some way. I chuckled to myself for having such bizarre thoughts, and glanced over at mom, for a reality check.

Her eyes were partially closed, and glued on Lillian. I looked over at Angie. She had the same look on her face and also looked entranced. As a matter of fact, everyone I could see in the dimming light, looked entranced. I found that strange.

One of the incantations we recited, was a thing called the "Declaration of Principles". It seemed to be some kind of Spiritualist creed.

In it, one of the principles said, "We believe that the existence, and personal identity, of the individual, continues after the change called death."

I thought about that one, for a minute. Some change. As far as I believed, death was far more than a simple change. It was permanent, and it was final.

The organist began playing softly as the lights went dimmer, and dimmer. While the music quietly played, one of the elders carried a candle lighter to the front of the church and lit a large candle, sitting on a table, in front of the podium.

Immediately the candle came to life, its light dancing around the corners and fixtures of the small sanctuary. I couldn't help but notice the eerie shadows cast on the walls and ceilings by the flickering light. There was no question about it. I was definitely getting spooked.

"Focus your gaze on the flame," Lillian led.

"And on the spirit," the congregation responded in unison.

"Dear heavenly father, we approach you this evening, in behalf of the spirit of Cameron Thomas. Bless his spirit."

"Guide his spirit," the congregation replied.

Lillian continued, "We pray your love and blessings on our service. Shield us against any negative vibrations, or spirit entities, and bring to us, our guides and teachers. Be with us now, our spirit friends."

The organ grew louder, and played an old favorite song of mom and dad's, *"I'd Rather Have Jesus"*.

Members of the congregation sat quietly, eyes closed, hands, palms up, on their knees, seeming deep in thought, listening, middle fingers touching thumbs in some sort of ritualistic positioning.

Finally, the music stopped and it was silent. The only motion in the room, was the motion of the flame from the candle flickering about in the darkness, still casting grotesque shadows on the ceilings and walls of the church.

Lillian spoke again, startling me.

"Please call to your guides."

What the hell did she mean by that? All around me people began mumbling names in the darkness. There seemed to be an intensity in their calls that I did not understand.

Mom joined in. Eyes closed, hands palms up on her knees, she whispered softly, apparently speaking to no one.

"I call, Perk, Bear, Big Horse, Sister Sarah, Princess Lotus Flower, Jane, Valar, Mahai, Dr. Watson, Dr. Thomas, Dr. Drake, St. Jude, St. Thomas, Paul, Red Eagle and any other spirits of truth that may wish to come in."

I moved away slightly, figuring that, with that many more people coming into the church, we would need more room in the pew.

The darkness made me a little nervous. My experience in dealing with people from the dead consisted of mainly what I had seen on TV and at the movies.

Now, here I was, sitting and listening to people calling spirits at will. Interesting, I thought, but not my cup of tea. I wanted a smoke.

As quickly as the murmuring began, it stopped, and it was silent once again. Two figures, dressed in hooded robes, walked quietly, down the center aisle, hands folded and motionless, except for the movement of their feet. Their walk from the rear of the church, coincided with music being played softly in the background. When they reached the front of the sanctuary, they turned and took their seats, sitting in front of the podium, near the flickering candle, facing the congregation.

I tried to focus my eyes in the dim light, but I couldn't see who the people were. It was too dark. Once again, the organ began playing a soft background tune. Lillian turned, walked to her seat and sat down.

After a short interlude, the young guy walked to the podium. He stood quietly, motionless for a moment, and then spoke.

"Bring to us, oh Lord, the spirit of our recently departed brother, Cameron. Allow us to properly bid him farewell."

It once again fell silent. It seemed like an interminable period of silence passed before he finally spoke again. This time he addressed those present.

"Brothers, and sisters, I sense the presence of a troubled spirit. God bless this troubled spirit. Guide him to us and let him speak."

I got this new feeling, a strong feeling. Brother or not, I wanted to get up and leave, but I couldn't move a muscle. I said to myself, That's it. I'm outta here. In spite of my desires, I sat there unmoving, waiting, listening, watching.

I tried to convince myself, that if I could have gotten out of there without falling and busting my ass in the dark, I would have done it.

The truth is, I was there for the duration, just like everyone else. I reasoned that, I too, had to pay my respects to Cam. However, I had figured I would take care of that responsibility at the funeral services.

Now, here I was sitting in the dark, calling to a bunch of spirits. I didn't have the slightest idea why. I just was.

I sat lost in my thoughts for a short time, but was brought back to reality by the voice from the person sitting on our side of the aisle, near the candle.

"Greetings, my friends, and may the blessings of the infinite be on you and yours."

Okay, I thought to myself, voices from nowhere, right? I am open minded in some things. And, I hadn't smoked dope in ten years. But, I felt like I was on some kind of bad drugs, as I listened to the voice. The voice I heard, was Cam's.

Jonathan spoke from the platform.

"Welcome, brother. Peace be with you in your new life."

I squinted real hard to try and see who was doing the talking. She was definitely a she, but the voice was definitely a he.

I thought to myself, Sean, you have no one to blame for this one but yourself. You should have left when you had the chance.

I almost crapped my pants when the voice said, "I call Sean Thomas".

My first reaction was to yell back, "He's not here tonight". But, I remained silent. I didn't know what I was supposed to do. Cam's call had startled me. When I looked around, everyone was looking in my direction. Mom leaned over and whispered,

"Give him your voice."

"What?" I whispered back.

"Say something," she snapped.

I was dumbfounded. I looked up and said the most important thing that came to my mind at the time.

"Yes?"

My voice cracked, barely audible. I mean, let's be real, what does a person say at a time like this?

The voice spoke again.

"My brother, I bring you greetings from the higher side of life. Relax and enjoy. Don't worry so much. The answers you are looking for, are near. Find my car, and if you are as good as I remember, you will find the answers."

"Thanks for the clues, mystery voice," I mumbled, chuckling inside. I didn't know whether to get scared, or laugh out loud. Everyone else took this stuff seriously. I decided to do neither, and listen to the voice.

"When you have found the clues, come and call to me again. Remember, follow your instincts. Also, all that is perceived, is not as it seems. Enlighten yourself, then enlighten others, and I will come again."

The voice had stopped. I sat stunned. What could I say? I didn't really think that it was actually Cam's voice speaking. I had never known Cam to be philosophical. Yet, the truth is, I had found a different brother, than I had remembered. Cam had changed in a lot of ways.

The medium sagged down in her chair, and the lights began to come up ever so slightly. Jonathan handed down a glass of water to one of the elders, who gave it to the speaker.

After a moment, the lights came up more, and I could see that the medium was—believe it or not—Carolyn Flowers. That fact won't mean much to any of you who didn't grow up in our neighborhood. But, Carolyn Flowers was to Catholicism, what "Carter's" is to little liver pills.

In all the years that I had known her, no one would date her, and you didn't dare talk to her about any other religion. We knew that she was going to grow up and be a nun. She talked about it, her mom talked about it. We were all convinced.

I remember on one visit home, I had talked to a friend of my mine who was also Catholic, and who had tried to date her. He said he was afraid to even ask her out because he was scared she would put a religious hex on him if he tried anything.

Now, here she was, working as a trance medium in a Spiritualist church. I felt like Dorothy in The Wizard of Oz. "We're not in Kansas anymore, Toto".

I had many early fantasies about Carolyn. She was always gorgeous, even in elementary school. In spite of my admiration of her good looks, I gave her a wide berth.

We all used to talk about what a waste, it was going to be—to lock that beautiful form up in a nun's habit.

Mom nudged me slightly, and then grabbed my arm, and held it tightly. Her smile radiated with bright energy in her eyes.

"Oh Sean, you're so lucky. I was hoping he would call to Angie or me."

Her voice trailed off, then after a moment, she continued, "I guess it's only right that he should talk to you. After all, you are twins. Do you know what he meant?"

I shook my head. I had no idea, and said so. After the funeral tomorrow, I would have to try and find out.

As we were leaving the church, I saw Gale. She walked over to me.

"Pretty far out stuff, huh?" she asked.

I nodded. "Like nothing I have ever seen."

Raven was at my side.

"Gale, this is Raven. She's the person I was telling you about."

"Hello," Raven said, extending her hand.

Gale reached out and took it, shaking it in a typically feminine handshake.

"I like your name," Gale said, with a smile. Then turning to look at me she said, "You're right Sean, she really is beautiful."

Raven looked at me with a smirk, then turned and looked back at Gale. "It really is nice to meet you. Sean has told me a lot about you."

Raven now held Gale's hand in a reassuring way.

"Gale is Kyle's girlfriend," I said. "She thinks he's a creep, but she can't seem to get away from him. I figure you guys can help her out."

Raven laughed.

"Oh yeah, like now I'm an expert, right?"

Raven looked at Gale who was six or seven years her senior, and said, "Don't worry honey, we'll fix you up. No need to tie yourself up to an asshole like him. Why don't you come and stay with us tonight. Tomorrow, we'll get you started."

Raven's confidence didn't surprise me. She had always been confident beyond her years.

"Does she always work this fast?" Gale asked.

"Only when she likes you."

Both girls laughed.

Jerry had already paid for the night at the Holiday, so he was explaining to mom, that he and Raven would come and stay a night with her before they left to go back to Frisco.

Angie put her arm around mom's shoulder.

"Come and stay with me and the kids tonight, mom. We're lonely too."

Mom looked at me and just nodded. Angie and mom left the church, disappearing through the door, and into the cold night air.

I felt a warm hand on the small of my back, and turned to see who was hooked on to it. Carolyn stood behind me. I turned all the way around to face her. The look on my face must have told her of the questions I had.

Almost on cue, Carolyn began answering them even without my asking.

"I hope I didn't startle you," she said.

I shook my head.

"Startle?" I began, "I was startled when they turned the lights down. What you did, frankly, was scare the crap out of me."

"Sorry about that." she said softly.

"Carolyn, tell me the truth. How did you make your voice sound so much like Cam's?"

Carolyn was very matter of fact.

"Sean, I don't control that, Cam and the spirit guides do."

I stared at her for a long moment.

"Can we be a little real, here? Are you trying to make me believe that was really Cam talking through you?"

"That is absolutely correct. Cam and his spirit guides used my vocal cords to speak to you. Wasn't it wonderful?"

She was excited. I was confused.

"Who the hell are these spirit guides everyone is talking about?"

Carolyn smiled the same smile everyone else seemed to be smiling these days.

"They are your very best friends. Their job, is to help us get through this life."

"And, they made it possible for Cam to talk through you."

Carolyn smiled again, and nodded.

"Yes, that's right. What did he say?" she asked, thoroughly confusing me.

"Why are you asking me?" I snapped.

Carolyn laughed at my anger.

"Because a medium generally can't hear or remember what the controlling spirit says when she's entranced."

"Entranced? What do you mean entranced?"

"It's the term we use to describe what happens to us when we relinquish control of our physical bodies to a controlling spirit entity."

"So, you have no idea what went on when you were—"

"—Entranced. No, not really. I lose my identity as the spirit enters me. My body becomes a vessel through which the spirit's voice passes."

Carolyn was obviously either very sincere, or a few strokes short of a par round. She was also on a roll, so I figured I get all the info I could from her.

"Now what about these spirit guides?" I pressed.

Carolyn was still somewhat deep in thought, but answered absently.

"Huh? Oh, the guides. Well, like I said, the guides are spirits from the higher side of life, who have been sent to the earth plane to help, and guide us through our existence here."

"Guide us?" I repeated.

"Yes. Some religions call them guardian angels. We just feel that they do more than just guard. They guide and teach us how to get through this existence."

I stared at her stoically.

I tried to think of something intelligent to say, or ask.

"Right," was the best thing I could come up with.

Her story sounded plausible. Too plausible. If I believed her, I could find myself in situation where I was at a serious disadvantage.

Everyone else knew more about this spiritual crap than I did. That disturbed me. I also wasn't sure there was enough time left to learn what I needed to know.

On the other hand, if I didn't believe her, I was back at square one. The only real chance I had was to trust her, God, help me.

"So what about the message," Carolyn asked.

It was my turn to be deep in thought.

For a reason that I have yet to figure out, I began recounting the dissertation given while Carolyn was entranced, whatever the hell that means. When I finished, Carolyn's face became serious and she nodded understandingly.

I reminded myself of my mental note to shake this town, this church, and this group of weirdos. I promised myself I would do this, just as soon as I could book my young ass a flight out of here.

Murders, rapes, muggings, infidelity, these are my bag of tricks. These are good, honest, down to earth crimes. Crimes that you can put your hands on. This spirit crap was something else, and as near as I could figure, not for me.

The frightening thought was, what if Cam really could come through and talk?

I was puzzled as I rethought Carolyn's story. There was no way that she could have known about the car. That fact alone, piqued my interest.

Carolyn brought me back to reality.

"A penny for your thoughts," She said.

"Oh yeah, right, a penny," I mumbled.

Carolyn took both of my hands in her own.

"Well, at least it sounds like it was a good message. Will you let me know how it turns out?"

I nodded. "I will".

I took a chance. "Do you have plans?" I asked.

Carolyn smiled. "Kinda," she said.

Then looking to my right she said, "Sean, this is my fiance' Jack. Jack, this is Sean Thomas, Cam's brother."

Jack extended a well-manicured hand, and I shook it.

"Nice to know you," I said.

I'm sure both of them noticed my surprise. I did my best to mumble something about needing to be somewhere, but frankly, I was so stunned, I'm sure that it showed.

I went out on a limb.

"Carolyn, how did you get into all of this, after the way you were raised?"

Carolyn smiled. I think she knew what I was talking about.

"It was easy," she began. "I had studied Catholicism so much, that I found it had a lot of flaws. When I met Jack, and he introduced me to Spiritualism, it was obvious almost immediately, that this is where I belonged."

It may have been, my teenage thoughts showing through, but I felt uncomfortable in their presence.

"Well, that's interesting and different. I would never have expected to see you here."

Carolyn laughed,

"That makes two of us. You also didn't seem destined to be a Spiritualist."

Her statement caught me off guard. Me, a Spiritualist? That thought had never crossed my mind.

"I'm not yet. I do have to admit, that it is a different way to worship."

"You'll learn to love it, as we all have," she said.

I was as polite as I could be,"We'll see. I'll see you guys at the funeral. Nice to meet you, Jack."

Jack and I shook hands.

Carolyn added her goodbyes, "We'll see you at the funeral."

I was a little dumbfounded as I watched them turn and leave the church. I muttered out loud, "I must be losing my friggin mind."

I mulled over my thoughts. *Isn't anybody straight, anymore*? Don't get me wrong. I was glad that everyone was interested in Cam, his death, and his spiritual development, or progression, as Lillian had called it. Even that, was something that I could live with. But the women, were they all—, nuts? Spirits this, and spirits that. Had they all lost their minds?

This whole Detroit trip had made me think of women in an entirely different light. I am sure that this attitude doesn't apply to ALL women, but look what had happened to me since I arrived in town.

I don't consider myself to be a Don Juan. That's not my style. Oh sure, I have my lucky moments, like most guys. But, since I had been in Detroit, I had hosed my brother's wife, stoked an old flame, and saw a situation that I never thought I would see in Carolyn Flowers.

I looked around to see who was still here. I was thankful for my friends. At least they provided me with some sense of sanity. Jerry was walking in my direction. I watched him approach, and was momentarily lost in my thoughts about the events of the day.

Jerry put his hand on my shoulder.

"See you back at the ranch," he said.

His touch startled me out of my deep thought.

"Huh? Oh, yeah, okay, stop over later," I said, trying to come back to earth.

Raven, Jerry and Gale left together, the chill air blowing in the door behind them, and then passing as the door closed once again.

I turned around. Jonathan and Lillian were straightening up, and looked in my direction. I must have looked a little bewildered. Jonathan said something to Lillian, and then walked in my direction. As he neared me, we shook hands.

"I appreciate your help," I said, not really knowing why.

"Jonathan, isn't it?"

"Jon, is okay with me," he said. "Sometimes people get a little formal with me."

We both chuckled, and then Jonathan continued.

"Sean, did you know that your brother was a great force in our church, a strong medium? He became a leader here in a very short time. He was a very good friend of mine, both in the worldly sense, and the spiritual sense."

"No kidding?"

"Really. Cam was quite gifted. He had great aspirations that you and he might work together on the platform one day. He believed, that by channeling your energies, you and he could literally perform miracles."

I nodded like I had some idea of what he was talking about. I kept reminding myself of my mental note, to eighty-six this place at the first opportunity.

The more I thought about it, it wasn't the people. I was comfortable with the people. It was what they were doing, that gave me the willies.

Lillian shuffled up beside us. Her body reflected the eighty-plus years she had lived, but her eyes were, crystal clear glinting a sparkle I had not seen in a long time. She was carrying a small book.

"Cam, wanted you to have this. Please read it, so that you can understand."

"Understand what?"

"You'll see, just read the book."

I reached to accept the book from her. When I extended my hand to take it, she placed her other hand on top of mine and held it for a moment. Her hands were warm and soft. I felt a sense of real peace and calm from her touch.

I looked at the book. "Understanding the Principals of the Spirit and Spiritualism". I slipped it into my pocket.

"Thank you Lillian. I appreciate your help too. It means a lot to me and my family."

Lillian laughed.

"Sean, the only person having trouble dealing with this, is you. Your family is fine. Come and see us again, soon. Cam, will want to speak with you again."

Then, turning to Jonathan she said, "Jonathan, take me home."

Jonathan picked up her coat and helped her on with it. We turned out the lights, and walked into the night.

* * * * * * * * * * * * * *

For the first time since I got here, I felt truly alone. I needed smokes, so I made a mental to note to pick up a pack. I lit one of the last two in the pack, turned the Ford onto Nine Mile Road and headed for the Holiday Inn.

My mind tried to piece together the events of the last few hours. I put my hand in my pocket, and then on the book.

"Spirits and Spiritualism", my ass. I decided it was all too deep for me. I just wanted to blow this place off, and head back to my scrungie, dirty office, my never cleaned apartment, and my buck-two-ninety eight, PI job. I was out of my league here.

I rolled the window down to throw the book out, wound up to fling it, and then, thought better of it. I had a feeling that I couldn't explain. Though I didn't hear words, or voices, I sensed that I was to keep the book, and read it.

I thought to myself, hell, if you want me to keep it and read it, who am I to argue. I flipped the book up onto the dash, and rolled the window back up.

I stopped at Annis' Market and bought two packs of Reds, and a pint of Cutty. Sitting in the cooling darkness of the Escort, I unscrewed the cap of the small bottle, and threw it out the window. That done, I took a hefty pull on the bottle, and lit up a smoke.

What had I gotten myself into? I sat in the Escort, thinking over the events that had occurred in the last few days. I had made so many mental notes, that I needed a mental note to keep track of my mental notes. If this kept up, I would actually have to start writing things down. I shivered at that thought.

Since I have been in Detroit, I have gotten laid by two women who have absolutely no interest in establishing any type of a long term relationship with me. I have smoked a month's worth of cigarettes in less than a week. I have drank enough booze to keep a sailor drunk for an entire liberty. And, most importantly, I have felt like I was losing my mind, almost from the moment I got off the plane.

I took the last drag on my smoke, rolled down the window, and flipped the butt into the parking lot. I shook my head. I needed a chaser. I decided to go for broke, and went back inside the market to grab a "40 Ouncer". Goebel, was the beer of choice for the evening.

Sitting in the dimly lit darkness of the parking lot, I drank deeply from the bottle, letting the carbonation erase the slime in my mouth and throat. After a polite belch, I hit the key, and fired up the Escort.

I drove the short distance back to the motel in silence. When I pulled into the parking lot, I shut off the lights, and left the engine running. I enjoyed the few moments of quiet, while I finished the pint and the quart.

I couldn't seem to organize my thoughts about this spiritual crap. I was picking up bits and pieces of it, but why was I so fortunate to be brought into it in the first place? I didn't need it. I didn't ask for it. What purpose would it serve?

I didn't know the answers to these questions, yet. But, what I did know, was that I needed to take a whiz, and get some sleep. I gave up my solitude, and went inside the hotel.

* * * * * * * * * * * * * *

Almost as soon as I closed the door to my room, there was a soft knock. It was Raven.

"Up to some company?" she asked.

I just nodded, and swung the door open. I didn't really want company, but maybe a little sanity from some friends would help. Raven took a seat in the chair in the corner, and watched me take off my coat.

"Long day, huh?" she asked.

"Long day," I said, dragging out the long.

Jerry came through the open door, followed by Gale. Gale had changed clothes, and put on a lounging dress that I had bought for Raven some time ago.

Now, Raven is a beautiful woman in every aspect of the word, but Gale's fair skin against the black lounging dress was almost too much. She looked gorgeous.

"Sorry, friends," I said. "I don't mean to seem inhospitable, but I drank up all the goodies."

I laughed. I was drunk. Jerry laughed, too.

"That's OK pal, we brought our own." He held up a fifth of Jim Beam, and a two liter Coke.

I fell back into the other chair.

"Jerry, you gotta straighten me out on all this. My mind is totally frigged."

I told him some of the events that I had faced since I had been in town. Jerry listened intensely, occasionally sipping the J.B., and chasing it with the "Real Thing".

By the time I was done, it all seemed so ludicrous that we were roaring with laughter. We passed the bottle for a long time, talking. I skipped the intimate details of what actually went on with Angie and Debbie, in order to spare Gale's feelings.

Jerry knew me, and he got the gist of my stories, and knew what I meant. The time passed quickly, and the next thing I knew I was sleeping in the chair with a blanket over me.

Gale was tucked in the bed, breathing softly, and my friends were gone for the night. I didn't remember passing out, but my guess was that all the extra oxygen that I had taken in laughing, had put me over the edge.

I got up and walked to the bed. I pulled the covers back and got in. Gale was sound asleep, and fully dressed. When I got in bed, she instinctively snuggled back against me. I put my arms around her and we slept.

CHAPTER 18

One beam of light cracked the curtains, and hit me right in the eye. Gale slept, curled in a ball in front of me, my arms around her, my face pressed in her hair.

I lay quietly, thinking. I must have really been drunk, to get in bed with another woman, even if we were both fully clothed. Gale stirred.

"I hope you don't mind," she said, "I was cold."

I forced my eyes all the way open. Knowing that nothing had happened, I didn't really mind.

"No, I don't mind. As a matter of fact, I kind of enjoyed it."

I looked around my room. It looked like a tornado—no, worse—it looked worse, like someone had partied in it all night. If you've ever had a good party going in someone's hotel room, you know that not even a tornado, could do as much damage.

I put my head back down, and quickly dozed off again. The bed was cold when I finally woke up. Jerry was at my side.

"It's time to get up, your royal friggin' highness," he laughed.

I looked at my watch, and tried to focus. It was ten-forty a.m. It was also time to roll.

"Where's Gale and Raven?" I asked.

"Getting ready," Jerry anticipated. "Angie, your mom and the kids are riding with Sandy. They'll meet us at Spaulding."

I nodded. "Thanks for your help, Jerry."

I put my arm around him. Friends like Jerry come around only once in a lifetime.

The shower helped clear away the cob webs, but answered none of the questions that still lingered in my mind. Hopefully, I would be able to gain some information today, that would help provide me with much needed answers.

I grabbed a quick cup from the barf-machine at the end of the hall, and walked into the brisk cold. It was too cold for a funeral, I thought. But, I guess they have to have funerals, even in the winter.

They can't keep the bodies stored somewhere until spring now, can they? The thought amused me. I can see them now, they'd be stacked like cord wood all over the cemetery. I chuckled at the morbidity of my thoughts, but let them continue—"Sure, Mr. Thomas, your brother is over here, cord two, level four, face down."

I had another thought come to me. Did you ever wonder how they dug the graves in the wintertime before power equipment was invented, or if the bodies stay perfectly intact, until the spring thaw? I shook my head, laughing. Sean Thomas, you are losing your friggin' mind.

I made myself a mental note to limit my all night drunks in the future. After a second thought, I laughed, and erased the mental note.

* * * * * * * * * * * * * *

After a brief and non-discript funeral service at the funeral home, the immediate family and friends, all boarded the "Pope Mobile" for the ride to the cemetery. The "Pope Mobile," as J.J. called it, is a highly outfitted travel home, that funeral parlors are using to transport whole families from the funeral home, to the grave site. I guess it reminded J.J. of the vehicle the Pope traveled around in, when he visited the U.S. a few years ago.

We rode together, and talked softly on the way to the cemetery. Mom mentioned that Debbie had called to offer her further condolences, and apologized for not being able to attend the funeral.

In my drunkenness, I had forgotten to even call her about the funeral. This would be another situation that she would probably get PO'd about.

However, I was relieved that she had decided to avoid conflict with the other family members by finding something else to do. I made a mental note to try and catch up with her again later when this mess was finally over.

After we had ridden for a short way, Raven asked mom about the service the night before. Mom didn't answer but just looked at her. She was deep in thought, her mind miles away.

Noticing mom's distraction, Raven turned to Angie.

"A long time ago," she began, "my mother knew someone who was a very spiritual person. They did a lot of things with spirits and spiritual stuff. Their goal was always to do something they called, "Le change", or something like it. I guess they were supposed to do it when they died. I never understood it, but I heard my mother talk about it with this lady when I was younger. She was trying to teach my mother how to do it.

At the time, it seemed interesting to me, but I didn't really understand why. They said something about, how you had to vibrate or something, to make it work."

Angie nodded slightly, but didn't say anything back. With that, Raven simply shrugged her shoulders, and looked out the window.

I looked over at mom. She had stiffened noticeably, and was staring right through Raven. Then after a moment, she smiled softly, turned her head slowly to also look out the window, and said, "Thank you, my child. Thank you."

CHAPTER 19

After the burial service, everyone went back to the church for the wake. I decided to go along, and make my presence known, though I really felt like being alone.

It's funny what funerals can do to you. I've never been one to flock to death rites or rituals, but when a family member is involved, especially a twin brother, the effect on the mourners is tremendously magnified.

The took the long way back to the church, and by the time I got there, the church parking lot was nearly full. I pulled the Ford into the back of the lot, shut the engine off, and got out.

I was amazed at the number of people that had taken time out of their busy schedules to pay their last respects. I guess Cam was tremendously popular, even though he was always quietly modest.

Mom and Lillian were waiting for me on the church porch as I walked from the car. After the initial pleasantries, we went inside, and I made my way through the crowd, finally going downstairs for a smoke, and a coffee.

Walking into the dankness of the old basement, I looked around the room for Jerry and Raven, but they were nowhere in sight.

Over in the corner, Kyle stood with his back to me talking to Gale. I headed their way. As I neared, I noticed an unmistakable look of anxiety on Gale's face.

I reached up and put my hand on Kyle's shoulder.

"How you doin' Kyle?"

Kyle immediately went into character.

"Sean, nice service, wasn't it? How are you doing? You, OK?"

My first reaction was to puke right on the spot, but I was stoic. I put my arm around Gale.

"What are you doing here, Kyle? You weren't invited."

Kyle flashed his shit eating grin confidently, and then answered.

"Sean, ol' buddy, of course I was invited. Angie invited me."

Then he laughed, half turning away. "You just don't get it do you?"

We stared eye to eye a minute, and then I spoke slow and directly.

"Oh, I get it alright, ass-wipe. And what I get, is this. I get, that this is my brother's wake, and that it is now time for you to leave."

Then, moving a step closer, I added, "And if you still don't get the gist of what I am saying, I would look forward to the opportunity to show you how strongly I feel about it."

I respected the propriety of the moment, and Cam's memory. As much as I wanted to erase Kyle Washington from our lives, I was glad that he hadn't taken me up on my offer. Certainly there would be another time, and another place.

Kyle never took his eyes off of me, nor did he react to the rancor in my words, but looked at Gale.

"Coming?" he asked. Gale looked at me just the least bit uncertainly, and then shook her head.

"No, Kyle, I don't think so."

Kyle shrugged and smirked.

"Suit yourself. I'll see you later," and turned to leave.

On his way out the door, he stopped to pick up a piece of cake, went up the stairs, and out into the cold. Sandy and Angie were in the doorway looking around the room. I waved, and they walked in our direction. Angie looked at me with my arm around Gale, and her arm around my waist.

"Cozy," she said.

I ignored her statement, knowing she didn't really care what I was doing with my time, or with Gale.

"Ladies, I need to talk to Angie," I said. "Alone."

Gale nodded, and gave me a polite hug, and then she and Sandy excused themselves before going over to greet Jerry. I turned to Angie.

"Angie, what the hell is the deal. Did you invite Kyle to the wake?"

Angie stared blankly at a spot on the wall, for a moment, then slowly turned her head to look in my direction.

"I honestly don't know," she said. "I get confused when I'm around him."

I pressed her for more information.

"Did you see him last night?"

Angie snapped her head to look straight at me.

"What are you my keeper or something?"

"No, I'm not your keeper. But, if you're going to keep on seeing that asshole, then maybe you need a keeper."

Angie knew I was serious. But, I also knew I couldn't control her. She was a grown woman, and a free moral agent. Just because I didn't like Kyle Washington, didn't mean that she would actually stop seeing him. Angie also knew the intensity of my feelings. She knew that I wouldn't rest for a second, if I thought Kyle had something to do with Cam's death. Angie's attitude softened, smiling calmly.

"No, I didn't. I was with mom, remember?"

"Yeah, now I remember. I'm glad Angie. Kyle Washington is a dangerous man. You need to get a grip on yourself, and keep him the hell out of your life."

"Believe it or not Sean, I really am trying to do just that. It's not as easy as you think. You just don't understand."

Angie was right. I didn't understand a lot of things.

On one hand, I felt a small sense of relief remembering that Angie had stayed with mom last night. On the other, I didn't understand squat about the vibrations I kept hearing the Spiritualists talk about. One thing I did understand was Kyle. I got real bad feelings when I was around him. Maybe these feelings were the vibrations everyone felt.

I made myself a mental note that I was gonna check him out thoroughly, and also check out the word "Vibrations" in the spiritualist book.

Sandy flashed me a look of despair and frustration.

What the hell is her problem, I thought.

"Angie, will you get me an ashtray, please?" I asked.

"Sure, I'll be right back."

Angie turned and headed to the church kitchen to get the ashtray. Sandy walked back over in my direction.

Angie had experienced both good and bad changes in her life and her personality, even since I first arrived in Detroit.

Sandy had taken on the responsibility of being Angie's guardian, and now, she was feeling the pressure of trying to keep up with Angie, and keeping her in touch with reality.

I nodded to Sandy and lit up a Red.

"Sean, she's really out of it." Sandy gasped. Every time he comes around, she loses her grip. You can't talk to her. You can't reason with her. She just does what he wants. Kyle this, Kyle that."

"What really pisses me off, is that since you've been here, he has put increased pressure on her. I'm afraid she's going to lose it altogether."

I nodded like I understood. I didn't. I was, however, putting the picture pieces together so that maybe there would be some degree of understanding eventually.

"Do you think that he drugs her?" I asked.

Sandy thought for a minute, then shook her head.

"I don't know. She, sure gets weird sometimes, but she doesn't always act the same, like she might if she were drugged.

Before we could come to a conclusion, mom and Raven walked over to where we were standing.

"Sean, I've got something I want to talk to you about," mom said, excitedly.

Instinctively, I looked for Angie. Jerry appeared to have her under control in the corner, talking with Gale and Lillian.

He saw me looking in his direction, smiled and raised his eyebrows in acknowledgment. I gave him the high sign, signaling for him to look after Angie for a while. Jerry nodded in agreement.

Mom, Raven and I went upstairs into the sanctuary. Once there, mom turned and faced me. Now, she was solemn.

"Sean, earlier today on the way to the funeral, Raven reminded me of something I had heard about, a long time ago. I want to get your opinion on it. If you agree it's worth a try, then we will all need to work together."

Well, here I was again. People were always talking in riddles to me, and expecting this poor dumb PI, to figure out what was going on, without any clues. I smiled idiotically.

"Sure mom, whatever you say."

Mom reached over and took Raven's hand in her own.

"Let's sit down."

During the next half hour mom and Raven recounted how in the olden days of Spiritualism, and voodoo, it was possible to bring a person back from the dead.

The Cajuns, relying heavily on ancient voodoo rituals, and French ancestry, often talked of the "Living dead".

For them, "Le change", was their way to escape from the grave. Mom mentioned that the Spiritualists had utilized a similar program during the seventeenth and eighteenth centuries, but only a few mediums in modern times had commanded the spiritual energy necessary to perform a physical transfer from death, back to life. I began to feel nervous.

When mom and Raven finished their explanation, I leaned back in the pew, and let out a deep sigh. I laughed silently to myself, thinking, That's it. I'm out of here. This situation was getting more and more crazy with each passing moment.

"Well, ladies, this has all been very interesting." I said. "Let me see if I understand this correctly. You are suggesting, that we could pull off some voodoo bull shit, and bring Cam back to life. Right?"

"It's not like that, Sean," Raven said.

I stood up to leave.

Mom hissed an angry reply, commanding, "Sit down, Sean!"

I slowly sat down, crossed my arms, and legs, and leaned back. Mom continued.

"Other cultures have done it for centuries. Cam was your brother, for Christ's sake. Don't you want him back?"

I mulled that one around in my mind for a few moments before I answered.

"Mom, you know I want him back as bad as anybody does. But I don't think that dealing with the devil, is the road we should be walking on. Too much weird shit happens when you start messing around with voodoo and stuff like that."

Mom's face was an inch from mine.

"Read your book, Sean. There is no devil! He's a fabrication. There's only life and after life. It can be done, and we can do it. Think about what this means."

I was thinking about it. Out of a courtesy for her feelings, I felt it best to keep my thoughts to myself. My thoughts certainly didn't follow her thought pattern.

I leaned my head back away from her. I had never seen her act like this. She was enraged, and appeared obsessed.

"Mom, calm down," I said. "I will think about it. I just don't want to get my ass burned by being somewhere I don't belong. You know I don't understand this spirit stuff, but I will think about it."

Raven looked at me supportingly. I shrugged, raised my eyebrows, and found myself muttering to myself, "Maybe, just maybe, it might be worth a try." I decided I would have to read the book.

Lillian came up the stairs. "Oh, here you are, Norma," she said. "Jerry told me you wanted to talk to me." Mom started the explanation again.

About halfway through the second presentation, I got a funny feeling that someone was looking over my shoulder. I felt like I was being watched. You could call it a feeling of guilt. Guilt, for even thinking sane thoughts about the possibilities of "Le change".

I don't know what the emotion was, but one thing was certain, I wasn't anxious to hear the presentation through a second time.

When mom was finished, Lillian looked at me.

"What do you think, Sean? You would be the key."

I suddenly got real interested.

"Me? Why me? I don't know the first thing about this stuff, Lillian."

Lillian showed her best grandmother side, and spoke calmly.

"Sean, you are the key, because you are the only person close enough to Cam, to make it work."

I shook my head, adding "I don't know."

And really, I didn't know.

"I came to Detroit to try and see my brother before he died. Then that turned into a funeral. Now—?" I paused in my thoughts, shaking my head. "I guess, I don't even know enough about this stuff to decide, or comment," I said. "I will honestly consider it. I'll let mom know."

"Time is very important," Lillian offered. "Please don't wait too, long."

I nodded. Some consideration. If I went for it, then I was at the center of something that made me very nervous. If I didn't, then I let everyone else down. Great choices. I felt a knot in the pit of my stomach. I knew there was no way I could let mom down. "Le change". Voodoo. Where was it all going to end? This stuff was not my style.

Everyone shuffled around, and got up to leave. Sandy came up to my side.

"Can we finish our talk?" she asked.

"Sure," I said. "I'll see you downstairs, mom."

Raven took mom, and Lillian towards the stairs leading to the basement. I turned to Sandy.

Sandy wanted to finish our conversation from earlier. I was vulnerable, so I figured I'd give her, her best shot.

"Sean, I think we need to do something for Angie on this Kyle thing."

I sighed, remembering our earlier conversation.

"You think she's out of control, right?" I asked. "What do you mean, when you say, out of control?"

Sandy was quick to reply.

"Just what I said Sean, out of control. She can't say no, to this guy about anything, and now it's getting worse."

I needed some fresh air and I needed a smoke.

"Let's go outside for a minute," I said, heading for the door. We walked through the door and into the cold. I gave her my jacket, fishing the long red pack from the pocket as I slipped it around her shoulders.

The air was cold and crisp. I lit up a Red, and turned to Sandy.

"Now, what do you mean, worse?

"Sean, you asked me if I thought he was drugging her. I don't know about drugs, but how about some kind of mind control or something."

"Mind control?"

"It's possible. I've known her for a long time, and I've never known her to act anything like she's acting now. Plus, she drinks like a fish these days. Angie never drank in any quantity before. She used to get drunk on one beer.

Since El creepo, has been around, she drinks hard stuff, and lots of it. I took a sip of her drink the other day, and it almost made me puke."

"Sandy, mind control seems a bit far fetched. I will agree that it is possible. But, anything is possible. I'll try and keep an open mind, and I will look into it. Okay?"

Sandy nodded. Sandy was beginning to shiver, and I was certainly freezing my ass off, so I doused the butt, and flicked it into the driveway.

"Let's go inside," I said, reaching for the door.

My mind was a little scrambled. Drugs? Booze? Mind control? I guess it was all possible. If the guy knew what he was doing, it became all the more possible.

Sandy's suspicions sounded a little spooky at first, but I knew Angie was not a drinker. Booze was just not her cup of tea.

Once inside, Sandy gave my coat back.

"I'm going to be doing some checking," I said. "It is feasible. Hard to believe, but feasible."

My first real thoughts were that drugs wouldn't seem to be causing the sense of obedience, or loss of self control. Dependency yes, but involuntary obedience, not possible. There was more to this than simple mind games. I had an idea.

"Keep Angie and the kids at your place for a couple of days. I've got some things I need to check out. I'll call you tonight. No matter what, don't let that bastard near either one of you or the kids."

I went downstairs, and again bid my adieus, I looked around for Gale. Jerry met me on the stairs,

"Take Gale with you Sean. She's got some stuff you need to know."

I nodded, "Keep your eye on the rest of the girls for me? I may have a lead on this whole scheme."

"No sweat," he answered. "I've got them covered."

Gale was at the coat rack, putting on her coat.

"I understand that I am going with you," she smiled slyly.

I looked at her. She looked softer, more demur than the last time I saw her, and she looked awfully sharp dressed up. I helped her finish putting on her coat.

"I'd like that," I said, waiting for my little voice to jump in. It didn't.

Outside, it was blistering cold. We crunched through the light snow, got in the Escort, and started it up. I was almost out of windshield washer fluid from defrosting the windshield. I would have to get another gallon at the store tomorrow. I turned out of the church parking lot and headed for a pay phone.

Once we were under way, I shook out a Pall Mall, and hit it with a flame. Gale shook her head.

"I thought you wanted to quit smoking."

I shrugged, and looked at her.

"Who, me?"

"Yes, you, Mr. Smart Ass."

"I guess I do. But, not now," I said. "This is a smoker's paradise. I've been a PI for eighteen years, and I have never had this much crap, in any case I've ever handled before."

Gale just looked at me, not saying anything. I took a deep drag, exhaled, then rolled the window down, and threw half of a cigarette into the street. It had been a long time since I'd done that.

I found a phone, turned into the lot, slapped the gear shift into "Pee", and lifted the receiver. My twenty-cents clinked into the coin box and I pushed the buttons.

"Ferndale Police."

"John Stephens, please."

The phone rang, again and again.

"Detective Sergeant Stephens, can I help you?" came the familiar reply.

"John, it's Sean Thomas."

John was quick to reply.

"Sean, it's good to hear from you. Sorry about Cam."

"Thanks. John, I need to talk to you about Cam's incident."

"Anything I can do to help," he said. "What do you need?"

"I need two things," I started. "First, I would like you to run a wants and warrants on a guy named Kyle Washington. As far as I know, he came here from Phoenix a couple of years back. Then I need to know where Cam's car is."

John was rustling through papers.

"You mean what's left of it, right?"

"Right", I answered.

"Hang on, I'll be right back.

After a second he was back on the line.

"Crews Towing, Nine and Hilton. See Kenny, he'll help you out."

I wrote down the info.

"Thanks John, I appreciate your help."

"Anytime," he answered. "Call me later on this Washington stuff."

I hung up the phone. Kenny Crews was a school acquaintance that I remembered from my youth. He was always in with the tough crowd. It would be interesting to see him again. I turned the Escort in the direction of the storage yard, and drove in silence.

CHAPTER 20

The sun was cooling in the West as I pulled the Ford into the parking lot of "Crews Fuel and Storage". I turned into one of the spots that were cleared of snow, killed the engine, and Gale and I got out.

After the warmth of the car, the outside air, seemed extraordinarily cold. We walked in silence as we headed for the office.

The bell jangled against the back of the door announcing our presence when we entered. Gale and I walked into the small storage yard office. The office was scattered and disorganized, the smoke-tinged overhead light, barely winning it's battle over the increasing darkness of the late afternoon. The smell of grease and old car parts hung heavy in the air.

Fitting, I thought. The office was empty, save for a small nine inch black and white TV, which was broadcasting mostly snow, and a slowly rolling, picture. Probably made by the same bastards that made my phone, I thought.

Gale looked around, and then looked at me.

"Are you sure you want to do this?" she asked.

That was a good question. I hadn't really thought about what I wanted to do, or not do. Certainly it wasn't a time to be squeamish, but I found myself answering honestly.

"No, I'm not sure," I said, "But, it's got to be done sooner or later. I've at least got to check out Carolyn's story, even if it is only to reassure myself."

"Sean Thomas," came the voice from behind us. I turned around, and looked in the direction of the welcome. There in living color, stood Kenny Crews. Now, balding, and pot bellied, he looked the worse for life's wear. We shook hands.

"Sorry to hear about Cam," he said.

"Yeah, thanks," I responded, dutifully. "Can I see his car?"

I think we both knew that small talk would not be our forte', so we just looked eye to eye for a moment, and Kenny turned towards the door.

"Sure, its out back. I'll show you," he said.

As we walked through the yard, the guard dogs romped around us, their breath blowing smoke in the cold air.

"There it is," Kenny said, pointing to a pile of scrap metal sitting in the corner of the yard. Gale gripped my arm.

"Oh, Sean," she said, her voice trailing off.

At least she could say something. Personally, I was speechless as I looked at the silent monument to Cam's memory. I wondered how he could have lived at all, after the crash.

"You need me?" Kenny asked, shivering. I didn't look at him, but shook my head.

"No. Thanks for your help," I said. I couldn't take my eyes off the wreckage. Kenny said nothing, but turned and walked back to his office, the dogs running along behind him.

I took a few halting steps forward, and peered into what was once the driver's compartment. The seats were bent, and blood spattered. A light covering of snow masked the magnitude of horror I felt, as I walked around the car.

The odometer was stuck near eighty, the ignition keys were bent and still hanging down from the steering column, the windows were all gone, save one rear side window on the passenger's side.

I looked for a message, but saw nothing. Damn, it was cold.

"Nothing here that I can see," I said in Gale's direction. Gale had crossed her arms across her chest, and stood a silent vigil, watching me move around the twisted metal.

I was freezing and about to give up my search for a message. As a last minute thought, I decided to take the car keys with me. When I reached in to take them from the ignition, I noticed the cassette door was open on the tape player, indicating that a tape was still inside. I pushed the button, marked "Eject", and the tape popped out into my hand. I slipped it into my coat pocket, and turned to walk away.

"What was that?" Gale asked.

"A message, I think."

I needed a tape player, bad.

It was starting to get dark as we made our way past the junked, and impounded cars in the lot. I pushed the office door opened, and we walked into the dim light of the overhead incandescent.

Kenny called from behind a row of used parts.

"Any luck?"

"Not really," I lied.

"Can I use your phone?" Kenny walked into view.

"Sure Sean, just dial nine."

The phone was scrungy, but it was available. I dialed the number and waited for an answer. Gale looked tired. A hot bath, and a warm bed would do her a world of good, I thought.

"Detective Stephens," came the answer.

"John, Sean Thomas. You find out anything?"

John laughed. "Yeah, you're gonna love this guy. Evidently he used to be a pharmacist, but he lost his license. Now, he makes his living off of women.

He's got breach of promise suits pending from all over the country. He's got suspicion warrants in several cities for everything from fraud, to murder. Most recent was a murder in Salt Lake City. He evidently goes after the women's insurance money. You know where I can put my hands on this guy?"

I thought for a moment.

"Yeah John, I do. Let me sit on him for a couple of days. I'll keep him close. He's a link I need right now to some problems Angie is having. When the time is right, you got him."

"Sean, you're not in any trouble, are you?"

"Do I sound like I'm in trouble?"

"Yeah, you do."

"No trouble, John. Just staying close to the edge."

John laughed out loud.

"You were always close to the edge. Just don't fall over."

"Thanks for your vote of confidence Detective Stephens. I'll stay in touch."

"Good enough," John said. "Remember, stay in touch."

I hung up the phone, thanked Kenny, and we walked back to the car.

Gale put her are around my waist, and drew us close together.

"What is it, Sean?" Gale asked.

I looked at her. "Gale, darlin', we need to have a serious heart to heart. You hungry?"

Gale smiled, "Starved," she said.

I knew just the place. We pulled into the small parking lot of Commo's Pizzeria. I had been coming to Commo's since I was a freshman in high school. Excellent pizzas, a little greasy, but heavy on taste. We took a seat in one of the plastic booths. Gale wasted no time getting to the point.

"What's going on, Sean?" she asked honestly.

I lit up a smoke, and took a deep drag before answering. I was teasing her with my apparent disinterest. The look of anxiety on her face told me it was time to drop the games.

"Gale, this may be bigger than both of us."

The waitress came to take our order. I wanted food of substance, so I ordered thoughtfully.

"We'll take a large with the works, two large Cokes, and an ashtray."

"Rhonda," her task complete, turned and headed for the kitchen. We now had a moment of privacy.

"How long have you known Kyle?" I asked. Gale thought for a moment.

"Is it important?"

"Trust me. It's very important."

"Maybe three years, all together. I met him in Phoenix. He bailed me out after my fire. He literally took care of everything. Why do you ask?"

"Did you know him before the fire?"

Gale shook her head.

"No, not really. He used to come into the store where I worked. One day he asked me out, the next thing I knew, we were living together. He treated me real nice, except for the sex."

"I'll bet."

"Look, Sean, I'm not a whore. You might think I'm a whore because of the Cam and Angie thing, but I'm not. That's not me. I'm really a lot more reserved, and together than that."

After a short wait, the waitress finally brought our food. I suddenly realized that I was starving too. I reached for the triangular slice, put it on my plate and added the crushed peppers that were necessary to make any pizza complete. We ate in silence, listening to the soft sixties music which was oozing thoughtfully from the juke box.

The restaurant had soft yellow lighting, and it cast a mellow glow on Gale's features. She was a very pretty woman. As I looked at her, I figured that she was right. Maybe I had misread her because of what I had heard. Gale wiped her mouth, and set the napkin down. It was obvious, she wanted to continue our earlier conversation.

"Don't get me wrong," she volunteered. I'm no prude either. If I see something I want, I go after it."

I smiled, and answered sarcastically. "And when you're cold?"

Gale laughed. "When I'm cold, I warm myself with only the best warmers I can find."

"Like yesterday?"

Gale caught her breath. She snickered just a little, and muttered, "sorry".

Gale's face turned colors. She was obviously embarrassed for falling asleep in my bed the other day.

"I guess I should have asked first."

Now, it was my turn to laugh.

"I can't imagine why you would worry about that. I was fully dressed."

Gale looked straight into my eyes.

"Yeah, I noticed," she said. "Are you a prude or something?" she asked, laughing and dragging out the word you.

Gale's laugh was infectious. We both laughed, and I just shook my head.

"No," I paused, "No, I don't think I'm a prude."

We continued to eat in silence for a while, and then I spoke.

"Did you ever know Kyle to use drugs?"

I had hit a nerve. Gale got real serious. She put down her pizza, and nearly choked on the piece she was chewing. Her face turned pale and then became real serious. After a small drink, she regained her composure, and continued.

"He drugged me, that bastard. And, I'll bet he's drugging Angie now. He's a pharmacist you know?"

I shook my head, lying my ass off again. I needed her to go on.

"I don't know how he's doing it, exactly, but for me, he told me it would relax me. Well, it didn't relax me, it knocked me out. After a while, it didn't work so well, and I used to get sick, so he offered to hypnotize me instead."

"Hypnotized? Like real hypnotism?"

"Sort of. He said it would still relax me like the drugs, but it would be harder, and would take longer to work, so up until the other day, he used to hypnotize me every day.

When we moved here, he started this sex thing. He told me that I was repressing sexual urges, and that's why I was having emotional problems."

"Emotional problems," I asked. "What kind of emotional problems?"

Gale was matter of fact. "I was depressed over losing my house, and the fact that I had only gotten about half of what they say my stuff was worth. I was crying all the time. When we started having sex with everyone, I did feel better for a while."

"What about Cam?" I asked.

Gale furrowed her brow.

"Cam, was real sick," she said. "One day Angie came in the store to pick up some food. Kyle was there. After he talked to her for a minute, he brought her home. At the time it seemed okay, so I went along with it."

"So, that seems simple enough," I added.

"Not really. Cam, came looking for her, and after they had words, Kyle told me to screw him, so I did. Cam, was so hurt. I tried really hard to make it important to him, but he felt so guilty. He had tried to pay Angie back, but it wasn't his nature.

Even though Angie had done it first, he just wasn't ready for it."

That part seemed logical. Cam, always led with his heart, and it caused him a lot of emotional pains.

I nodded. "So now what's in store for you?"

Gale looked down, and slowly shook her head."

I don't know," she said. "I certainly want to stay away from Kyle. Since I haven't been around him, I feel good again."

I figured she was telling me the truth. What would she gain by lying to me. Her face said, believe me, and I had no reason not to.

I ordered another Coke and lit up a Red. I wanted to talk more, but time was against me today.

"You want to stay at the Holiday again?" I asked. Gale nodded.

"Jerry and Raven said I could stay with them."

I took a deep drag. "You are welcome to stay in my room," I offered.

Gale and I both laughed at the same time.

"Sure, Raven told me all about you. You'll take advantage of me in my weakened state."

I laughed again. "So, Raven told you all about me, huh? Wait till I see her again."

"Really though," I said, probably lying my ass off again, "You're safe with me." I handed her the key. "At least Kyle won't come looking for you there."

Gale reached out to take the key from me, a smile on her face, her eyes focused on my eyes. "If you promise not to be such a prude."

"I promise," I answered.

I held her hand in both of my hands for a moment as I gave her the key. Gale leaned forward, and gave me a soft peck on the lips, the moistness of her full lips gently teasing both my mind, and my mouth.

"Then, if you will take me home," she said, slowly standing, turning and heading toward the door.

We rode in silence for the few minutes it took to get to the Holiday. I pulled up in front of the lobby, and turned to look at Gale.

"I've got a couple of stops to make before I come back for the night. Jerry makes a terrific Margarita. Have him make you one, and I'll see you in a little while."

Gale leaned over and gave me a kiss that sent chills down my back.

"Maybe I'll have two," she said.

She then reached out her index finger and gently touched my lips.

"Hurry back," she said.

I nodded. *Hurry, indeed,* I thought.

I watched Gale disappear through the door of the Holiday, and then turn down the hallway towards the room. I thought to myself, I didn't need the distractions of another woman right now. Yet, somehow Gale seemed different, more of a help than a hindrance.

For now though, I needed a tape player. I stopped at a pay phone and dialed mom's number, Sandy answered.

"Hello Sandy, this is Sean."

"Hi, Sean," came the response.

I noticed a little ice in the greeting.

"Where are you?"

"I'm out," I answered. "Do you have a cassette tape player?"

Sandy thought for a minute.

"Sure, why?"

"I've got a tape I need to play."

"It's at the house, but I don't want to leave Angie alone, Kyle's been calling all night. I keep hanging up on him, but he calls about every 15 minutes."

"Whatever you do, don't even let him talk to her. I've found out some weird shit about him, and it's important that he has no access to her, okay?"

Sandy answered. "Okay. Stop by my house and see Jeff. I'll call him and tell him you'll be coming by. We need to do something soon. It's about time for Kyle to call back again."

"I'll be there as soon as I can," I said, and hung up the phone.

* * * * * * * * * * * * * *

After I picked up the recorder, I headed to mom's. Sandy, Angie, and mom were already there. I pulled into the drive. Kyle's car was across the street and it was empty. Shit, I thought, grabbing the tape player and the tape and heading for the house.

Fortunately, Kyle was not inside. Angie was sleeping in mom's bedroom, dead to the world. I picked up the phone, and called John.

About ten minutes after my call, a patrol car, and a tow truck showed up in front of the house. Hopefully that would keep Kyle out of circulation for at least a little while. I put the tape in the player, sat down at the dining room table, and hit the "Play" button.

The tape whirred.

"Congratulations, brother. If you are listening to this, it means that you have done your usual outstanding job of investigating. It also means that I have fallen on my ass trying to resolve my situation."

I pushed the "Pause" button, stopping the tape. I wondered to myself, was this a set-up? A trick perhaps, to distract me, or worse, disarm me. I sat thinking for a moment, mulling over the possibilities.

Logic said, that neither Cam nor the Spiritualists had anything to gain by deceiving me, and thinking further, Cam was dead. What purpose would my distraction serve for him? I chalked it up to an over imaginative PI mind, and hit the "Pause" button a second time. Cam's voice returned.

"Life sucks, really," he said. "It looks more and more, like I have lost control of anything that is important to me. It seems that, well . . .," Cam paused, his voice trailing off, then after what seemed like an eternity, Cam composed himself, and continued.

"I guess, the first thing is to say that I didn't plan for all this to happen. Everything just seemed to get out of hand. This fiasco, this mess, this shit."

Cam, was drunk. He was obviously drinking tequila. He coughed, cleared his throat, and went on.

"This shit, it's more than I can handle. It's not like I ain't trying or something. But think about it. What would you do?"

My attention to the tape intensified. Listening to the sounds of my brother's voice had convinced me that this was not a hoax. Cam, had recorded the tape, and was pouring his heart out in it. Cam's voice continued.

"Don't get me wrong, I think I've got the rest of life in perspective. But shit, everyone has limits, and I've got mine."

Cam, chucked softly. "Limits," he, said, and then laughed again. "Even the great Cam Thomas, has limits. Well, at least now you all know I have limits. I'm not really embarrassed, just drunk." Cam, laughed again. "Don't misunderstand me. It's not like this shit was ever an avenue of choice. My choice would be to turn the clock back and get my wife and family back, and rid myself of this agony."

Cam, sighed deeply. "All this shit, and I mean shit," he continued spitting out the word, "started out great," he said, his thoughts controlling his speech, "Any man's fantasy, I guess you might say."

I thought to myself, this is Cam's confessional, and he went through hell to make it.

"The truth is," Cam's voice continued, "this mess is so confusing, even I'm not sure of what happened. I don't know how it all started, really." Cam paused, taking another drink. "Once it got rolling, it got real crazy. Anyway, after a while I lost track. Angie got hooked up with that bastard Kyle, and I tried to act cool and said, screw her too, I'll get even."

Cam laughed again. He was really drunk. His slurred words causing me to listen even closer.

"Hah, the joke was on me. I tried to get into it, but my mind went A.W.O.L. See, I wasn't really interested in these other women. I only wanted to maintain my sense of masculinity. My mind and body knew better."

"After a while, I don't know how to say this, but I couldn't get it up for these women. Do you know what it's like to lose the use of your pecker?" Cam laughed again, sounding like he might puke. He was slurring his words so badly, that his words were almost impossible to understand. Cam was crying softly.

"Might as well already be dead, right? But life goes on for some. Just so you know, I'm feeling like I should finish this off so that I can end the agony I feel. At least that would save me the embarrassment of a long and difficult failing. Look, Sean, if you have dealt with the Kyle, Gale and Angie issue, you're probably as confused as hell by now. Try not to look down on Angie or Gale. They are only reacting to situations."

The tape was nearly out. There appeared to be only a minute or two left on it.

"As for me, I am confident that if anything should happen to me, that life on the other side will be better and more peaceful than it is here. Truly, if death is nothing more than darkness, and a hole in the ground, it will be better than this." Cam paused while he apparently took a swig of Jose' Cuervo.

"Do me a favor and take care of Angie and the kids for me. Do what you can to get her away from Kyle. He really has got a hold on her you know?"

"She may tell you a story about me screwing someone at work, but don't believe it. It's a crock. It was planted in her mind by Kyle. She and Kyle were screwing from the first day they met. When I found out, I tried to beat his ass, but that didn't work out."

"I remember dad saying, don't fight when you're drunk, you'll get your butt whipped. Man, he was right. I thought Kyle and Gale were married, so I figured I'd get even with him and Angie by popping her. Once again the joke was on me, because no one cared, one way or the other. They just stood around and watched. Talk about a bunch of kinky bastards."

"Sean, I tried to make Angie jealous, but it didn't work. It breaks my heart, because I've lost her, and there's nothing I can do about it."

Cam paused before continuing. "It's been a wild time," he laughed dryly, "but, I would give it all up, to have Angie love me like she used to. The only person who knows how I really feel is Susan. She may not tell you, but she does know."

Only seconds remained on the tape.

"I may be way off base, but from the things I've heard, Kyle is some kind of con man or something. I figure you're better at figuring out that kind of stuff, than I am. I wish I knew where to look for answers. Maybe then, life would still hold some future for me. Just for safe keeping, I took all my insurance, and stock shit, and put them in the kids name with you as the executor.

If you can figure all of this out, and get Angie back on track, then you can switch it back. I gave you power of attorney. Whatever you do, don't change anything back if Kyle is still around. I think he wants to get my money through Angie."

"Gale said something about an insurance policy on her house. I checked with a guy named Ron Tippen at Homeowner's Mutual. They cut a check for seventy-five g's, Gale got thirty. Near as I can figure, Kyle kept the rest."

Cam sighed heavily, "Sean, if something should happen to me, please take care of my family." Then as an after thought, Cam added, "Oh, by the way, if you get a chance to meet Gale, I think you'll like her. She seems very down to earth."

The player clicked off, and I heard myself breath for the first time since I started the tape. My thoughts were a bit confused. Why couldn't Cam have called me and talked about this problem? Had I distanced myself that much from my family? I shook my head. A distant voice from behind startled me back to reality.

"Who was that?" Angie asked, looking sleepily around the corner.

Mom answered for me.

"It was Cam, honey. It was his last tape."

I didn't even know that mom had been listening. I guess I should have assumed that she and Sandy were listening, since there were no other sounds in the house as the tape played.

Angie asked, "Can I hear it?"

Mom looked at us with a helpless look before turning back to Angie to answer.

"Do you think you are ready for it?" she asked.

"I don't know what I'm ready for anymore." Angie answered honestly, shaking her head.

The sounds of chains on metal and someone swearing at the top of his voice caught our attention. Mom, Sandy, and I went to the front window to watch Kyle make a total ass of himself. He was calling the police officer, and the tow truck driver every profane name in the book.

Once secure, the truck driver began driving down the street toward the impound yard. Kyle jumped into the moving truck still swearing.

After about a hundred yards, the tow truck stopped, and Kyle got out, cursing and slamming the door.

Once free of his vile cargo, the truck driver proceeded, Kyle flipped the driver, the bird, and looked back towards the house swearing.

After he had vented his frustrations, he began walking in the direction the truck had taken, presumably to try and get his car back.

We all laughed. When I turned around, Angie was just finishing up the tape. She pushed the "Stop" button, and sat silently, staring straight ahead.

We all looked at each other, and then back to Angie. She slowly got up, and walked back into the bedroom. Angie looked dazed. That frightened me. After a few minutes, I went in and sat on the side of the bed. Angie lay curled in the fetal position sobbing.

"I killed him, Sean. I killed him."

I leaned over and kissed her softly on the cheek.

"Angie, he chose this path."

As I said that, I felt a chill go down my spine. Drunk as Cam was, depressed as he seemed to be, checking out via suicide, was not his style.

I felt this surge of energy that said, "There's more to this than meets the eye, or in this case, the ear."

I made myself a mental note to figure out just exactly what that was.

Angie had stopped crying, and lay quietly. Her deep sigh, told me that she was trying to regain some composure.

I think the tragedy of Cam's death was beginning to sink in. Angie spoke haltingly.

"But what I did. Sean, I just didn't know, honestly. I can't believe I even slept with you."

Hearing those words brought me a measure of relief, but you can imagine the blow to my ego. Angie continued.

"I mean, I do love you Sean, but not like that. You are too much like Cam, it wouldn't be right." I patted her softly on the back.

For once she was right, and it was refreshing to hear someone coming back to their senses, if only momentarily.

"Let's not dwell on what was, Ang," I said, "Let's look forward."

I took a deep breath before speaking. Now, was the time to start putting the pieces together, and I needed Angie's help to do it.

"Angie?"

"What?"

"Mom and Raven have an idea. If we're lucky, we may be able to pull off something I can hardly even understand. Just let us handle it, and stay away from Kyle until I tell you different, got it?" Angie nodded, rolled over, and smiled a small smile.

"Got it," she said.

I walked back into the front room, and made sure that someone was going to stay with Angie and mom. Conveniently, my Aunt Lou showed up just before I left. I felt secure in the number of people who would be with her.

"Mom, call Lillian and see if we can get together tomorrow in the evening," I said. "Tomorrow morning, Angie and I are going to see Susan. I'll call her and set it up."

Mom nodded, "I'll see that she's ready."

I kissed them all good-bye, and went outside.

I didn't know what to expect. Kyle had been out there a long time.

Fortunately, the Escort seemed intact. I started her up, and reached for my pack. As I did, I remembered Gale's harassment earlier in the day. Maybe she was right. I passed on the *Red.*

When I turned on the headlights, I saw the business card stuck in the wiper. It was John's. On the back of the card, it said simply "Call me", and a phone number.

* * * * * * * * * * * * *

I stopped in the lobby of the Holiday on the way in, and dialed the number on the card. After several rings the phone clicked.

"Yeah?" It was John.

"John, this is Sean."

"Yeah Sean, I got an update on our friend. He's a crazy dude. He's screwed up a lot of people's lives. Don't let him get away from you."

I listened with interest to what John was telling me.

"Okay, is there anything else specific I should know?"

John was rustling paper in the background. His voice trailed off for a moment before coming back, loud and clear.

"Yeah, but you're not going to believe this."

"Try me."

"Do you remember that I told you that he's got at least a dozen aliases, and he's wanted under most of them?"

"Yeah."

"Well, he's formally wanted for extortion, illegal prescription drugs with the suspicion of intent to deliver, breach of contract, practicing medicine without a license, and there are two more pages on the list. He's also got, attempted murder warrants pending in three states. Don't turn your back on him, even for a minute."

I had no intentions of letting Kyle get the upper hand, if there was any way I could prevent it. I planned to be on the offense from now on.

"John I've got a plan that may put him out of commission for good, but you've got to trust me."

John was quiet for a minute, then answered.

"I'm listening," he said.

I stalled. "I can't tell you yet. Just trust me."

John was very matter of fact.

"Sean, for some reason I feel real bad about this plan, real bad."

I laughed, "John, you're gonna love it, I promise."

I hung up the phone, picked it up again, and dropped in two bits. The voice at the other end of my phone sounded like melted caramel.

"Sue, this is Sean."

Susan cleared her throat."Sean, do you know what time it is?"

I didn't, but looked at my watch.

"Twelve-twenty," I mumbled, "Sorry to be so late, but this is important. I got new information today. Cam, said that you knew his whole story. The information I got today says that maybe you didn't tell me the whole story."

Susan sighed, "That's right, I do know more of the story. There are some things I didn't tell you, but it's not like you think," she said, "I told you most of the facts, and I would have told you the rest eventually, after I got to know you better. It's not like I left out any of the major facts."

Susan was groping for support or forgiveness. At the moment, I decided not to give it to her. I had only asked for honesty. Susan had decided to play games with me. Why, I didn't know. I figured that she may have just been trying to protect Cam's image.

"It doesn't matter now," I said, "But I do need your help. You do hypnosis don't you?"

"Sure, why?"

"I'll tell you when I see you," I said. Then as an afterthought, I added "Can you use hypnosis to de-program someone," I asked.

Susan's words became measured. She spoke slowly, choosing her words carefully.

"I'm not sure what you mean by de-program, but if you mean what I think you mean, it depends on what was said, how it was said, the way it was received by the receptor, and a lot of other things. Who did you have in mind?"

"Gale and Angie," I answered.

"What makes you think they were hypnotized?"

"Cam, said they were."

"Cam's, dead."

"Yeah, I know. But, before he died, he made a cassette tape. On this tape, he said Kyle was hypnotizing them. After talking to both of them, I think they were too. Do you think you can help?"

"I can sure, try. Come in tomorrow at eleven."

I repeated the time back to her.

"Sean?"

"Yeah?" I answered.

"I make no promises."

"None expected," I said to reassure her.

I started to hang up the phone when I remembered something.

"Susan?"

"Yes," she answered sleepily, "What now?"

"Did Cam seem like the type of person that would walk away from a fight?"

Susan was quiet.

"What do you mean?"

I continued, thinking aloud as I talked to her.

"Knowing what you did about him, did he seem like he had the personality to take his own life"?

I sensed that Susan knew what I was leading up to. Susan was obviously waking up a little. She yawned before replying.

"I'm sorry. Now, what did you ask?"

"Do you think Cam would take his own life?"

"Sean, that's a good question. Now, that you mention it, most of the time, he didn't, but things do change you know?"

I did know. I also knew that if Cam had that type of a change in his personality, it probably wasn't by accident.

"Do me a favor," I asked "Think, on it for a while. I'd like to talk to you more about it tomorrow."

Susan didn't answer my request.

"Good night, Sean."

"Good night Susan," I said, and finally hung up the phone.

* * * * * * * * * * * * *

The room was dark, and smelled of a shower. Gale looked asleep, so I took a towel and some clean skivvies into the john and turned on the light.

The card stood on the back of the sink faucet. I opened it up. It was a nice card, with a silkscreen cloth insert in the cover. It said, simply "Sometimes words are not enough to say, thank you."

Gale had written below, "Sean, I may be cold when you get here. Please come and keep me warm."

I lost my breath for just a moment. Gale was something special. My attraction to her, was not just some flash in the pan. I also felt that Gale felt the same way about me. It was possible that we were heading to something more than a spur of the moment relationship. That thought made me feel a little uncomfortable. I had no intentions of becoming involved. Also, Gale was involved. Did I want to become part of that?

For the moment, I decided to put my concerns on hold. Wherever Gale and I were headed, time was not an issue. I understood the risks, but I also could see the potential. All things in good time, I thought.

I quickly got in the shower, and turned it on high. The water felt good, chasing the cares and the trials of the day.

As I rinsed off, my thoughts went to Gale. I quickly cut the shower short, stepped out, and dried off. I skipped the skivvies, turned out the bathroom light, and walked to the bed.

Drawing the covers back, I could see the beauty of her nakedness. Gale stirred, and reached her arms up to me. As I lay down, she kissed me softly on the mouth.

There was a decided, contrast between the cool sheets and the warmth of her body. I too, was chilled. When my skin touched the coolness of the sheets, I shivered. It looked like I was also going to need some warming up. I slid over next to Gale and put my arms around her, pulling her close to me.

The heat of our bodies, joined at that moment, with a final shudder, chasing away the cold and its shivers.

Gale turned to face me, and without a word, explored the depth of my touch, and my kiss. Responding was automatic. My skin tingled with anticipation. I sensed that Gale had also heard the melody of love. We kissed again, deeply, and then spent the rest of the night in warmth and mutual admiration.

CHAPTER 21

"Sean Thomas," I said into the phone, clearing my throat, and trying to wake up. I looked at my watch. It was still early, only nine forty-five.

"Sean, this is Carolyn. Did you get the tape?"

My first thought was, How did she know that the message Cam had mentioned was on a tape?

"Yeah, I got it," I said into the receiver.

"Who is it?" Gale whispered, her silky skin gently rubbing against my naked body. I turned to her.

"It's Carolyn," I answered.

"What did you find out?" Carolyn continued into my ear.

"I'll let you hear it later. What's your schedule like today?"

"Do you have company?" came, the inquiry.

"Yeah, I do," I said, evading the issue. "Why do you ask?"

Carolyn mused on the other end of the line.

"Just wondering, that's all. I'm sorry you didn't know about Jack."

My thoughts were, why would you be wondering what I'm doing, and I really don't care about Jack. I kept those thoughts to myself.

I didn't know if she wanted me to say something cute, or what, but Gale started rubbing my back, and at this point I really wasn't concerned about her opinion or her relationship with Jack. That was from another place and another time.

"Don't give it another thought," I said, and turned to put my hand on Gale's shoulder. "Life does go on".

"I guess you're right," Carolyn said. "I guess now is not the best time to talk about it either, right?"

"That's right," I answered. "Why don't we all get together for lunch?"

"I can't," she said. "But, I'll see you later at church."

I hung up the phone and turned to look at Gale. She looked stunning in the morning light.

She modestly kept the sheets pulled up, covering over her body. I thought to myself, this is supposed to be the lady, that everyone says would screw anyone? I didn't know who started that rumor. But, somebody was way off base.

Gale gave me a hug, and a kiss, then swung her legs out of bed, got up and went to the shower. I watched her walk, and thought how beautiful she really was.

I felt uncomfortably contented. I certainly didn't want to get involved with Gale, but for some reason our developing relationship seemed normal. I resigned myself to let things ride.

Normally, it would have been against my better judgement to get involved with a woman who was involved in one of my cases. Gale had caused me to question my own judgement, but for now, I wasn't going to worry about it.

I got out of bed and the movement in the mirror, to my left, caught my eye. Gale was drying off. I watched her for a minute. I realize that I was being a voyeur. But, the beauty of her body mesmerized me. I simply couldn't look away.

I also realized the effect that Gale had already had on my life, and I decided that I wanted to stay close to her.

When we were finally dressed, I walked across the hall and knocked on the door to Jerry's room. Raven, answered the door. They too were just starting to move around.

"What's happening?" Jerry said, more as a statement than a question.

I smiled, "Same ol' shit, buddy."

Raven, shook her head, and muttered something about, "Even the first thing in the morning," or something like that.

"I want you guys to come to the therapist with me at eleven," I said.

Jerry nodded, "OK, but what's up?"

"First of all," I said "I want you to meet her, but really, I've got an idea that she can help us get Angie and Gale back to reality."

"How's Angie doing?" Raven asked.

I shook my head.

"Actually, she's crashing, bad. As it stands, I'm really concerned about her mental state. Hopefully, Susan can help her."

Raven walked over and got in my face.

"And, how is Miss Gale doing?" she sneered, jokingly.

We both laughed.

"Miss Gale, is doing just fine, if you really want to know the truth," I answered somewhat sheepishly.

Jerry and Raven both howled, "Whoooooo," and then broke up, in laughter. Jerry got serious for a moment.

"Sean, no kidding, she really is a beautiful girl. Now, she's not as beautiful as my ebony sweetheart here," putting his arm around Raven, "but she is beautiful."

I'm sure that somewhere in my deep subconscious, I had actually heard what he said, but at the moment it didn't register. I opened my eyes wide.

"Are you guys trying to tell me something?" I asked.

They both laughed.

"Hey," Jerry said, hugging Raven tighter, "We're talking. You'll be the first to know."

I shook Jerry's hand. "Well, hey, good luck, or something," I added.

I never have been one to be eloquent with words, especially at sensitive times. But, if they decided to become an item, they would do so with my blessings. They were my best friends, and I loved them both.

I gave Jerry, Susan's address, and some basic directions. When I felt comfortable that he knew where he was going, I went back to get Gale, and headed to breakfast.

I was completely famished, and ate like it. I had to recharge my batteries, and it took the "Farmer's Special" and a side order of hot cakes, to satiate my hunger pangs.

After breakfast, we stopped and picked up Angie, and the three of us drove, to Susan's office. Raven and Jerry were already there when we drove up.

"What are we doing, here?" Angie asked, emphasizing the word Here.

I parked the car, killed the engine, and turned to face her.

"Ang, Kyle hypnotized you and Gale."

"What?"

"He hypno—"

"I heard what you said. What do you mean?"

"I mean, like, hypnotized. Put in a trance? Under a spell? Kyle hypnotized both you and Gale to get you to do what he wanted. You may still be under his spell."

Angie had a very sarcastic look on her face. She didn't believe me.

"You mean that he could make me bark like a dog or something, right?"

I laughed. "In a sense. But, it was much more sophisticated than that. That's why we're here. I want to find out how sophisticated. Susan knows hypnosis as well as anyone. She thinks she can de-program Kyle's input."

Angie nodded silently, as though understanding the concept for the first time.

"I have felt a lot better since I haven't been seeing him, you know, stronger." Then Angie shook her head in disbelief. "But, even now, I have the strongest urge to see him, you know, to be with him."

I did know what she was saying.

"Trust me through this one, ladies," I offered. "I think Susan can help all of us." I mentally crossed my fingers.

Soft music played from the ceiling somewhere, as we sat waiting for Susan to finish up with a client. I wondered if Susan was servicing her client, or merely doing psychological work.

I probably had no right to even think such a thing, but at least I'm honest. After a few moments, the office door opened and a mother and her teenage daughter, maybe fifteen or sixteen walked out.

"Then we'll see you again on Friday," Susan said, stepping into the waiting room. She waited until the mother and daughter had left, and then turned her attention to us.

"Hi Sean," she said, extending her hand. "Why don't you all come on in."

I stood up, shook her hand, and turned to look after the mother and daughter.

"Intimate Assistants?" I asked questioningly.

Susan smiled. "I/A is only one aspect of our business. We do general psychological counseling, troubled children, marriage counseling. You know, everyday, head shrinking stuff, in addition to I/A."

I suddenly felt real stupid for asking. Susan detected my uneasiness, and spoke first.

"How can I help you?" she asked.

I reached for my pack.

"Mind if I smoke?" I asked. Susan shook her head. I lit up a Red, took a hit and exhaled.

"Cam's tape, said that he thought Kyle used drugs, and hypnosis to control both Angie and Gale. He took Gale for forty grand, and I think he's trying to get Cam's insurance money from Angie."

Susan grimaced. "One thing I can do for sure, is to find out if Kyle told them anything, and if so, what it was. Whether or not I can change it," she paused, and shrugged, "well, that's another story. We'll just have to wait and see."

I looked at Angie and Gale with a smile, and a shrug.

"Well, it's a start, isn't it?"

"Who's first?" Susan asked. Gale and Angie both looked at each other. Neither wanted to be the guinea pig. After a moment, Gale spoke.

"I'll go first," she said.

Angie looked frightened, and then relieved. Gale got up and walked to the recliner sitting near the center of the room, and sat down.

Dirty old man that I am, I had always wondered what a guy could tell a woman, that he had hypnotized, to make her his love slave. Okay, so maybe I was looking for pointers. Certainly, Susan would have my undivided attention.

I was brought back from fantasyland by the sudden dimming of the lights.

Susan began speaking softly.

"Gale, just sit back in the chair and relax. Listen carefully to my words. Listen to nothing else."

Silence overtook the room. After a short pause, Susan began again.

"Gale, you are beginning to relax. I want you to repeat after me, and count backwards from the number ten. I am beginning to relax."

Gale repeated the words. "I am going deeper and deeper, asleep. Number nine. I am beginning to relax. I am going deeper, and deeper, asleep. Number eight."

At number five, it was obvious that Gale was no longer consciously repeating the statements. She was off in the ozones.

Susan proceeded. "Gale, can you hear me?"

Gale nodded, and whispered softly "Yes".

"Gale, I want you to go back to the day when you met Kyle Washington. Do you remember that day?"

Gale nodded again. The next fifteen minutes covered the development of their relationship. I was amazed at the details that Gale could remember. Simple things like the weather, the clothes she wore, the people that were around.

Shortly thereafter, they got to the point in the relationship that just preceded Kyle's moving in with her, Gale told of a wild party where she and Kyle drank heavily until she passed out.

After we passed that point, Gale's demeanor took on a totally different attitude. One of flippancy, and devil-may-care. Susan stopped, and looked at all of us uncertainly.

It was as if Susan wanted our approval to keep digging into her subconscious. I figured, We've come this far, so why not? I nodded for her to continue.

Susan continued, "Gale, I want you to go back to the party. What are you drinking?"

Gale thought for a minute.

"I'm drinking Sea Breezes," Gale smiled.

"Is that the only thing you have to drink, Sea Breezes?" Susan asked. Gale nodded affirmedly, and then proceeded to review the rest of the day.

"Later on, Kyle fixed me a drink. I don't know what it is, but it is real bitter. Mixing it with the Sea Breeze is making me sick."

Gale's face turned white. She swallowed rapidly a couple of times as if re-experiencing the nauseating taste in her mouth. She rubbed her stomach, as though feeling sick, or upset. Susan jumped in quickly.

"Gale, I only want you to see the events of the day. You don't have to feel them. You can watch everything that is going on, but nothing can hurt you, or make you feel uncomfortable in any way."

Susan gave Gale a moment to compose her self, and then seeing her calm down, she proceeded.

"Gale, please continue."

"I told Kyle that I don't want it, but he says it gets better as you drink more. I just don't like it."

Susan continued. "Gale who else is at the party?"

Gale paused, again looking around in her mind. She answered softly.

"I am there—, and Kyle is there—. That's all. I feel sick, I've got a tremendous headache, I'm going to throw up."

Susan went on. "What happens next?"

Gale laughed "Kyle is trying to keep me from barfing. He says he can get rid of my headache by hypnotizing me. I don't believe in that stuff."

Susan took a deep breath, sighed and continued cautiously, "Do you let him hypnotize you?"

Gale laughed again, "Sure, why not. I feel like shit anyway. Besides, it might be fun."

Susan asked, "Can you remember him actually doing it, actually hypnotizing you?"

Gale shook her head. "No, not really. I just feel real sick."

Susan looked questioningly at us and got serious. She raised her eyebrows signaling us she was on to something. Susan seemed to intensify her concentration. Her questions became more serious.

"Gale, listen to me. Is Kyle talking to you?"

Gale sat silently, not speaking.

Susan continued.

"Gale, is Kyle talking to you?"

Gale nodded silently.

"What is he saying?"

You can imagine that all of us were sitting on the edge of our seats. It was so quiet that you could have heard a pin drop on the carpet.

After what seemed to be an interminable period of time, Gale began speaking again.

"He says I am the most beautiful woman in the world. All my life, I have looked for a man just like him. Now, that I have him, I will do anything he asks to make him happy. I don't ever want him to leave me."

Susan, questioned again. "How do you feel about that, Gale?"

"Kyle is like a father to me. I don't want to hurt his feelings. He knows what is best for me. There is no man who is a greater lover."

Susan looked questioningly at all of us again. I shrugged, nodding further approval to continue.

"Are you happy with these thoughts, Gale?"

Gale shook her head. "I do want to make him happy, but I also want to be on my own. Kyle tells me to do just what he wants me to do, and to just listen to him. I don't like that, but I've got to make him happy."

Susan got up and walked around behind Gale, and gave us one of those I don't know looks, then leaned forward, and spoke softly into Gale's ear.

"Gale, I want you to listen to me very closely. Can you hear me?"

"Yes," Gale answered softly.

"Kyle Washington is a fraud. He is not your dream man. He lies to people, hurts them, drugs them. Do you understand?"

Tears ran down Gale's cheeks, but she nodded that she understood. Susan spoke directly to Gale. Repeat the thought to me, Gale.

"Kyle Washington is a fraud. He is not my dream man. He lies to people, hurts them, drugs them," Gale repeated softly.

Susan now planted the hypnotic virus.

"Gale, I command your subconscious to continue to repeat this thought every time you think of Kyle Washington. When you do think of Kyle, you will instantly feel sick. You will never want to see Kyle Washington again. Do you understand?"

Gale nodded, speaking softly. "I understand."

After a short pause, Susan continued.

"Gale, when I count to ten, you will wake up from your sleep. When you awake, you will be just like you were before you met Kyle. His words will no longer influence your life. You will be free to think, and control your own life. Do you understand?" Gale nodded again.

Susan finally turned her hands palms up in an expression of uncertainty, and softly mouthed "Here goes nothing." She then began counting. "One, Kyle's words are leaving your memory. Two, you feel yourself gaining control of your life, three. . . . "

The counting continued, each number bringing with it, a new affirmation, until finally, "On the next number, the number ten, you will wake up, and be in total control of your life. Ten."

Gale stirred softly, sighed deeply, and opened her eyes and stretched her arms out over her head.

"Well, are we going to do this or not? Damn, I was tired, I must have dozed off." Then she looked at me. "If some people wouldn't keep me up all night."

Everyone laughed. "How do you feel?" Susan asked Gale.

"Fine, why?"

Everyone laughed again.

"You're done," she added. Gale looked a little surprised.

"Did it work?"

Susan shrugged, and shook her head. "We don't know for sure, only time will tell."

We all felt light-hearted for the moment. In spite of our levity, we all knew that the last laugh would be on us, if the deprogramming didn't work. We held our breath as Susan administered the test.

"Gale?" she asked, nonchalantly, "How's Kyle?"

Gale looked surprised—no stunned—at the question. Her face turned white, and she appeared as though she might either throw up or pass out. Gale gasped for air, swallowing rapidly, and looking at me in desperation.

"I feel sick."

Good, I thought. We were one step closer.

Susan reached out and placed her hand on Gale's shoulder, and the sickness seemed to pass. The color returned to Gale's face, and her breathing returned to normal.

"Boy, that was weird. I felt like I was going to throw up. Kyle is a bastard. I hate his guts. If I ever see him again, it will be too soon."

Two steps closer, I thought.

The whole process had taken over an hour. Sue looked at her watch.

"Do you want to go on?"

Angie nodded. "I'm here. If it's all the same to you, I would like to get this over with."

The next hour and a half was filled with more of the same, except that Angie told of introducing Kyle to Cam, and how Kyle twisted Cam's life.

Susan appeared to do an outstanding job, easing the pain of Cam's loss while freeing Angie from Kyle's rule.

When Angie woke up, she looked at us as though she had never seen us before. Susan had given Angie the same cue, nausea, anger, and then release by touching the left shoulder.

In order to ensure that the post hypnotic suggestion had worked, Susan repeated the test given to Gale. Right on cue, Angie turned white, but unlike Gale, actually had to hit the toilet. After a moment, she reappeared, looking shaken. I placed my hand on her shoulder.

"Kyle Washington is a blood sucking, son-of-a-bitch," Angie sneered through clinched teeth. "I wish someone would blow his friggen' head off."

I thought to myself, don't sugar-coat it Ang, tell us how you really feel about Kyle. I laughed nervously to myself, hoping that maybe we were finally making progress.

Angie took a deep breath, sighed deeply, and seemed to regain some of her composure.

"Let's eat," she said. "I'm starved."

"Great idea. Lunch is on me," I offered, looking at Susan. "How about the China Star?"

Susan smiled, begging off.

"Sorry guys, I would love to, but I have an I/A client. I will take a rain check though."

I pointed a finger at her in the gun position and smiled.

"You're on, I'll call you."

The China Star was within walking distance, so I decided that it was still a great idea to go there for lunch. After thanking Susan for her time and efforts, we all mosied on down there for chow.

Growing up, the China Star Restaurant, was always a favorite place for oriental food. Over the years, I had forgotten just how good the food really was there until Susan and I had lunch earlier in the week. I ordered with mouth-watering, anticipation.

While we waited to get our food, I went and called mom. Our plans were to meet, at the church for the "Le Change" stuff later on, and I needed more details about it.

"Hello," mom's voice cracked into the phone.

"Hi, mom, it's Sean. Are you guys alright?"

Mom became more assertive. "I, am fine," she said with conviction, but that damn Kyle's been calling for Angie all morning."

"The last time, he said he wanted to talk to you too. He left a number."

I reached for my pen. The line was quiet for a second while mom went and got his number. When mom came back on the line, she warned me.

"Sean, don't chase him away, we need him. Watch him, but whatever you do, don't chase him away."

"Okay mom, I'll just call him," I said. Mom slowly read me the number. I wrote it on the back of one of the business cards left by the phone by the local cab company, and slipped it in my pocket.

"Sean, there's one more thing. Somehow we need to get him to one of the seances. I'll tell you more about it later."

"Seance?" I asked. "Do you mean that we are going to hold a seance, with ghosts and spirits, and stuff?"

I found that idea to be distressing. I was still afraid of spirits, and didn't relish the thought of being part of any attempt to bring them into my midst.

Also, the thought of having Kyle there, was not appealing. I only had one thought about being around Kyle, and that thought, involved rearranging his face.

There must be some special reason for this, I thought.

"Ma, can we talk about this, first?"

"Sean, I said, we'd talk about it later."

I certainly didn't want to give in carte' blanche, but I decided I had no choice but to agree.

"Okay, mom," I answered obediently, "I gotcha," and hung up the phone.

Seance, I thought, what a waste of time. I figured I'd call Kyle once the girls were set, and I had a full stomach.

I sat down next to Gale. She was bubbling.

I felt like I had walked in on a group of people I didn't even know. Angie was doubled over laughing, and Raven was laughing so hard, she couldn't talk, tears of laughter streaming down her face.

Gale put her arm around me, and kissed me on the cheek, and then said to God and everyone else within earshot, "Now, here is a real man.

They all cheered, and we all broke up laughing at the spontaneity of her humor. It was refreshing. I waited for my little voice to jump in and warn me. Nothing happened. No voice. No warning. I was on my own.

CHAPTER 22

The church was still chilled from the thermostat being turned down all day. Now, with the activities about to begin, the ancient furnace struggled vainly to chase away the cold and dampness in the air before everyone arrived. The smell of heat was strong in the air.

Gale and I hung up our coats, and headed downstairs, to where the group had already begun to gather.

Lillian and Jonathan, had arranged thirteen folding chairs into the shape of a circle. On each chair sat a small glass of water.

With Jonathan's assistance, we each picked a spot to sit, and sat the water glasses on the floor beneath our chairs. As other members filed in, they also took their seats. We awaited the arrival of a few members who were running late, and to pass the time, we began idle conversations.

The seating alternated male and female. Gale sat to my right, Angie to my left, then Jerry, Raven, Jack, mom, another older gentleman who had come with Lillian, Carolyn, Jonathan and Lillian. One chair was left empty. I presumed this was to symbolize where Kyle was to sit when he joined us at the next session.

"Are you nervous?" Angie asked.

"No, not really," I lied. "Don't you know, I do this all the time."

If the truth were to be known, I didn't lie to Angie. I wasn't nervous, I was beyond nervous. I felt like a sixteen-year-old drug pusher, who was about to ask the police chief's daughter to the prom. I was petrified. Of course, a big, tough, private investigator is never supposed to be afraid of anything, so I kept up my front, hoping that this would be over soon. Finally, everyone had arrived and taken their seats.

Lillian sat at the head of the circle, and led us through an outline of the evening's program. As she did so, Jonathan slowly began dimming the lights, causing unusual shadow formations to begin forming on the walls and the ceiling of the basement. In just a few minutes, the room was totally dark.

We sat silently in the blackness for a few moments, and then Lillian spoke.

"Place your feet flat on the floor, and join hands."

There was some shuffling as we complied. After a momentary pause, Lillian took a deep breath, sighed, and began.

"Our Infinite Father, friends in spirit, loved ones, be with us now. As we seek the vibrations of spirit, shield us, guide us, help us."

My eyes remained closed through most of the prayer, but as Lillian droned on, I opened them into the darkness. My eyes had become accustomed to the absence of light, and I was able to see reasonably well. That thought brought a measure of relief to me, as I would at least be able to see what was going on.

I glanced around the room, straining to see if anyone else had their eyes open. I couldn't see anyone very clearly, except Jonathan. He sat in such a position, that I could see him in the glimmer of light, which shone through a crack in the paneled basement walls. The light was faint, but visible. As it shined on him, it cast an eerie glow across his face.

To my surprise, his eyes were opened too, and he was staring straight at me. I wondered if he could see that my eyes were opened. I figured that maybe he was really a cat that had been changed into a human, by an evil spell or something.

I looked away, and made myself a mental note not to watch so much late night television in the future.

The prayer finally ended, and with the vibratory song behind us, Lillian spoke with conviction, her voice deep and throaty.

"Infinite intelligence, which we call God, bring to us, those spirits of truth that wish to speak. We call for the spirit of Cameron Thomas."

Silence once again consumed the room. I sat wondering what to expect for a few moments, and then it began. One by one, people around the circle began speaking spontaneously, citing contact with disembodied spirits in spiritland or wherever they were supposed to be.

I stared at them. Were these people possessed, or perhaps caught up in the emotion of the moment? Was it really possible that they were in contact with spirits?

I didn't think so.

As much as I tried to believe, I found it hard to keep a straight face. I envisioned all these "Casper the Friendly Ghost-like" figures dancing around in an invisible land, waiting for a phone call from the land of the living. Right, I thought.

I looked over at Jerry and Raven. Their faces appeared intense, and they seemed to be mesmerized by the events that were taking place.

After what seemed like an hour of singing and praying, everyone seemed to give up, resigning themselves to the fact that nothing was going to happen tonight. I laughed to myself. So much for the great "Le Change", caper.

* * * * * * * * * * * * * *

The ride back to the Holiday was quiet. Gale said virtually nothing the entire way. The only sounds to break total silence, were those of the heater fan, striving valiantly to chase away the chill in the Escort, and the soft music of the Pillow Talk radio station, playing on the car stereo.

The music was nice. It's oval tones created a relaxing and mellowing mood for the evening. I was amazed at how tired I was. I'm talking drained, I looked at Gale.

"Tired?"

She nodded softly without answering. After a moment she leaned over, resting her head on my shoulder.

"Sean, I think I'm more confused now, than ever. What exactly, are they trying to do with these meetings. They scare the hell out of me."

Her statement and the way she said it, implied that she already knew what they were trying to do, but didn't want to acknowledge it. I didn't blame her.

"What do you mean?" I asked.

"I mean, why are we holding these seances, anyway?"

"Why do you think?"

"I don't know. I guess, to try and get in touch with Cam's spirit."

"Hm-m-m," I mused, "You may be right, but I don't think so."

"So, what then?"

I chuckled, but my laugh was a nervous one. I also, was more than a little apprehensive at the goings on, and I needed some better answers too.

What I really didn't need, was to have Gale all up in arms over the meetings or their intent. I tried to calm her down.

"Gale, I'll be real honest with you. I haven't the foggiest idea what the program is. I trust a lot of those people, and I'm sure that their interests are sincere."

"I always try and play it safe. Since I'm not sure exactly what is happening, I will be asking a lot of questions in the next couple of days. If you want to be with me when I do, you're more than welcome."

Again, Gale just looked at me and nodded, a smile crossing her lips as she saw through my ploy.

"Okay, wise-guy," she said. "Assuming that you really don't know what is going on, what do you think, is going on?"

We both laughed. I may have misread her level of understanding.

Gale was staring straight at me, saying nothing, so I figured I would be straight with her.

"I don't know the plan in its entirety, but I think you're right. I think it is some kind of attempt to get in touch with Cam."

Gale pursed her lips, almost mocking me.

"Do you think they can bring him back?"

I almost ran a red light, swerving at the last minute, and turning right, so as to not have to go through the intersection. The Escort slid slightly as I careened around the corner.

I thought to myself, "Oh great. Here we go again." Just as quickly as the car skidded, it returned to control. Gale breathed a sigh of relief.

"What happened?" she, asked.

"Patch of ice," I replied.

"I know that. Why did you turn the corner like that?"

"Gale, I almost missed the light. What did you mean, do I think they can bring him back? Bring who back?"

"Cam. Do you think that the Spiritualists can bring Cam back from the dead?"

"What the hell is that supposed to mean?" I asked.

For the first time, I was addressing the reality of what I had only feared. Gale laughed softly at my question, and then slowly looked away, shaking her head from side to side.

This was a habit she had, that pissed me off to no end. I'm sure she knew that it irritated me, because she had begun doing it more frequently, after I told her it drove me crazy.

"You're doing it again."

"Doing what?" she asked, still looking away.

"The head shaking thing."

She finally turned back to face me, smiling wryly.

"Sorry," she said. "Certainly you don't really believe that this is just a simple case of spirit communication, do you?"

I turned into the Holiday Inn parking lot, pulled into a parking spot and killed the engine.

I sighed "I don't know what I think, at this point. But, I do intend to find out, soon."

I looked at Gale again, absorbing her femininity, and softness. She was beautiful in the dim light. I felt romantic, and had the strong need to be close to her. Not necessarily sexually, just close.

"I wonder how we got ourselves into this mess, don't you?" I asked.

Gale laughed, "Baby, it was our destiny."

I laughed back, bursting in laughter. "Yeah, Right!"

We both laughed in unison, "Some destiny."

"Seriously, Sean. If it weren't for this mess, I wouldn't have met you. I realize it's a little early yet, but as near as I can see, its gonna be worth the challenge."

With that said, Gale leaned over, and touched my lips with her own. The touch was so light, that there was almost no contact, but the electricity that I felt shot through me like a bolt of lightening. Gale was some lady.

I slipped the key in the lock and clicked the door open. There was a note under the door from Jerry, "Gone to eat. Back at ten, let's get together."

As I sat on the bed reading the note, Gale sat to my side, and behind me, and put her arms around me, resting her head on my back.

"Aren't you tired?" she, asked.

She knew I was. I had been exhausted since we left church.

I nodded, "Yes, I am, but I need to talk to Raven, and get some facts on this "Le Change" stuff. If you're tired, you can sleep here, and I'll just go over to their room."

Gale sat up, and ran her hands up and down my back, it felt good.

"No," she said, "if I'm going to be part of this, and it appears that I am, then I need to understand it too. Plus, I want to be with you tonight. I feel the need to be close to you."

That was fine with me. I turned and kissed her softly on the mouth, gently cradling her face in my hands. I made a mental note not to make any more mental notes about Gale until further notice. I felt like a teenager for the first time in many, many years.

CHAPTER 23

I figured tequila would be as good a way as any to get back into the swing of things, so Jose' Cuervo, was the liquor of choice.

I took great pains to cut the lemons, and limes just so. Gale had ripped off a salt shaker from "Mickey D's," and we were about to be in business.

There was a soft knock at the door. Gale opened it. Raven and Jerry stood waiting for an invite in.

"Come on in," I yelled. "I'm just about ready for the unveiling."

That said, I took the "Spirit of Detroit" souvenir shot glass, filled it with amber liquid, licked the back of my hand, shook the salt onto the moisture, drained the glass, and sucked on the fruit in typical shooter fashion. The tart bite of lemon mellowing the thick taste of the tequila.

I passed the small tray to Jerry, and he followed suit. Some people don't like the taste of tequila, but it's my favorite. Unfortunately, I am not tequila's favorite. Tequila seems to dull my logic. I once walked fifteen miles home from a friend's house, after an argument concerning which color stripe was on the top of the American flag, red or white.

Since then, I drink my favorite, only in the comfort and privacy of my own home. That way, if I am going to make a total ass of myself, I can do it where the only walk I have to make, is to the bedroom.

The fact is, I like tequila because it not only gets the edge off the day, but it keeps you awake doing it. For me, that means more party time.

After the second pass, we all crashed to somewhere comfortable. The music was playing from the radio in the television set, trying its best to stay on a single station long enough, to get through an entire song.

Gale and I, sat at the top of one of the beds, leaning back against the headboard. Jerry and Raven each took a seat in one of the reddish, wine colored, high-backed chairs.

I took out my pack, shook out a Red, and fired it up.

"Raven, tell me more about this "Le Change" stuff," I began.

Raven laughed slightly, looking at me like a disobedient child.

"Sean, what are you worried about? Why don't you just go with the flow?"

That pee'd me off.

"Un-uh darlin'," I said. "We are not dodging this issue, that easy."

"Sean. Why don't you let it rest? We'll take care of the details."

"Because," I continued, "this is important, and I am involved. I need to know exactly what I'm getting myself into."

Raven picked up the bottle, and took a strong pull. She gently set the bottle down, took a piece of lemon, and put it to her lips.

"The other night," she began, "We just touched on "Le Change". What we didn't talk about, were the dangers."

The word, dangers, piqued my interest to a new high. I knew there were going to be risks, and needed to know what they were.

Raven paused, took another swig from the square bottle, and continued talking. The time passed quickly as she talked on and on, recounting details and personal experiences, occasionally stopping to take a drink from the bottle, and then passing it to us when she was through.

After an hour, I was drunk, but I knew what "Le Change" was. I thought to myself, maybe I should have kept my mouth shut, and not asked any questions. At least now, I knew what I had to do, and why. I was going to be a very busy guy for a while.

Jerry got up, walked to the door and crooked his finger to Raven in the come hither fashion. Raven slowly got up and followed, offering a weak wave good-bye, as she left.

The room became very quiet when the door shut behind them. I looked at Gale, she was coasting along, eyes half open, showing the effects of a wonderful tequila drunk. I bent over and kissed her mouth. Her lips parted slightly, and the tip of her tongue caressed the edge of my lips.

I forgot about "Le Change," and about Cam. I even forgot about San Francisco, as I drifted in the jet-stream of love, feeling the warmth, the love, and the ecstacy that only a mellow drunk and a fine woman can bring.

The light of day was just breaking, when I finally reached over and turned the radio off. It had been a near-perfect evening. A glove that fit the hand, that it was made for. I hoped I had remembered to put the "Do Not Disturb" sign on the door. After a night like this, I did not need to be disturbed.

CHAPTER 24

The brash ringing of the phone startled me to a heavy, wakefulness. I could barely open my eyes. The phone rang, and rang. Somehow, I pulled my arm out from under my body, and worked my way from beneath the covers to reach for the phone. I fumbled for the receiver.

"Yeah?" I croaked, coughing, and clearing my throat.

"Sean?" It was Carolyn.

"Yeah, hi," I managed, rubbing my eyes, trying to focus. "What's up?"

"I just talked to your mom. Kyle left a note for Angie. He said he was leaving town. Sean, it's you he's running from. You've gotta stop him. We need him to be at the first sitting."

I held the receiver away from my ear, thinking out loud. Damn it, this is just what I need, right now. I glanced at the dial on my Rolex. It was only ten o'clock in the morning.

"Where are you?" I asked.

"I'm at your mom's."

I forced my mind to focus my thoughts.

"I'll call him."

"Call me back," she ordered.

I dropped the receiver to the floor without answering. At this moment, I couldn't even remember where I had left the sombitches number. God, was I hung over.

* * * * * * * * * * * * * *

"Hello," came the syrupy reply.

"Kyle," I said.

There was a long pause at the other end of Alexander Graham Bell's favorite invention, and then Kyle answered

"Yes . . . ?"

I hated this wimp-shit. I also hated what I had to do. I didn't want to be sociable to Kyle, but the events of the day demanded my passivity.

"We need to have a talk," I ordered.

"About what?" he asked.

I took a heavy drag from the half burned Red, held it deeply for a moment and then exhaled as I answered, "Everything," I said, somewhat at a loss for words. "I'll fill you in when I see you."

Kyle was noticeably silent. After a few moments of silence on the other end of the line, I asked, "You still there?"

"Yeah, I'm here," he finally answered, "but no trouble, right?"

I shook my head at the thought.

"Kyle, would I give you any trouble? Really, I need to ask you a favor."

"You need to ask me a favor?" he said. "What kind of favor?"

I wasn't letting him off the hook that easy.

"I'll tell you when I see you. Meet me at the Rialto at noon. I'll even buy," I added, hoping that the chance of a free meal would ice the cake.

Kyle thought for a minute, then he said, "But no trouble, right?"

"Kyle, you worry too much. I'll see you at noon."

The line went dead. I laughed. "Trouble?" Kyle, my man, you don't even know the meaning of the word.

I looked at Gale, she was a goner. I had the strongest urge to check her pulse. I laughed at myself. Check her pulse? I should check my own pulse. I looked for the bottle of Coke from last night.

Knowing the thirsties that follow a tequila drunk, I figured Jerry had taken the rest of it back to his room.

Screw it, I thought. It only had a swig in it anyway. I looked for my pants. They must have got up and walked out sometime in the middle of the night. I did find my skivvies. I pulled them on, and picked up the change on the night stand.

There were just enough coins for two cans from the machine. I headed out the door, and down the hall to the vending area.

Even the clang of the quarters dropping through the mechanics of the machine seemed loud. I hit the red, white and blue button of the "New

Generation". The can dropped to the bottom of the machine. I picked up the can, pushed the tab back, and following the soft hiss, sucked the caramel liquid over my parched pallet.

Now, twelve ounces of Pepsi is a drop in the bucket when you need a gallon. I tossed the empty into the "Pop Cans Only" box and hit the slot with another six bits. The orange light next to the Pepsi was glowing, indicating "Empty When Lit".

I opted for "The Real Thing", and was gonna kill that one too, until I heard,"***Aye, Corumba".***

I turned toward the voice and there stood Carlotta, one of the hotel maids.

I smiled my best shit eating grin and said, "Good morning." Then with the red and white can in my hand, I eased past her and walked back to my room.

Carlotta was laughing and telling the other housekeepers about me, in Spanish. I just shook my bootie at them and closed the door behind me to their uproarious laughter.

Gale had rolled over and pulled the blankets with her, baring one of nature's most perfect forms. I decided to sip the Coke and take in the view. After a few minutes, I thought, Kyle, I'm gonna be a little bit late.

I made the toss and the empty made a heavy clunk as it dropped into the oval, fiber, waste basket. Gale stirred, turning to look at me.

"Hey, buster. Keep it down will ya?" she said smiling and looking at me, and then added "Oops, too late,"

* * * * * * * * * * * * *

Kyle was waiting in a booth near the back of the restaurant when I walked into the Rialto. He looked nervous. I slid in across from him, and called the waitress over. "Kathi" sauntered over to our booth. Her pad in hand.

"Want something," I asked Kyle.

He shook his head negatively. I looked up at "Kathi".

"Give me two large Cokes and a black coffee, and keep them coming."

I turned back to look at Kyle. He really didn't look hungry. We sat in silence for a minute while I fired up a Pall Mall.

Kathi was back with the drinks, setting them carefully in front of me.

"You want cream?"

I shook my head negatively, and emptied my lungs of blue smoke. "No thanks, Hon. Black will do today."

Kathi left to serve another table, and I turned my attention to the closest Coke glass. I lifted it and took a heavy pull from the glass, returned it to the table, and offered a polite burp.

"Kyle," I started. "I've learned a lot about you, and about your past in the last few days."

He looked up at me, a puzzled, like what, look on his face. I gave him a disgusted look and shook my head. Kyle screwed up his face.

"What do you mean?" he said.

I blew smoke in his face.

"Kyle, cut the shit. You forget that I make my living getting rap sheets on assholes like you. Unless you're a lot more stupid than I think you are, you know that I already have yours."

Kyle stared straight at me, eye-to-eye. He became stoic.

"So what?"

"So," I said, "Let's talk man to man. I don't give a rat's ass about what has gone on before right now. But, I do know all about your past escapades.

For now, the only thing I really care about is what happens next. My responsibility, is to do anything I can, to be sure that everyone in Detroit, is allowed to get their lives back to normal."

I snuffed out the butt, drank about half of my coffee, and continued.

"Now, you can help me, and then in the end, maybe you take a walk," I continued, "Or you can fight me, or try and run, in which case, I will personally hunt your ass down, and make sure you know how much I really dislike you. The option is yours."

I finished the first Coke, and slid the glass away from me.

Kyle stared straight past me at the traffic on Woodward Avenue, saying nothing. After a minute or two, he looked back at me.

"Okay," he said, "What do you want from me?"

I explained that mom and Angie were crushed at the loss of Cam. I told him that I needed him to sit in on the seances, just to help mom and Angie, ease their feelings about him. I explained, that since he was so closely involved with them all, that it would only be natural for him to help out. I reminded him that I would be there too.

Kyle shook his head.

"Seances, I don't know. I don't really want to do this shit anyway, but seances. . . .," his voice trailed off.

I quickly jumped in.

"Kyle, if you really didn't have anything to do with Cam's death, then this is one way you can show it."

I finished the last of my refreshments, and Kathi was back. I ordered a large double-double to go, and stood up.

"Well, the choice is yours. If you make the right choice, we'll all be meeting at Flower Memorial, tonight at seven-thirty."

I fired up a Red.

"If not," I continued, exhaling, "Then, I guess we'll just have see what happens next."

Kyle was looking down.

"And Gale?" he asked.

I just laughed. "Kyle, just forget it. I'll see you tonight."

Kathi returned with my reinforcements. I slipped her a fin, and walked into the cold. As I walked to the Escort, I saw a cop in the process of ticketing my car for a parking infraction.

I thought to myself, shit, this is just what I need. As I got closer, I could see that it was John Stephens. He smiled.

"Hello Sean," he said, dragging out the Hello.

"Are you seriously giving me a ticket?" I asked.

John smiled again.

"No, but I could have, you forgot to feed the meter."

I looked at the red "Expired" tag showing through the arched glass window of the meter. I thought about making a mental note to remember to put money in the meter in the future, but decided, screw it.

"I'm here for our friend," I said to John, motioning with my head in the direction Kyle had walked when he left the Rialto.

John nodded. "I know, we've been staying close."

"How'd you know we were here?"

John looked at me like I was stupid.

"I figured that you would be in touch with Mr. Wonderful, so I checked you out."

I feigned surprise. "You didn't trust me?" I smiled.

John was quick to respond.

"Buddy, I don't even trust my own mother. I want to be sure this guy doesn't sprout wings, and fly away."

I didn't blame him. I wasn't sure of Kyle's real intentions either. The only thing I was sure of, was my ability to find him if he did leave.

"Feel free to stay close," I said, "But for God's sake, don't spook him. My family needs him. If everything goes well, in a few days, Kyle Washington will be simply a flicker in the de'jevu of every person that knows him.

John looked disinterested.

"Just keep it clean, Sean."

I nodded, "I will. Stay in touch," I said, and hit the key.

John turned and walked back to his black and white. I leaned back, tore the sipping tab off the white lid of the coffee cup, lifted it to my mouth, and burned the piss out of my upper lip with the hot coffee. "Damn it," I sputtered to myself.

I set the cup in the built-in cup holder, and hit my pack. The first smell of burning tobacco reached my nostrils, and I inhaled deeply. Well, I thought, the first step was in motion. I clicked the Escort in gear, and began looking for a phone.

A lot of questions were beginning to form in my mind. After talking to Raven, I figured I was all set. Man, was I wrong! The more I thought about

"Le Change", the more I realized that I had a lot of questions that couldn't be just passed off. I was going to have to do a lot more asking, before we got to a critical point with this thing.

CHAPTER 25

"Good morning," came, the reply, to the incessant ringing. I cut the preliminaries.

"Carolyn?

"Yes?"

"I planted the seed. Now the rest is up to him."

I could tell Carolyn was smiling at the other end of the wire.

"Good, boy," she said, "Do you think he will come?"

"Hell, I don't know," I answered honestly. "John Stephens is tracking him too, so our worst case scenario, is that Kyle's at least gonna be punished for his legal misdeeds."

Carolyn laughed dryly.

"From what I hear, the only punishment that would fit the crime, would be to cut his nuts off."

I winced at the thought, and made myself my first mental note of the past few days–, to never cross Carolyn.

I answered thoughtfully.

"If we can make this happen, it may be worse than cutting his nuts off," I said, again wincing at the thought. "I'll see you tonight."

I figured it was time to read The book. I reached over, picked it up off the seat, and thumbed through the pages. It looked like easy reading. I slipped it in my coat pocket, and headed back to the Holiday.

The hall was empty and quiet as I neared our room. I stuck the Swiss cheese looking piece of plastic into the slot. When the green light flashed, I pushed the door open, and quietly stepped inside.

Gale rolled over and looked at the door when it opened. She smiled and pulled the sheet up to demurely cover her femininity.

"Hi" she said.

"Hi, yourself," I answered, leaning over for a soft peck. "How do you feel?"

Gale was contrite, and laughed softly.

"I feel like I got hit by a truck. But, other than that, I feel fine. Your mom called. She said we were all set for tonight. Is Kyle coming?"

I shrugged. "I hope so. We'll just have to see tonight. Get dressed, and let's go get some chow."

Gale pouted. "But I want to sleep," she whined.

I laughed, pulling her playfully out of bed.

"Get up, and let's eat."

Gale's resolve quickly ebbed, and she trudged toward the shower. I followed her contours until she disappeared from view, and then reached into my pocket for the book.

As I read the different descriptions of a medium and mediumship, trance, and transformation, spirit and spirit possession, I learned that a great many sane, and noteworthy people in our society have been Spiritualists.

I thought, so what. Their interest or participation, did not prove the authenticity of the Spiritualist philosophy. Yet, reading the names of some of the famous persons who were involved in Spiritualism, intrigued me.

Don't read anything into this. It's not like I'm giving into this crap, carte' blanche. But, many of people that were very close to me, people that I respect a lot, are active believers.

Where I'm from, a smart PI has to follow his instincts. My instincts now said, check it out. Gone were the mental notes, gone was my small voice of reason, and on their way out, were many of the inhibitions that had influenced my judgment for so long. I was in this for the long ride, God, help me.

The "Who's Who" of famous people included, Abraham Lincoln, Sir Arthur Canaan Doyle, and Oliver Wendell Holmes. I figured, if these prominent people can believe in spirit communication, et el, then the least I could do, is check it out and play devils advocate, no pun intended.

One of the things that impressed me the most, was the fact that these Spiritualists were deeply religious, deeply respectful of God, and deeply committed to helping their fellow man.

I watched Gale dress. As I did so, my thoughts went back many years to Debbie. Boy, we were a hot couple then. It made me a little nervous that I was developing the same comfortable feeling about Gale, that I had experienced with Debbie.

Frankly, I rationalized, I didn't have the time or energy to be in love with anyone. I halted my thoughts at the "L" word. However, I did have to admit that Gale made me feel, well, special.

If you were looking at the events of the past few days as an outsider, you probably wouldn't put much stock in my feelings. Yet for me, the past few days had brought the most important women in my past, back into my life, and Gale had out-shined them all.

I suddenly thought that I needed to call and have my apartment cleaned, just in case Gale wanted to come back to Frisco for a visit when this was all over.

"You're daydreaming," Gale said, bringing me back to reality.

I laughed, "Yeah, about you."

Gale smiled. "Oh my, is the big tough PI daydreaming about little ol' me?" she said, fluttering her eyelashes. Then after a moments reflection she queried, "Like what?"

I laughed again, "I'll tell you later. Let's eat."

* * * * * * * * * * * * * *

"Peppy's" was a greasy spoon that specialized in coneys, and Greek food. I turned in the driveway, parked the Escort, and we went inside.

We asked for the smoking section, and sat down in the wooden chairs. The table wobbled appropriately, and when "Bunny" came to take our order, I realized the full ambiance of this long-standing landmark. I had long since forgotten most of it.

I lit up a *Red*, and ordered some heavy dogs to kill the hangover.

"Gale, what are you gonna do when this is all over?" I asked.

Gale looked up, a little stunned, then turned and looked around herself, like I was talking to someone else. "Are You talking to moi?" she, asked, pointing to herself with a questioning look.

I nodded.

Gale shrugged, being serious for the moment. "I don't know Sean. I haven't thought that far ahead, yet." Gale looked down, turning her water glass in her hands for a moment, and then looked back up at me. "I really haven't had much time to think about it."

Gale became pensive, thinking and then added, "Without Kyle, I really don't have anything here or anywhere else, to tie me down."

"What about your house?" I asked.

Gale laughed. "My house? Our house? We were renting it month to month. Supposedly, Kyle was gonna try and buy it. But, like everything else, as far as I know, nothing ever happened."

Gale, looked me straight in the eyes. I hate it when a woman does that.

"Why do you ask?" she said.

Normally, this directness would make me shuck, jive, and skate, but instead, I stared back at her, and I heard myself calmly respond.

"Well, I've got this place in Frisco. It's not much, but if you were interested, I'd be happy to have you, uh, you know, come and stay with me till you find something better."

Gale continued to search my eyes with her own. After a moment, she smiled and started to answer. Before she could answer, "Bunny" was back with our food.

"Will there be anything else?" she asked, absently.

I shook my head. "No, thanks." Bunny turned and left.

I lifted one of the dogs to my lips, and savored the fragrant aroma of the chili and onions.

Gale was silent, though she was still smiling, and looking straight at me.

"Well?" I mumbled through a mouthful of Oscar Mayer.

"You're serious, aren't you?" Gale asked.

I took a slug of the watered down liquid that Peppy's tried to pass off as Coca Cola, and washed down the taste of sauerkraut, chili and onions.

I nodded, "Hell yes, I'm serious."

"I don't believe you."

"Why not?"

Gale shrugged, "I don't know. I guess I figured it would be too good to be true."

I looked straight into her eyes.

"Gale, I don't believe that I have ever been more serious about anything in my entire life."

Gale laughed nervously. "Well, if I won't be in the way, I'd love it."

I reached over, and placed my hand on top of hers. "Gale, I assure you, you won't be in the way."

The rest of the day we were like high school kids, laughing and acting like we had discovered some unknown feeling. These heightened emotions were disarming, and a cause for me to be concerned.

A PI lives by his instincts, and to be at your best, your instincts have to be razor-sharp. Love has a funny side effect. It dulls your sensitivity, your awareness, and your objectivity. This can make you vulnerable. I made a mental note to keep my senses about me, and to stay focused on the situation at hand.

Finally it was time to head to Flower Memorial. As we drove in the cold, I felt uneasy. I wondered if Gale did too.

"Are you ready for this?" I asked.

Gale was solemn. "I don't know. It kind of scares me."

I nodded. "Yeah, me too. I just hope it works. I trust ma, so I'll give it a shot, but I will have to see some real proof before I truly believe."

CHAPTER 26

When Gale and I got to the church, the wind was blowing light snow all around us, biting us with the cold. Gale and I hurried towards the church door, and quickly pulled it open.

The heavy wooden door screeched open, and then slammed shut behind us. The voices coming from the basement led us there.

As I stepped off the bottom step into the basement, I heard Kyle's voice. I was surprised to see that he had actually shown up, and even more surprised, that he had actually come early.

I searched the basement for him, and was pleased to see that he had pretty much isolated himself off away from the ladies, talking to Jack. I lit up a smoke.

The door opened again, and after a brief pause, once again slammed shut. We looked to the stairway to see Lillian and Jonathan walk in. Mom and Debbie walked over and greeted them. Debbie took their coats, and left to hang them up.

Lillian looked around the room.

"Are we all here?" she asked.

"I think so," mom said.

Lillian nodded, and said matter of factly, "Well, then let's get started."

Carolyn had said that tonight, it was important that we sit in the proper sequence, so Jonathan had set up the room exactly like before.

While we waited to be directed to a seat, I couldn't help but notice the musty, dankness, of the old building. The furnace was struggling gallantly to warm our space, and it seemed to be making eerie noises, noises which sounded to me like voices calling from some unknown or unspoken point of origin.

My imagination was beginning to give me second thoughts about participating in this facade of sanity. I made a mental note to call my shrink when I got back to Frisco, and have him count my marbles.

Finally, Jonathan touched my arm, and sat me down. We sat, male, female, male, female, with Kyle seated next to Lillian.

As before, we began with a series of protective incantations. This time, while we mouthed the words, I sensed a higher level of urgency, a stronger sense of electricity in the air, and a feeling of certainty about the upcoming events.

After the incantations, the others called to their guides. This time, I sat quietly, and respectfully in the darkness. Lillian repeated the call to Cam.

With that done, I gradually opened my eyes, not really sure what to expect. I looked around the room. It was alight with sparkling stars of light. In truth, sparkling, is a misnomer. Dancing, is a more appropriate analogy.

The room was filled with small balls of light which seemed to travel around the space, like the electrons of an atom, darting here and there.

I looked at Kyle, he was surrounded by a dark-yellow, light. The book said that the light was an aura. An emanation of energy which was an extension of the soul.

As near as I could remember, the book also said that an ideal aura was to be a deep blue, or violet color, if it were pure. The color of Kyle's aura would mean that he was in deep shit, spiritually.

We began to softly sing the hymn "In The Garden". About halfway through the second verse, Lillian began mumbling, and I felt a rush of cold air flow past my left ear.

Just then, Lillian began to speak. As with Carolyn, it was Cam's voice.

"Good evening friends, good evening, Sean."

In unison, we all said, "Good evening, Cam."

I looked at Lillian, and in the soft glow of her aura, I swore I could see Cam's face. If this were true, this was what is called a "transfiguration".

During a transfiguration, the face of the medium takes on the image of the controlling entity. As I stared at Lillian, she looked like Cam. I was surprised, because the book said that transfigurations are a rarity in modern mediumship. I stared as hard as I could.

"Sean, thanks for coming, and thank you all for your efforts," Cam, said. "You have done well. Please thank, your guide Dr. Richard Andrews for his help. "As I asked, you sought, you taught, and you returned. Yet, there is still much to do. Please balance your energy, and reach for the higher vibrations. When you have accomplished this, I will come to you again."

"Angie, I do love you. Till I can hold you again, my dearest. Sorry, but my time is short today. Call for me again, soon. Good-bye."

With that, the voice went silent, Lillian's aura flashed, and dimmed. She was once again the image of herself. I looked around the room, and heard everyone breathe a deep sigh of relief as though everyone had been holding their breath.

When the voice began speaking, I had noticed a definite change in Lillian's features. She actually looked like Cam. Now, Cam's voice was gone, and so was his image. Lillian sat as stone, unmoving, and silent. Now, life seemed to again be returning to her face.

Jonathan arose and went to slowly begin raising the lights. Everyone except Kyle and Gale, reached for the water glasses which were sitting on the floor beneath their seats, and took a drink.

I reached for my own, and tasted the cool liquid. It tasted odd. Not bad, just odd.

"What happened to the water?" I asked Carolyn.

Carolyn smiled. "It was ionized by the spiritual energy. Drink it all. You'll feel refreshed."

I followed the advice, and was a little surprised to find that I did feel better, more energized.

I looked over at Lillian. She looked drained.

"Why did Cam pick Lillian"? I asked in Carolyn's direction. Carolyn was a little distracted, and turned to look at me.

"What did you say?" I mouthed the words slowly, thinking of all the "Blond" jokes I had heard in the past.

"Why did Cam pick Lillian to speak through?"

"I thought you said you read your book."

I shrugged. "I did. What did I miss?"

"Oh, nothing much, just the crux of the whole program here." Carolyn shook her head. "What is it, that constitutes all spiritual activity?" she asked, making me feel like a total asshole.

I didn't have the foggiest idea, but I took a stab at the answer.

"Vibrations?"

"Yes, that's right."

I was pleased that I had passed my first test. Carolyn seemed amused at my naivety. I continued confidently, though thinking the entire time that I was probably wrong.

"So Cam and Lillian's spiritual vibrations were very close tonight. That's why he chose her. Right?"

"I'm proud of you, Sean." Carolyn said. "You did your homework."

I made a mental note to get myself a copy of "Wylie's Notes" on Spiritualism, so that I could cram for my next exam.

Carolyn continued.

"That's the way a spirit chooses its channel. The medium that possesses the vibration level closest to that of the spirit entity coming through, is the one who is chosen as the channel."

I nodded knowingly like, "Shit, I knew that all along."

Kyle was talking softly to Jack. I couldn't hear all of what he said, but I overheard the words "weird" and "stupid". Talk about the pot calling the kettle black.

Mom and Angie were up, and seeing Kyle, began walking in his direction.

"Thank you for coming, Kyle," mom said, glancing slyly at me. "If all goes well, after just a few more sittings, Angie and I, and everyone else, will be OK again."

Mom looked at Angie.

"What do you think, honey?"

Angie looked away and nodded. She all but ignored Kyle. I imagined that it had been tough on her. Even if Susan's hypnosis passed all the tests, there was Kyle in the flesh. It must have been hard.

"Please come back Thursday," mom added.

Kyle shook his head. "We'll see," and then turning to look at me added, "I think I can make it."

CHAPTER 27

With two days before the next session, it was prime time to get some rest. I put my arm around Gale, and said "Let's go sleep in."

Gale smiled, "I thought you'd never ask."

Ah, yes, I thought. Two days, glued to my soft, comfortable bed, with Gale at my side, would be just what the doctor ordered.

Our joy was short lived however. Mom came over and spoke directly.

"Sean?"

"Yeah, ma?"

"Please don't relax too much. We made a significant breakthrough here tonight, but now we must prepare for the next step."

"What step is that, ma?" I asked, thinking to myself, "How bad do I really want this to happen?"

Mom looked around the room for Lillian, as she spoke to Gale and I.

"We need a full materialization before Thursday. We've got to get together again tomorrow night, this time without Kyle."

I began to feel more than a little uncomfortable again.

Mom continued, "Get Raven and Jerry to meet all of us at my house tomorrow afternoon at three o'clock. There are some things we must cover so we can be stronger."

Mom hadn't noticed my uneasiness, because she was so intent. I also felt that this was not the time to mention it. I answered confidently for everyone.

"Don't sweat it, ma. We'll all be there."

Mom nodded, turned around slowly and walked over to Lillian. I stood there for a moment thinking. I'm sure it doesn't take a genius to know that PI's are constantly questioning everything going on in their world. But, I had questions, serious questions, that no one had even tried to answer.

I made a mental note, that before I put my ass on the line again, I was getting answers to all of these questions, and I meant all of them.

"What do you think?" Gale asked, jogging me from my thoughts.

I shrugged, "Hell, I don't know. You know as much about this as I do. I guess we'll just have to wait and see what happens."

I really didn't know what was going to happen next. I knew one thing for certain, it seemed to me that an awful lot of people were in an awful big hurry to make something happen that I didn't completely understand.

When things like that happen, my PI personality yells "Whoa, wait a damn minute." This time, I felt like I had no control over what was happening, or going to happen.

Here I was, right in the middle of things, and I was being carried along, like a stick floating in a fast rushing tide.

That's not the way I was accustomed to doing things. I controlled the case. I never let it control me. This case was beyond my control. I was simply a participant in the events that were unfolding.

Even though it was against my normally better judgement, I listened to my little voice. It said, "You'll never know unless you show up and find out."

Jerry and Raven were standing near the stairway door talking to Carolyn. I looked around for Kyle. He had already left. For a moment, I had a fear that he might be headin' on down the highway. Interestingly enough, Carolyn sensed my fears.

"Don't worry Sean, he's not going anywhere," she said. I looked puzzled.

"How do you know?"

Carolyn laughed, "Because he's staying with Jack and I for the next few days."

Gale frowned, looking at me. "Is that safe?"

Carolyn laughed again, "Trust me. It will be the best thing for all of us. Jack and I will school him on how important his spiritual growth will be in restoring the lives of those his inconsiderate acts have harmed."

I sighed deeply and nodded.

"Well, if you think it's alright, I'll trust your judgement. I will tell you, that it doesn't feel completely safe to me."

I was being honest. I've been doing a lot of that lately. Don't get me wrong. I'm no saint by any stretch of the imagination, but it concerned me that I didn't know enough about all of this, book or not, to know how to twist things to my advantage even if I wanted to. That really did make me feel uneasy.

"Sean, I appreciate your concern. But, have a little faith. Jack and I know what we're doing."

"If you say so. Just be careful."

Angie and mom were ready to go. Sandy was still keeping the kids, so we didn't have to worry about them, at least for the night. As we drove mom and Angie to mom's house, both of them were quiet. Perhaps a little too quiet, for my feelings. I turned into the driveway, dropped the gearshift into "Pee", and turned to face mom.

"Mom, how long do you think all of this will take?"

Mom was quiet for a while. At first, I thought she didn't hear me, but just as I was about to ask the same question again, mom sighed, and began to speak slowly and deliberately.

"Sean, I don't know."

"Well, how long do you think?"

"Sean, please," she interrupted in a shallow voice, sounding drained. "If all goes as I understand it should, it could be over in a few sittings. If not, well—"

"Well, what?"

"Well, Sean, I really don't know. I've never actually participated in a "Le Change". I've only heard about them."

Mom's voice trailed off. She was silent for a few moments before she continued.

"If it doesn't go as planned, then I really don't know."

Mom seemed tired, worried or uncertain. This made me feel like I wanted to avoid further discussions, but a good PI learns to ask questions when the opportunity presents itself, so I continued.

"Mom? Why do you seem so. . . . . "

I couldn't finish the sentence. Mom seemed different, and for the life of me, I couldn't put my finger on the reason why. I searched for the right word, failing.

"Whatever. . .?" I finished.

Normally, it was not like me to be at a loss for words. Mom smiled politely.

"Sean, just being involved in this makes me feel—, well, like I'm doing something wrong."

"Sometimes I think I would do anything to get Cam back, but I'm a spiritual person. Our religion teaches love and life. Even though I want Cam back, this just seems wrong somehow."

That was refreshing to hear. At least now I knew that mom was not a zealot. She hadn't totally lost her marbles to this spiritualistic crap. She was still skeptical. That was encouraging.

"Thanks for sharing that with me mom. It makes me feel better to hear you say that?"

"Why?"

"Because, I haven't bought into this spiritual program totally. A little uncertainty is refreshing."

Mom nodded. "I hope it's all worth it."

I made a mental note to ask Jonathan and Lillian about what mom had said and a lot of other things, tomorrow.

It seemed to me, that we were all placing a lot of trust in people that I hardly knew. Even though mom and the family knew them and even though they seemed relatively normal, I was still having some second thoughts.

I guess mom's feelings were the same as mine. As big of an asshole as Kyle Washington was, I didn't honestly feel it was right to sacrifice one life for another, even if it was Kyle's.

I watched the porch light go out and backed the Escort out of the driveway. The orange glow of the cigarette lighter spelled impending relief for the nicotine fit I was having. I fired up the Red took a deep hit, held it for a while, and then exhaled slowly.

It surprised me that Gale hadn't said anything. Maybe she was just trying to be neutral. I didn't know. Gale leaned over, and put her head on my shoulder.

"Tired," I asked.

"Uh-uh. I just want to be close to you."

CHAPTER 28

At two o'clock on Wednesday, Gale and I got in the Escort, and began to follow Jerry and Raven to ma's house. It had been a quiet and romantic period for Gale and I. Personally, I loved it.

Women in my recent past had always tried to change me. They didn't understand my business, or my work ethic. Sooner or later, they would start nagging me about my time commitments, and the relationship would be on the way out.

That's one of the reasons why I was happy when I met Gale. She took me for what I am. When it came to issues that she didn't understand, we discussed them. Gale accepts my personality for what it is, and she accepts my opinions as valid.

Through these discussions, I have recognized some aspects of my life that need changing. But, these will be changes I choose to make, not changes which are forced upon me.

Our relationship was good for Gale, too. She is starting to develop a confidence that is changing her attitude from one of "I think I need to do this", to one of "I'm doing this because I want to".

For me, she was becoming a soul mate. Someone, that I felt would share in, and inspire me to, greater heights.

As she felt more comfortable about her role in our relationship, I felt better about having her around.

"Have you ever studied this Spiritualism stuff before?" I asked Gale.

She shook her head in the negative.

"Uh-uh, but for some reason, I think I'll be good at it."

I looked over at her. She was smiling and looking right at me.

"Why is that?"

"I don't know. I kind of identify with the spiritualists-–, their feelings, emotions, and thoughts. I guess all of it. Maybe I'm just sensitive, and it comes naturally."

"Does that mean that you believe it?" I asked, somewhat surprised.

Gale was very "polite," almost condescending.

"Maybe. Sean, something happened to me the other night. While I was praying, I uh, well, I think I saw images in my mind, and I sensed things, I wanted to say out loud."

The light turned red, and I stopped the Ford. Jerry finally drove out of sight.

"You're kidding, right?

Gale shook her head again. "No. Actually, I'm not kidding. I really can't explain it. All can say is, it was so exciting that I just can't wait for tonight."

I checked the light, it was now green. I hit the pedal next to the brake, and started forward. As we cleared the intersection, I looked over at Gale. Our eyes met. She smiled somewhat sheepishly.

"Didn't you feel anything?"

I thought for a moment about lying to her, and telling her that I hadn't felt or sensed anything, but as I looked at her, I realized that she was being honest with me, and that I didn't want there to be any lies between us.

I was deep in thought. I guess my distraction was causing me to drive too slow, because the guy behind me was leaning on his horn. I flipped him off, and pushed a little harder on the gas pedal. We sped up, putting some space between us and the other car. I turned to look at Gale.

"Yeah, I felt something."

Gale was jubilant. "Like what?"

I told Gale about the rush of air, the tingling I felt, the light balls and seeing Kyle's aura. I steered the car onto mom's street.

"Wow," Gale said, "You really got into it, huh?"

I looked at her and laughed.

"I think saying, it got into me, better describes, what really happened. I wasn't asking for this you know."

Gale smiled at me as I continued.

"But, now that you ask me, I guess secretly, I wanted it to happen. Honestly? I'm as excited about this, as you are."

"What I felt and saw seems real to me. I guess I'm also excited about what the future holds. I mean, what if—, and, I don't know how the hell they are going to pull it off, but just what if, they can somehow or other bring Cam back?"

We both laughed nervously.

"Now, you're talking" Gale said.

I had a fleeting thought that Gale might be thinking about her good times with Cam when she said that, but I tried to quickly dismiss my feelings of petty jealousy.

I pulled into mom's driveway. Jerry, Raven, Angie and Carolyn were already there. I shut off the Ford, and turned to look at Gale.

"Gale," I began cautiously, "What if Cam does come back?"

Gale had been looking out the windshield. When I finished asking the question, she turned to look at me. My insecurities had caused me to ask a very stupid, but valid question.

Gale's first look was a pissed, offended, look. At first, she said nothing. After a moment, she paused and softened.

Instead of cajoling me, she reached over, cupped my face in her hands, and kissed me softly and deeply on the mouth.

The rest of my unasked questions were completely answered in that brief moment. We broke, I nodded, saying nothing, got out of the Escort, and went around to opened Gale's door. Together, we walked up to the house where mom stood waiting to let us in.

Carolyn sat with Jerry on the couch near the window.

"Where's Kyle?" I asked Carolyn.

"Jack has him covered," she said. "He'll be out of circulation for today. Tonight I get to be his guard. Rest assured, he won't be out of our sight, even for a minute."

I wasn't sure I was comfortable with Kyle's being alone with Carolyn, but she was a mature and in-control lady, and I'm sure she knew what she was doing. At least I hoped she did.

Right at three o'clock on the nose, the doorbell rang, and Lillian, Jonathan and Sandy showed up.

Over the next two hours, we discussed every aspect of spirit contact. We revealed our feelings, our hopes, our fears, and our past experiences. I began feeling like I was becoming a part of it all, and I looked forward to that night, and our next meeting.

CHAPTER 29

I was excited about the upcoming session. But, first things, first. I decided that before I got knee-deep in this spiritual frenzy, that it was time for some peace of mind.

I had been carrying questions around in my mind about this whole process almost since it was first mentioned. Now, I intended to get them answered.

Several of my concerns were passed off as silly by the rest of the group. I wasn't sure if that was because they really were silly, or because they didn't want to answer them for fear that I wouldn't like the answers. My repeated rephrasing of the questions, brought no further progress. I was on my own.

These "Le Change" questions, seemed to be very complex questions. But yet, they were all so basic, that I couldn't believe no one had thought to ask them before. Maybe everyone was scared a little shitless by this whole process, just like me.

I was curious, to say the least. For example, didn't anyone wonder what happened to the physical body of the person transferring out? And what exactly was this transferring out process, anyway?

In this case, what would actually happen to Kyle Washington? For all I knew, maybe it just dried up and blew away like dust. I laughed. No, that would be too easy. The way things were going, we would probably have to cut the sombitch up, and eat his ass or something.

What about all the people that knew him? What of his family, his friends, if he had any? And, what happened to the lives of everyone he screwed over. Was all of that simply forgotten?

Probably not. Nothing was ever that simple. The one lesson I had learned in this business, was that nothing is that easy, and nothing is that simple. There are always details that continue to surface, right up until the very end.

I let my mind wander. Kyle Washington was only half the problem. I had the same questions about Cam.

PI's are a little funny sometimes. We don't tend to like half-painted pictures. As far as I could see, there was an awful lot of this picture, that was incomplete.

I wondered, did we have to go out and dig up Cam's body? Maybe all the weird thoughts I had when we were buying the casket weren't so far fetched after all.

That'll teach me, I thought. Maybe I should have paid a little more attention to what was being said when we bought Cam's coffin.

My investigative instincts were having a field day, playing with my wild imagination. The PI in me, said that none of this was possible. Yet, my logic also said, that if so many people were convinced that it could happen, then someway or another, "Le Change" was possible.

I concluded, that I was not educated enough in Spiritualism to know how or what would actually happen, or how they would do it. But, I figured that as hard as mom and everyone else, was working to make something happen, it was probable that they would do it.

This conclusion brought me a very strong blast of paranoia. My fear was, that the people who were in the know, were keeping something from me, something I would later regret not knowing.

I also didn't like the fact that no one else had raised my questions.

Leaving mom's, I told everyone that I had a lot of running around to do, and asked Gale to ride to the church with Angie and mom.

It wasn't that I didn't want to be around the folks, but you gotta' believe, that thinking in PI, was tough with all these other people around me all the time.

As a rule, I generally don't like crowds. This whole experience was too different, even for me. In Frisco, I had a lot of, alone time, on my hands. This was time that allowed for free thinking, "blue skying" as I guess the establishment calls it. I needed some of that time right now.

Two questions burned in the back of my mind as I turned the Escort towards the "Ferndale Public Library". One, even though Cam sounded like he was gonna jump off the deep end, why would he? I mean, he had been in tough spots before with no ill effects.

Also, Cam was at least as smart as I am. Why was he so totally lost? That part couldn't figure. He should have been able to get to the bottom of this case in no time. Sure, it was confusing, but in only three days, I had figured out the crux of the whole situation. Certainly Cam could have done the same.

My second thought involved the whole "Le Change" process. I said earlier, I was anxious to get to the next sitting. That much was true. However, before I got to that sitting, I had to feel comfortable that I would not be creating a future nightmare for myself and Gale. Since the others, could not, or would not, help me, I was convinced that I would have to find the answers on my own. I was tired of screwing around. This was serious, and this certainly was no game.

I couldn't get the thought out of my mind that this whole "Le Change" business is designed to bring Cam back from the dead, and that this was to be at the expense of Kyle Washington's worthless ass. Kyle would be our sacrificial lamb. I shivered at the thought, though I wasn't cold.

This whole spiritual quest had me spooked. Not because of the spiritual aspect of it all, but because of the moral aspects involved. Basically, I am a moral person. The morality of this whole issue was the last thought I had before I turned the Escort into the library parking lot.

I still had a lot of Christian influence in my background. Background, that kept echoing thoughts about devil worship, and evil spirits into my mind.

I've said it before, but each time this becomes an issue again, it makes me wish I hadn't watched so many episodes of the "Twilight Zone", when I was younger.

I pushed the glass door of the library open. The acid smell of many ancient writings burned into my nostrils. It had been so long since I had been in a library, that I felt totally lost. Gone were the card indexes, and sitting in their place was a computer terminal.

My first instinct was to dash for the Escort while it was still warm. I took a deep breath, walked over, and faced the colored screen.

Next to me there was a kid about ten years old, that was clickity-clicking through the screens like he owned the joint. Smart ass, I thought. I began to read the screen. "Enter book title or author's name and push, "Enter".

That was it. I was out of there. I looked left and right. I was alone. I thought to myself, now how the hell was I going to do that. I had no idea what I was even after, much less, a book title.

I decided to walk around a bit, and see if the answer would miraculously jump off the shelves into my lap.

I headed to the "Reference" area. After a few moments of wandering, I stood in the "Religious" section, pouring over the titles. There was a soft hand on my arm. It startled me. I tried not to show it, and turned to see who was hooked onto the other end of it. There stood the first love of my life, Thelma Hancock.

"Need some help?" she smiled, her soft southern drawl soothing my frustrations, and my anxiety.

I laughed, "How could you tell?"

"Librarians smell people in trouble," she said. Her smile never wavered, and neither did her gaze into my eyes. She looked good.

It had been more years than I could remember since I had seen her, and from the looks of it, it had been my loss. The years had done her right.

Looking at Thelma, I had a strange feeling. Maybe I was homesick, or maybe I was just getting older, but I thought to myself, I really had good taste in women when I was younger. I was amazed by the fact that the women that had been part of early life, still looked so good after all these years.

Thelma had been a case of her own. Cam, and I had tried to fool her many times, but never succeeded. As a matter of fact, she would play along with us right up until we thought we were getting somewhere, then, Bingo, she would pop our bubbles. We even went so far as to wear each others clothes, but to no avail.

She still looked pretty much the same as she had the last time I remembered seeing her, years earlier. In the late fifties, I used to walk her home after school from "Taft Junior High".

Ours was a traditional young teen relationship, filled with love and giggles. But, for me, it was also my first semi-sexual encounter.

I've gotta tell you, the intrigue caused by our chance meeting, was very strong. I mean, doesn't everyone want to go back and find out what has changed in the life of their first love, after so many years?

No, we never got to the down and dirty. But, we did get as far "you show me yours, and I'll show you mine."

It was also Thelma's pert body that first christened my hands and mouth into the pleasures of the feminine form. Looking at her now, I thought there may be some unfinished business here, but for now, that would have to wait for another day, and another time.

I came back to reality.

"Yeah, you can help. I'm looking for a book on ancient religions."

"Like voodoo?" she offered.

"Yeah, how'd you know?"

Thelma smiled and shook her head, softly swinging her long brown hair. "I just knew."

"No, really. How did you know?"

Thelma laughed. "Because you're the second person today that has been in here asking for the same thing."

I got a deep sinking feeling in the pit of my stomach. I was afraid to ask the obvious question, but I forged ahead.

"Was this a guy, maybe six one, or six two with a moustache?"

Thelma nodded and became serious.

"Yeah. How'd you know that?"

"Lucky guess," I muttered.

What this meant, was that Kyle was nowhere near as stupid as I had given him credit for. It also meant that somewhere down the line, the security system Jack and Carolyn had devised to keep tabs on him, had a very serious flaw.

I needed to find out if he had learned anything about our plans, and also about what had gone wrong at Jack and Carolyn's.

I decided, I would try and figure out the first question first. There would be time to check on security later. I returned to the matter at hand.

"Did he find what he was looking for?" I asked cautiously.

Thelma shook her head, "I don't think so. He seemed frustrated. We did have the book he wanted, but an older gray-haired lady had it checked out. She just brought it back a little while ago. Do you want to see it?"

I nodded, and breathed a sigh of relief. Lillian had conveniently beaten Kyle to the punch. I thought to myself, with luck like this, we may be able to pull this thing off yet." Thelma was back with the book. It looked ancient, and worn.

"Can I check it out," I asked.

Thelma smiled, "Do you have a current library card, Mr. Thomas?"

I knew there were all kinds of innuendos there. Instinctively, I wanted to follow them, but I opted to just figure out what I had to do to get the book into my hands. My having it, meant that it was out of Kyle's reach.

I would keep it, at least until I decided whether or not all this spiritual stuff was feasible, and whether or not I wanted to be part of it. That decision would be based on what I found out from the book.

CHAPTER 30

The book was tattered and old. After filling out a couple of forms, I checked out the book, took it into one of the reading rooms, and cracked it open.

After only a couple of minutes, I found a section on "Le Change Complete". Most of the preliminaries, I already knew. However, when my eyes caught the sub heading on "The Physical Presence", I slowed my reading to a snail's pace. "Spirit manifests the physical", it read.

This was the most profound concept of the entire writing. Seems as though we are, or were, spirit beings first. That is, before we became physical beings, we were spirit beings.

I always figured that the physical presence was the most dominant force in the universe. However, that principle had been shaken a lot in the past few days.

I read on. After reading a few more of the age-darkened pages, I found a section that covered the history of "Le Change". It seems as though, around the turn of the century "Le Change" was relatively commonplace.

At that time people would have get-togethers, like seances, and people would actually volunteer to go back into the spirit realm, simply to let another spirit become physical for a period of time.

I figured that if it was so common then, that it probably wouldn't be too hard to pull off now. It was interesting to know that the power of the spirit was all encompassing.

When the change was complete, virtually every aspect of the existence, both physical, and spiritual were altered to accommodate the new status.

This meant that when Cam came back, no one would really remember that he was ever gone. I wondered then, how people would be able to switch back to the spiritual from the physical, when the "Le Change" time was completed.

If everyone's memory changed, or we all forgot, who would say. OK, times up?" For all I knew, that was the job of the boogie man, or something. Somehow, there had to be a key to switching everything back.

The next page answered my two key questions. One person is designated as the "Concierge", or keeper-of-the-gate. They know, and remember all aspects of the change.

It is their responsibility to keep timing accurate and to call the group together again for the switch back. In the old days, this was simple, because everyone volunteered. Our situation would be quite different.

I wondered who would be chosen as our concierge, and how the selection would be accomplished. From what I understood, it was the physical spirit that made the choice, not the spiritual spirit.

I found it interesting to know that creating a new physical body, or eliminating one, was the easiest part of the whole deal. The spirits use a substance called ectoplasm. Ectoplasm is a combination of sixteen chemical elements drawn from the earth's atmosphere.

As the physical being begins to manifest, a few simple adjustments from the spirit side of life, finalizes the re-materialization.

I closed the book. It was getting dark out, and it was nearly time for me to head to the church. I had been so enthralled in my research, that I failed to notice that I was starving.

Thelma saw me leaving and came over to say good-bye.

She smiled, "Nice to see you again."

I smiled back and nodded.

"Call me up sometime," she added, handing me a slip of paper with her number on it.

"I will," I answered, routinely.

We shook hands, I turned and walked back through the glass doors, and out into the cold.

Sure, it was nice to see her again, I thought. But, now was not the right time. Too many things had changed, and I didn't have the time to catch up on old times now. Thelma would have to wait.

The Escort was cold, and struggled a little to get started. When it finally fired, I goosed it and hit the heater switch to high.

The gnawing in my stomach called for something out of the ordinary, so I pulled into "Top Hat Hamburgers" for a few sliders and a tall Coke. It had been a very long time since I had sampled one of the nutritional mainstays of my youth, and I was ready.

I gave my order to the voice in the box, and headed for the "First Window". Tonight would be interesting, I thought. Especially now that I had a broader understanding of what was going on.

After the exchange of a small amount of money, I headed to "Window Number Two" and picked up my food.

Top Hat Hamburgers had a smell like no other food in the world. My stay at the second window was also brief, and I was soon on my way, heading North towards the church.

My mouth watered in anticipation of the unique taste of the allegedly nutritious morsels. At least I always wanted to believe that they were nutritious.

One thing was certain, they quickly knocked out the gnawing hunger that I felt, and did other unusual things to the aroma of my breath.

I felt grubby. My instincts said that I should have taken a detour back to the Holiday, and cleaned up some. I laughed to myself. Hell, this was only a dry run. Certainly, I would have time to fix up, clean up, and dress up, later on. What I didn't know at the time, was that this was a decision that I would soon regret.

CHAPTER 31

The lights in the basement of the old church seemed very bright tonight, as if someone had replaced several sixty watt bulbs with one-hundreds.

I arrived at the church a little earlier than mom and the girls, so I got myself a cup of coffee, seasoned it with cream and sugar, shook out a Red and fired it up. I could hear someone moving around upstairs. I figured it was Lillian.

The smoke from the Pall Mall actually tasted great. At least it took the edge off the onion smell and taste of the "Top Hats". It was also nice to relax in the quiet, alone with my thoughts.

Perspective is a funny thing. No matter how you look at something, someone else will see the same thing, in different way. My perspectives on this whole issue had gone full-circle in the last few days. Now, I was an active participant, unafraid, almost anxious, to be part of it all.

I felt a sense of—well, for lack of a better description—arrogance, about the whole deal. That disturbed me. I had a feeling that the attitude of arrogance was off base somewhere. That I was supposed to still be afraid, and still want to get away from the spiritual influences.

For the first time in a long while I heard my little voice warn me to stay on guard. That really disturbed me.

"A penny for your thoughts." I turned towards the female voice, and there stood Carolyn.

I laughed, took the last hit on my cigarette, and snuffed out the butt in one of the well-worn aluminum ashtrays on the table.

"Yeah," I laughed, "A penny may be too much for my thoughts these days."

I stood up and gave her a polite hug.

"I thought you were Lillian," I offered.

Carolyn said, "Lillian usually comes a little later on. How come you're here so early?"

I shrugged. "I wasn't paying that much attention to the time. You know in California, its only four-thirty. I really didn't think I would be this early," I said. "Should I go, or something?"

It was Carolyn's turn to laugh. "No, of course not. You aren't that early," she answered, emphasizing the word that.

"Besides," she continued "The church is always open to those who are seeking."

My brief rest had almost made me forget a very important issue.

"Carolyn, who was watching Kyle today?"

Carolyn frowned, anticipating my question.

"I was, why?"

"Because, we nearly had a major problem."

I related the story of the library, and Carolyn's frown deepened.

"He only wanted something to read."

I handed her the book.

"This is exactly what he wanted to read. He even asked for it by name. I think we had better be doubly careful with this guy."

Carolyn's frown turned to a look of anxiousness. "I'd better call Jack," she said, heading for the stairs, and the phone.

She quickly turned the corner, and disappeared.

"Yeah, I guess you should," I said to no one, after she had turned the corner, and passed from sight.

Another thought crossed my mind. I had understood Carolyn to say that she was watching Kyle tonight. Yet, she was here and Kyle was not. When she came back, I would have to find out where he was.

The rush of cold air told me that someone had opened the outside door. Angie, Raven, and Jerry came down the stairs. Jerry looked around.

"Man, it's bright in here," he said.

I suddenly felt a little more sane.

"I thought so too, where's Gale?"

Jerry looked at me at me blankly. The blank look turned to an Oh, shit kind of look.

"I thought she was with you" he said.

"Uh-uh," I answered. "I was at the library all afternoon. Wasn't she at mom's?"

Jerry nodded, "She was, but right after you left, she wanted to go back to the hotel for a while, so we took her."

"We thought you were gonna stop by and pick her up," he added.

My stomach sank deeply. Now it was my turn to frown, and head for the phone.

Shit, shit, shit, I thought. If that bastard—." I let my thoughts end there as I turned towards the church office.

When I walked through the door into the small room, Carolyn was just finishing her call.

"Jack, be careful. Sean seems to think Kyle knows what's going on."

After the closing incidentals, Carolyn set the heavy black receiver back onto the base.

It was encouraging to see that not everyone had sold out to the cheap, Far Eastern imitation phones so prevalent these days. Without my asking, Carolyn offered a synopsis of her conversation with Jack.

I was relieved to hear that Kyle was still there, and under Jack's watchful eye. Jack had mentioned that Kyle was full of questions, but that he had avoided answering most of them.

"Good idea," I thought. "So how come you're here, and not Jack?" I asked.

Carolyn's attitude was serious. "Jack wasn't comfortable with the way things were going. I guess Kyle said something about being able to, take, anyone. That scared me."

I nodded, and this time I said "good idea".

I motioned to the phone.

"I've gotta find out what happened to Gale."

Carolyn looked puzzled.

"What do you mean?" she asked.

"She's not here," I answered. "Jerry and Raven haven't seen her."

"Wasn't she coming with them?"

"I thought she was. But, they thought I picked her up. I haven't talked to her since this morning."

Carolyn shook her head anxiously, adding, "I'll wait downstairs."

Carolyn left the office, turned the corner, and disappeared. I picked up the heavy receiver.

There was something nostalgic about using a rotary dial phone. As much as I hated the new technological crap that was forced upon us, the "Clickity-click" of the rotary dial, as it returned to "Zero", seemed almost melancholy.

The phone began ringing at the other end. I reached for my pack. The smell of the fresh tobacco was inviting. I put the Red between my lips, and reached for my lighter.

"Good evening, thank you for calling the Holiday Inn-East, this is Wendy, how may I help you?"

The intro was so long and syrupy that I almost puked, and nearly forgot what I was calling for.

I gave Wendy my room number, and thought to myself, What kind of karmic debt must someone have to have, to be forced to live their life as a desk clerk at the Holiday Inn?

The phone rang, again and again.

I resumed my "Quest for Fire". Evidently I had left my lighter in the basement. When you have the habit real bad, if you can't smoke one, you'll eat one, just to get a nicotine fix. After some serious thought, I passed on that idea. The phone kept ringing.

I was just about to hang up the phone when a very groggy voice whispered "Hello", in my ear.

"Gale?" I asked. The voice cleared her throat.

"Yeah, who's this?" I didn't like the tone of her voice.

"It's Sean" I said.

"Sean, who?" Gale asked.

Now I was worried. Gale didn't sound like she was playing.

"Sean Thomas, Gale," I snapped. "Were you sleeping?" My heart was racing.

"What the hell do you want?" Gale demanded.

Alarms went off in my head. We've been had, was my only thought. I figured my best defense would be a strong offense.

"I want you to get up and get your buns dressed. I'll pick you up in fifteen minutes."

"To go where?" Gale continued groggily. I started to answer, but thought better of it.

"Gale, are you OK?" I offered tentatively, suspecting the worst.

"I guess so. Why do you care?" she asked.

"Is this Gale Anderson?" I asked, thinking that somehow they had buzzed the wrong room.

"No, it's not. My name is Gale Washington."

Gale Washington? I wish I could put into words the thoughts that were crashing around in my head right now. I was tremendously anxious at this moment, and really didn't know where to start.

"Gale, do you know who I am?" The other end of the line was silent, so I prompted, "Gale?"

After a moment's pause, Gale answered.

"Yes," she snapped back, "I've heard of you. You're after my money. You and your friends want me to worship the devil."

The way she said, friends, was not friendly. There was hate and bitterness in her voice. Kyle had done his number well.

My only thought was to say "stay there," and I said so. Gale mumbled something about her husband coming home from work.

"Right," I said, and hung up the phone.

It was nice, that phone. I slammed it down hard and it still worked perfectly. If I had done that with my office phone, I'd have pieces all over the place, and be on my way to K-Mart to get a replacement. I headed for the stairs. It was time for a conference.

Everyone was freaked out by what I told them. Somehow Kyle had tripped a hidden switch. I left the others in the basement, and headed for the phone again.

The ringing at the other end was interrupted by a familiar voice.

"Susan?" I said, "this is Sean."

"Hello, Sean," came, the pleasant reply. I wasn't feeling very sociable at this point, so I cut the pleasantries.

Susan listened intently as I relayed the story, not saying anything until I had finished. The deep sigh, followed by her drawn out words.

"Well, well, well," she said. This alone told me that we had a formidable adversary on our hands.

Susan was quiet, obviously thinking.

"Sean, we need to get to her as soon as possible. Meet me in the hotel lobby as quick as you can get there."

I hung up the phone and headed for the basement.

After a short explanation to the rest of the folks, I headed for the Holiday.

* * * * * * * * * * * * * *

I had been waiting in the lobby for about ten minutes when Susan came in. Her face was solemn and determined. I guess mine was as well.

"Sorry to keep you waiting," she said. "I had to make some phone calls. We have a real case here. What we have is what is called a delayed thought transfer cue."

"Delayed, what?"

"Thought transfer cue. But, don't worry about it," she snapped. She took a deep breath, and then spoke rapidly.

"As we try and de-program one thought or level, another one kicks in. Kyle could trigger it with a word or phrase, simply from a phone call. He could call her up and say something as simple as Hello Gale, this is your husband Kyle, and the rest would be history."

I didn't speak for a minute. I guess I was overwhelmed at what I had heard. As cautious as we all had been, we had seriously underestimated Kyle and his vindictiveness. If he had done this to Gale, he may have also done it to Angie, and who knows how many others.

"How many levels could he have used?" I asked, hoping that the most he could use would be two levels. Since we were already at two, I knew that was a stupid question.

Susan shook her head. "I don't know. The most I have ever heard of was four. The bad thing," she continued, "Is that there's no telling what the next step is, without doing some heavy digging."

"I'm going to go down to the room, and try and tip her off the end, without her knowing it. If I don't come back in ten minutes, come down to the room, and be quiet."

I nodded and watched Susan walk down the hall. Great, I thought. And what if Gale refuses to participate? I envisioned, Linda Blair in "The Exorcist", her head spinning around, spewing pea soup. Somehow knowing the fact that it was only pea soup in the movie, didn't seem to help at this moment.

I wondered if maybe the last step of the programming was to convince Gale that she was destitute, and then when she got destitute, she was supposed to blow her brains out or something.

In all my life, I've never had the serious inclination to kill anyone, but if I ever did, Kyle Washington would be my first.

The ten minutes passed like an eternity. I realized that Gale was more than just another dame, and I made a vow. If Kyle permanently screwed up Gale's life, I would kill him.

While I waited, Angie, Raven, and Jerry walked into the lobby. I filled them in on what was going on, and told them that the ten minutes were up. It was time to go down to our room.

Jerry and Raven decided to wait in their own room, so we walked down the hall together. They stood and waited, while I pulled the room key from my pocket.

The plastic key was virtually silent as I slipped it into the slot. Susan had said for me to come in, so when Angie and I stepped through the doorway, Susan looked a little surprised.

After a momentary gaze of recognition, Susan turned her attention back to Gale, and said softly, "Gale, I want you to visit that special place in your mind again. When you are there, let me know."

A few moments passed and Gale spoke softly.

"I'm here."

Susan glanced in our direction, and gave us the hi sign. Without turning back to look at Gale she spoke softly, in a monotone.

"Gale, I want you to rest here. Visualize your life as you wish it would be. In a few moments, we'll talk again."

Susan stood and motioned towards the bathroom area. Angie and I tiptoed into the small alcove, and turned to face Susan.

Susan spoke quietly.

"Sean, I am at level five. I think I have her where she can function in the present, but if I were to try and go through all the levels, there's no telling how long it would take. It seems that he has planted a seed that generates new levels without further intervention."

"I told her that she had been having bad dreams. I don't know how well it will work, but for now it's all I can do. I want her to re-meet everyone, then I will plant a hypnotic virus in her subconscious, that I hope will erase the levels, and the seed, regardless of how many levels there are."

It all seemed like hocus-pocus to me, but I kept my feelings to myself.

"Are you sure the virus will work?" I asked.

Susan shook her head.

"No, I'm not. "I haven't even the slightest idea what the scope is that we are dealing with. If we are lucky, and there aren't too many levels, we should see a steady but gradual improvement. One thing is certain, she's going to need some extended care.

Angie and I looked at each other. I guess we all knew it was a crap-shoot, no matter how optimistic it seemed.

I had two objectives. One was to get Gale back to the way she was, and the second was to fix Kyle Washington's ass, once and for all.

Gale slowly opened here eyes. Her face had more color. She smiled when she saw me.

"I guess I overslept," she said.

I laughed, a little nervously.

"Just a little," I said.

"Sorry."

"It's no big deal," I reassured her, walking over to the bed, and leaning down to kiss her on the forehead. "We were worried about you, so we came to see if you were okay."

Gale pursed her lips.

"God, I've had some weird dreams in my life, but this one was the weirdest ever. I dreamed I even married Kyle."

I was seriously embarrassed. I mean, I do this for a living, right? Somewhere along the way, I had misjudged Kyle Washington. I had him pegged as a relatively harmless idiot.

Sure, you might figure that with his rap sheet, we should have expected that he might be up to something more than petty swindling.

I have found that many times, in cases like this, some of the alleged charges are drummed up, or hearsay. But not this time.

It was evident that Kyle had taken a turn away from the apparently, harmless, crimes, and into a field of more serious acts. Certainly the type of things he had done to Gale could have ruined her life.

When things like this happen, it adds credence to the probability that the other charges were not drummed up, but are authentic. Fact is, I'll bet everything that John said about Kyle's record was accurate. Kyle had made a mockery of all of us, especially me, and that pissed me off big time.

I was mostly pissed at myself. Pissed that I had let my guard down so much, as to be hoodwinked by the likes of Kyle Washington.

See asshole, I told you so, I thought, blaming my scatterbrained mind for falling in love. Perhaps this was the first time I had actually thought the

"L" word in a long time. But, Gale was worth it. I only hoped she was not permanently effected by Kyle's influence on her life.

All the pieces were finally coming together. I was feeling a lot like I felt when Jan was killed in San Francisco, so many years before.

I was thoroughly enraged. A great portion of my ire stemmed from the fact that I was mad at myself for being so stupid, but you can rest assured that I wasn't going to take my anger out on myself, Kyle Washington would bear the brunt of my feelings, period.

I turned to the girls, "Will you all look after Gale? I've gotta get out of here for a while, and run some errands. I'll be in touch with you guys later."

I headed down the hall towards the door. As I neared the lobby, I could hear the voices of the others.

When I turned the corner, the conversation stopped, and all eyes were on me. I felt compelled to update the rest of them. After a brief synopsis, I confirmed that the next meeting was on Thursday at seven o'clock, and I hit the cold air.

I was on my way to Carolyn and Jack's. It was only after I had backed out of the parking space that I realized, I didn't know where they lived.

I needed some smokes anyway, so I figured I would stop at a gas station, pick up a pack, and give Jack a call. My hope was, that Kyle would still be there, and wouldn't know I was coming. I had a surprise for him, and I wouldn't call it a pleasant surprise.

CHAPTER 32

I think it was the cold and the snow that kept Kyle from passing out completely. I mean, I did everything I could do to kill the bastard with my bare hands, but he still lay moaning in the snow. Maybe I should kick him and put him out of his misery?

Nah, I thought. He's not worth it. Plus, we needed him around for a while. Still, I hadn't felt that much rage inside myself, in a long time. It was not like me to be that out of control. Maybe I was just getting old, or maybe I should have kept training regularly, or maybe it was the cigarettes. I had wanted to quit for a long, long time. Maybe now.

I left Kyle laying face down in the snow and went back into Jack and Carolyn's house. I needed to put a bandage on my hand, and I wanted to make a phone call.

The hand? I hit ass-hole, so hard in the face that it split the skin on the back of my hand. It looked like I might need a little needlework, but it was worth it.

Jack, who normally seemed docile, was there with us, twisting and turning with each blow. I felt vented.

As I rested, I began to catch my breath, and to feel the pump, that can only be brought on by beating someone's ass. I made a mental note to start back in my karate training when I got back to San Francisco.

Like a lot of other things, my martial arts training had fallen by the wayside in recent months. I guess, looking back, I hadn't planned this portion of my life too well.

Jack and Carolyn had phones all over their house, I took the one in the kitchen.

The phone rang at the other end for what seemed like an eternity, and finally the voice told me that I had reached Detective Stephens.

John said he would have a squad car at the house in a few minutes. I looked out the window that faces the back of the house, and saw Kyle laying motionless, still face down in the snow.

I suggested to John that they bring a rescue squad also, but asked that they use no lights or sirens. I wanted to keep this episode, low-key.

Looking out into the backyard, I had a fleeting thought that maybe I had killed the

poor bastard. I figured it was no sweat if I did, after all he did swing first.

The paramedic looked familiar, but I couldn't place his name. John told me that the paramedic was Todd Hancock, Thelma's ex-husband.

Perhaps, he either didn'trecognize my name, or chose not to make an issue of it.

Kyle wasn't dead, but he was on a one-way to Beaumont Hospital for repairs. I had the small consolation of knowing that with his jaw being severely broken in a couple of places, I wouldn't have to worry about Kyle running his mouth for a while.

Some joke. I laughed a little, as I wondered whether the wire they were going to put in his mouth to wire his jaw shut, might act as an antenna to improve our reception from the spirit world. Maybe that would keep him on the straight and narrow.

Their task complete, the rescue squad moved slowly down the street towards the hospital. John was back at my side.

"You gonna press charges?" he asked.

I thought I had misheard him. I turned to face him.

"Say again?"

He continued, "Charges? Do you want to press assault charges against Kyle?"

I had heard him correctly, but I didn't believe what I heard, I just stared at John.

He continued, "Jack told he swung first."

I nodded, then shook my head.

"Yes, he did. And no, I don't want to press charges."

"What I would like, is for Kyle Washington to be out of circulation until

I finish up some business. Maybe a week at the outside."

My mind was working fast and furious. John figured with the broken jaw, the cracked or broken ribs, and the concussion, Kyle wouldn't feel like running around much for the next week or so anyway.

"Can you put him in medical custody?" I asked.

"Sure, no sweat," John answered. "With all the wants and warrants against him, he could be an old man before we even get to checking all of those out."

I chuckled knowingly to myself, "Not a chance, Detective Stephens, not a chance."

The paramedics had made quick work of my hand, no stitches, thank you very much, so I felt pretty good. I started to head for the house, but stopped.

"John?"

"Yeah," he answered showing the first signs of irritation.

"No outside contact. If he needs something, have them call me, I'll take care of it."

"You got it. But Sean, this had better be worth my effort."

"Trust me, John. You'll love it."

John walked towards his unmarked, and I headed for the house, I was freezing. Jack met me at the door. He smiled wryly as I entered.

"We've got to move fast, Sean. We really have no time to waste."

Jack was right. We did have to get moving. Kyle was a dangerous individual. He had proven that fact with his treatment of Gale.

The fact that he had set off some psychological time-bomb in Gale, and had tried to get his hands on the library book, told me that he may have even been a little ahead of us. That worried me.

The book had reassured me that the "transferee" did not have to be in attendance for the "Le Change" process to work. As Kyle was being whisked off to the hospital, I hoped the book was right.

We only had one plus on our side. Like it or not, Kyle's being in custody was our only advantage for the moment.

You may remember, I had questioned the morality of this whole scheme. Kyle's latest efforts had made me opt to discard the concept of "fair play", and replace it with an attitude of "win at all costs".

I remember our dad trying to teach Cam and I to play fair. He would always start out with his best radio announcer's voice, the one that he used when he got to the fire and brimstone parts of his sermons.

He would say "Boys, never hit a man when he's down." That was his idea of fair play.

I guess with ninety percent of humanity, that philosophy is okay. But, there is the ten percent of the population that doesn't understand reason. They only understand a fist in the face. Kyle Washington was one of those people.

As a general rule, I do my best to try and stay clear of those types of people. However, in Kyle's case, I was going to implement the "Lawrence of Arabia" theory. That is, "No prisoners and no survivors". It was time to contact the others.

CHAPTER 33

The static in the air of the basement seemed to crackle like damp wood in a roaring fireplace. This was not imagined energy. This was real.

I reached out to touch Gale on her arm, just beneath the sleeve of her blouse, and even before my hand made contact with her skin, a blue flash caused us both to jump.

Gale laughed nervously.

"Heh-heh," I offered, "Dry in here."

Both of us knew that the electricity which we felt, had nothing to do with the atmosphere of the church. This was spiritual energy.

I looked around the basement meeting room. The people there, were in small groups, talking softly. Gone was the gaiety and outspokenness of the other sittings.

The air seemed chilled. No one drank coffee, or joked, not even me. In all honesty, I was afraid to do anything out of the ordinary.

I laughed at that thought. I didn't know what ordinary was anymore. It appeared that everything was following the dictates of an unseen, unwritten agenda. I was scared.

Jonathan finished positioning the chairs, and placing the glasses of water on them, until all of the positions were filled.

Then, like a minister at an alter call, he stood up, looked in our direction, and said simply, "It's time".

I gave Gale's hand a final squeeze, and waited to be seated. The silence in the room was broken only by the slight scuffling of the chairs as everyone moved them to sit down.

I knew that the next step was the lowering of the lights. A slight sense of panic crossed my mind when I looked over at the empty chair where Kyle would have normally sat.

What I really felt like doing, was loosing myself from the tension, by jumping up and leaving this meeting.

Escape by any means possible, I thought. Fortunately, or unfortunately, I didn't get the chance to act. Jonathan had begun dimming the lights, and people moved around in their seats, trying to get in comfortable positions before the session began.

In only a moment, the room was totally dark. I opened my eyes, and waited for them to adjust to the darkness. Looking around the room, I saw that most everyone had their eyes tightly closed, hands, palms-up, on their knees, waiting patiently to begin.

I mentioned, that there was electricity in the air. It was so bad, that the hair was standing up on my arms.

I felt a chill, as though someone had left the door open. There also seemed to be a rushing sound, similar to how the air sounds when the wind buffets and trumpets on a March day.

After what seemed to be an eternity, Lillian spoke in a deep throaty voice that I had not heard before.

"Good evening friends, and welcome."

It was as though, she was already entranced.

I found that odd, since we had not done any of our incantations or songs. The voice continued.

"Lillian has asked me to lead you tonight, so that we may bring forth a manifestation of spirit into life. Please focus your gaze on the vacant chair."

Personally, I was afraid to look. I don't know why, but it was a real struggle to look.

When I finally did, I noticed an outline, almost as though someone, albeit without substance, was sitting in the chair.

"I am Dr. Watson. Please follow me with me in the preparation."

I couldn't help but notice the crackling sound in the room. It sounded very much like what you might hear on a record that had a scratch on it, but much sharper, and clearer.

Being the skeptic that I am, I tried to figure out if this might be a setup, or a trick of some kind. I vanquished the thought when a sharp crack occurred right next to my ear.

It startled me so much, that under the cover of the darkness in the room, I secretly checked myself, to see if I had pissed in my pants.

In the next few minutes, we said our normal prayers, and incantations. We sang our usual songs to raise our vibration levels. As we sang, I swear I heard music somewhere, accompanying our singing.

After we sang the last verse of "In The Garden", the room became deathly quiet, no pun intended. We all sat waiting.

After a moment, I realized I had been holding my breath. I exhaled slowly and quietly. Dr. Watson spoke again, this time in such a loud volume, that everyone jumped.

"Call now to your spirit guides," he said, "Call to your loved ones."

This said, everyone began mouthing the names of their guides and friends in spirit. I felt a little uncomfortable, so I called to Cam. I mean, who else did I have?

It really never crossed my mind to call dad. I guess maybe I figured he was in heaven or something, and out of range. I know that's contradictory, but at a moment like this, who has time for reason.

The room felt as though it was trembling, much like a small earthquake was centered right here in our own little space.

Out of the corner of my eyes, I saw flashes of movement, which I perceived were spirit travelers, answering their beckonings.

My skin tingled, and felt cold. I decided that I would make this my last session, and I meant it. I wanted to run, but I couldn't move. I was glued to the seat in this position, with my gaze fixed on the empty chair.

The popping or crackling I was hearing, resembled the sound that popcorn makes when it is beginning to pop. Not steady, but frequent.

"Spirit of spirits," Dr. Watson began, "Infinite Intelligence which we call God, bring to us the manifestation of Cameron Thomas. Say Amen."

We all softly repeated, "Amen". Dr. Watson continued.

"Please say after me. Spirit guides, loved ones, bring to us the manifestation of Cameron Thomas."

I mouthed the words out loud, as did the rest of the seekers.

"Repeat after me, Spirit of Spirits, God of Gods, bring to us the manifestation of Cameron Thomas."

I looked to my left and right, as I spoke. The room was alive with darting lights, like a hundred fire flies, juiced up on speed, with nowhere else to go.

As crazy as this sounds, my chair was rocking and rolling. Whether it was a perception on my part, or a reality, I didn't know. What I did know, was that I wanted to grab hold of the sides of my chair to hold on.

The tension in the room seemed to mount to a crescendo, and the rushing sound was now a roar, the popping sound now a concert. Dr. Watson spoke loudly.

"Release the spirit of Kyle Washington. Send his spirit home."

I looked at the empty chair. It was full. There before my eyes, sat Cam. Casually dressed, eyes closed, his hands also resting palms up on his thighs.

Now, you've got to believe that I hadn't breathed a breath in about ten minutes anyway, but the sight of Cam sitting there caused me to gasp. This time, I didn't have to check my pants.

I wondered to myself how long this session would last. I felt drained. Then, just as dramatically as it started, I felt a rush of warm air go past my face, there was one loud final crack, and the room was deathly silent. I looked at Kyle's chair, it was empty.

It seemed longer than it actually was, but after a few moments, Lillian whispered to Jonathan to turn up the lights. Angie and mom cried softly, others recited prayers. I was drenched in sweat. Though during the seance I was frozen, I now felt very warm.

"We almost had him," Lillian said, to no one in particular. "We were so close."

It seemed as though no one wanted to talk about our near miss. The vacant chair, still vacant, sat as an ominous reminder of our failed efforts.

I looked at my watch. We had been involved for more than an hour. I was drained. Gale came over, and we hugged closely and silently, for several minutes, consoling each other over our missed opportunity.

Lillian sat solemnly, looking exhausted. It was time to give her a perk for her efforts. I walked to where she was seated, drinking her water.

Before I could speak, she said, "We need another voice, Sean. We're not quite strong enough alone."

I wasn't sure what that meant, but I cupped her hand in both of mine.

"Lillian, we did good. We'll get him next time." I said.

Lillian nodded "I'll see to that, Sean. I'll see to that."

Jonathan came over to where I was standing with Lillian.

"Sean, there was a message on the answering machine for you to call the hospital. It sounded urgent."

"Thanks Jon," I answered and headed for the phone.

"Can I have the Medical Custody Unit, please?" I asked the pleasant voice on the hospital's end of the phone.

"One moment, please."

"M.C.U., Officer Hume, can I help you?"

"Sean Thomas here," I said. "I had a message to call."

"Yes sir, Mr. Thomas," he said.

"Dr. Jargon wants to see you as soon as possible. He said he'll be available until midnight."

"Okay. Do me a favor, and tell him that I'm on my way to the hospital. Ask him not to leave until I get there."

"Will do," Officer Hume said.

I hung up the phone. Jerry and Raven agreed to take Gale back to the Holiday while I went to Beaumont Hospital. Before I left, I looked around the basement. I was surprised to see how subdued the atmosphere was. I guess all of this was just a little too much for everyone, even the long-term Spiritualists.

* * * * * * * * * * * * *

Two hours later, I was back in the Escort, sucking on a Red and heading back to the Holiday. The trip to Beaumont had been informative.

Driving to the hospital, I was curious as to what the effects of our efforts had been on Kyle, and on the people at the hospital.

In spite of all my pre-conceived expectations, I honestly hadn't expected to hear the things I had heard when I talked to Dr. Jargon. But, then again, I hadn't expected many of the things that had happened to me since I had been back in Motown.

This whole scenario was beginning to wear on my nerves. I mean, I'm open minded enough to face many things, but tonight—well, tonight—I was faced with things that I thought only happened in the movies. Enough punishment for one day, I thought. I needed some sleep.

CHAPTER 34

I awoke laying flat on my back. Gale's head was resting on my shoulder, her arm across my chest, her leg over mine.

I consider myself to be a semi-macho kinda guy, if there is such a thing. But, I also think that one of God's richest blessings is the smell, the touch, and the warmth of a naked woman's body.

I didn't think much about such things last night, but what the hell, I had other things on my mind then.

I had done my duty last night, and had gotten a lot of valuable information. Information that we would need if we were going to be successful at this transfer.

I had found out what had happened on the other end of our efforts. That, was critical information. While this information was important, it was also very interesting, and from our vantage point, very encouraging.

I don't know exactly what time it was when I finally crashed out last night, but I do know, that I was too tired then, to do what I wanted to do now.

I reached over and nudged Gale.

"Gale honey—"

She didn't move.

"Swee-e-etheart, it's time to wake up," I teased.

Gale laughed at my brazenness, and played coy and disinterested.

"No, I'm still too tired," she moaned, "Later, okay?"

"Not later. Now," I whined playfully.

Gale lifted her head from under the covers to look at me. I leaned over as she did, and kissed her softly on the lips.

My kiss told her that if we were to wait until later, that she may be passing up a very special occasion. The second kiss was all it took. Gale and I had this thing. She actually wanted me for more than just a fling or a quicky. I felt like she wanted many of the same things I did. I felt like a lucky man.

* * * * * * * * * * * * *

Gale was just coming out of the shower while I finished drying my hair. I watched her form in the mirror. I guess for the first time in my life, I had to admit that I really loved this woman.

This was not merely passion or lust, and it surely wasn't infatuation, I was much too old for that. I wanted to tell Gale my darkest secrets, my deepest fantasies, my hopes, my fears.

Gale dressed the way I like a woman to dress—feminine, yet foxy. I felt very lucky at this moment, but I also felt a little insecure that this moment might pass too quickly.

The knock at the door told me that Jerry and Raven were up and about, and ready for some chow.

I walked to the door and opened it wide.

"You ready to go?" he asked.

"Yeah, come on in." I stepped aside. Gale was just finishing putting on her boots. The fashion "De' jour," was my very favorite, jeans and dress boots, my, my, my.

We decided to eat in the restaurant in the hotel. Generally the food served in hotel restaurants is either over priced, over cooked, or over rated. This was a pleasant exception. I had eaten breakfast there before, and their omelets were delicious.

We followed the pleasant breakfast smells down the hall and into the brightly decorated restaurant.

The question posed by "Dolly" brought a response of "Smoking". We followed her to a corner booth, near the back of the restaurant.

As we took our seats, I felt a little bit of overt arrogance, knowing that I could smoke without violating someone's space.

I shook out a Red and lit it. The first hit was great. I guess that was one of the main reasons why I never gave up smoking in the first place. It was the way cigarettes tasted the first thing in the morning, and following a sumptuous meal.

I filled the air with pollutants, took a sip of Hills Brothers, and read the menu. For me, the menu was simply a formality. I wanted a deluxe omelet, and potatoes. "Dolly" came back just in time to keep things moving.

Gale ordered a feast, which made me feel good.

She hadn't been eating too well. Maybe she was starting to feel like her old self again.

We had almost no conversation since we left our rooms. I was looking down at the place-mat on the table, and felt the stares of my friends. I looked up, and just as I suspected, they were all staring at me.

I smiled, rubbing the bottom of my nose.

"What?"

"Nothing," they said in unison.

"Do I have a booger or something?"

Raven spoke first. "It's just that—"

"What?"

Jerry jumped in.

"All of us—well, at least Raven and I—are very interested in what happened at the hospital last night."

"Oh, that?" I laughed and countered, "What happened at the church?"

Gale took up the slack, smiling and pretending to stand up.

"Okay, you guys. Let's go. We'll leave "Mr. I'm Keeping This Secret To Myself", here by himself, and we'll go somewhere else to eat."

I gave in reluctantly. "Sit down. Why is it so important?"

Raven answered. Because, we can't plan another sitting unless we know what happened to Kyle."

I wasn't sure that we had all the answers, but I am sure that we were on the right track. I also wasn't sure we had enough time to cover all the things that had happened in the Beaumont M.C.U., but I figured they were entitled to an update.

"When I got to the hospital," I began, "Everyone in the M.C.U. was running around like a Chinese fire drill. There was an old guy there who had killed his wife, and then tried to kill himself. I thought maybe he had died."

"What really happened, was that Kyle had undergone a major change. At one point, they thought he had died. When I talked to Dr. Jargon, he said that he had never seen anything like what had happened to Kyle."

All eyes were staring at me. I took the cue, continuing.

"Evidently at precisely the time we were in session, the monitors on Kyle were flashing on and off. Kyle had no pulse or respiration, but his eyes were open, and he was talking, fighting an unseen enemy, as Dr. Jargon called it.

Dr. Jargon determined that Kyle was having some kind of near-death or out-of-body experience. Then, I guess, after about thirty minutes, there was a large flash, which the doc said, looked like lightening, a loud crack, and then everything returned to normal—his pulse, respiration, the monitors, everything."

"No shit," Jerry mumbled, dragging out the word No.

"Yeah, no shit," I answered. Jerry had the same response I did when Dr. Jargon relayed the events to me for the first time.

"They spent most of the night running all kinds of tests on him to see if anything could be found."

"So what did they find out?," Raven asked.

"Physically, they didn't find anything. They didn't have a clue."

"What they did find, which baffled them, was that most of his injuries had almost disappeared, including the broken bones."

The food was back, so we ate. The chow gave me a few minutes to collect my thoughts. I had saved the best for last, and I knew my friends would all be astonished, when I told them about Kyle's near disappearance.

After we had all stuffed enough grub in our mouths to quell the hunger pangs, I set down my fork, killed the rest of my cup and continued.

"The most interesting thing that occurred, took place just before the flash of light in the hospital room."

"The doc said, that for almost two full minutes, Kyle became virtually transparent. He said that they could see the bed clothes beneath him, by looking right through him. He flashed brighter and dimmer for more than a minute, then, the flash, and the loud crack. The doc said that there were four people in the room, and they all saw the same thing. "From what I heard him say, the doc swore them all to secrecy because he figured no one would believe them."

"He wouldn't have even told me, if the nurse hadn't slipped and said something."

"What do they think happened?" Gale asked.

I shrugged. "I'm not sure exactly. Maybe they thought it was an alien abduction or something."

"I tried not to ask too many questions, or offer any information. One thing they do know. It wasn't your everyday hospital experience."

"What's that supposed to mean?" Jerry asked.

I shrugged. "I'm not sure what they really think. I know they're not too anxious to talk about it with anyone outside the unit." I laughed, adding "Do you blame them?"

We all chuckled at the thought of Dr. Jargon and his staff trying to explain the change they saw, to a conservative medical group.

"Did you talk to Kyle?" Gale asked.

"Yeah," I said, "We talked. He made as many threats as he could possibly squeeze through his teeth. He tried to tell everyone about "Le Change", but it sounded more like he was sneezing through his teeth." I laughed.

"We do have a problem, though," I continued. "Kyle is fully aware of everything we are doing. He said he will do everything he can to fight it. He also said that he would get us, one and all."

"He'd better hurry," Jerry said. Thinking out loud that the transition was close at hand.

I wasn't as comfortable as Jerry was with that thought. I continued.

"When Kyle and I were alone, and he had calmed down somewhat, he told me that he had done his own research, and that what we were doing was child's play.

He also reminded me, that he had developed his mental powers, and was stronger than any of us alone, and stronger than most of the group, combined."

I noticed that everyone had slowed their eating, and seemed to be having troubling swallowing. This is one of those times I mentioned earlier. The times where you realize that, like it or not, you may be in, way over your head.

I wasn't afraid of Kyle in a physical sense. But, I was a beginner in dealing with spiritual things. I conceded that he may have had an advantage in this area. This thought I didn't like.

Lillian had said that she had a plan to finalize this whole deal. I suddenly felt a real sense of urgency to get the change completed. I figured that once the change was history, we would all be safe.

Safe was a word that I hadn't used in a long time. For me, it indicated fear, and I usually am not afraid of anything. This time I was afraid. Afraid of Kyle, afraid of the spiritual shit, afraid of this whole unknown, untried process.

I finished my last "Tater Tot", wiped my mouth, and leaned back. I knew I would have to call ma, and update her.

We decided to not express our fears, but rather just stick to the facts. Hopefully, that's all we would need to do at this point.

CHAPTER 35

I had a lengthy talk with mom about the events at the hospital. She listened in silence, not asking questions, or offering input.

When I finished, mom said, "Sean, I need you to pick someone up at the airport. The Reverend Ada Stitch is flying in from Cassadaga, Florida, at five-thirty."

"Who?"

"Ada Stitch. She's a medium, and a good one. She's coming to help us out. Will you pick her up?"

"Sure mom. What airlines?" I asked.

Mom shuffled papers for a moment before answering.

"She'll be on Northwest flight two fifty-five. I told her that you would have a sign with her name on it."

"Good thinking, ma." I said. "I'll be there to get her. Do you want me to bring her to your house?"

"Yes. And when you get here, I'll tell you what our next step will be, and when we will be holding the next session."

Kyle was healing fast, so we, also had to act fast. Because of the close spiritual encounter he had experienced, Kyle had been subject to intense spiritual influences. In this case, healing influences.

If we waited too long, Kyle would be well enough to leave the hospital in a day or so. We had planned on his internment in the hospital lasting at least a week. I took a gamble.

I called John and asked him to be sure we had at least a couple of extra days. He said he would do his best, but made me no promises.

"What's the big deal, Sean? Even if he leaves the hospital, he's still going to jail."

I knew that and said so, but added, "We need him to be isolated, just for a couple of days."

John now seemed seriously irritated.

"Just how many days, Sean?"

"Just through the weekend," I said, fishing for a time that I thought seemed reasonable.

John agreed, but grudgingly.

I knew that I had set a timetable that I wasn't sure we could keep, but I figured if it was meant to be, we'd work it out. For all I knew, maybe Reverend Ada was the answer. Time was short, I knew that. One way or the other, we would soon find out.

John didn't sound real enthusiastic about wanting to keep Kyle in the hospital. I'm sure he would just as soon have had him locked up behind bars, in a jail, like any other ordinary citizen.

I certainly didn't disagree with that philosophy, but for now, I would follow the dictates of the moment.

I knew Kyle had to stay where he was at, at least until we were through with our end of the program.

As long as Kyle stayed in the M.C.U., he was in virtual isolation. In jail, he would be allowed out in the mainstream jail population, where just about anything was possible.

Mom had suggested that the ideal time for the next session might be the next night, which coincidentally was Friday the thirteenth. I thought to myself, oh great, all I need now is a witch, a black cat and a broom, and the whole picture would be just peachy.

This lady, the Reverend Ada Stitch, was supposed to be some hotsy-totsy medium of some kind. Ma told me that Cassadaga, Florida was like the Spiritualist center of the South, with a lot of active and retired mediums living there.

Before leaving for the airport, I had taken the time to make up a sign that said "Rev. Stitch". I held it in front of me, and stood patiently waiting for her flight to unload.

I had no idea what Rev. Stitch looked like, so as the arriving passengers walked by, I held up my sign. Since paper and such, weren't one of my forte's, I had made the sign on the inside of a Pall Mall carton. Hey, it was the right size, and it was my way of snubbing my nose at the "no smoking" establishment.

Don't ask me how, but I knew she was coming off the plane even before I could see her. The aisle-way cleared and I saw her, there was no mistaking who she was.

Ada was a short woman, maybe sixty or sixty-five years old, blond hair tied in a bun, and gnarly. She looked like a tough ol' woman that would chew you up and spit you out, if you crossed her.

She walked, stoop shouldered, taking short but determined steps, all the while, confident of where she was going. I lowered the sign, and walked to where she stood.

"Reverend Stitch?" I asked.

"Yes, hello Sean," she answered without an introduction.

She looked at my sign and laughed.

"Made a sign, did you?" I suddenly felt very stupid.

"I would have known who you were. You could have waited in the lobby and I would have found you. You know that, don't you?"

I nodded, not knowing the correct answer. I sure as hell wasn't going to say no. Ada laughed a little cackle, just as the courtesy gurney pulled up to give us a ride to the baggage claim area.

I wondered how the guy knew to come and pick us up. Without my asking the question out loud, Ada answered.

"How do you think?" she asked.

That was it. It was obvious to me, that all that we had been doing with this spiritual stuff, was merely playing around. Ada would offer us a new dimension.

I had enough problems dealing with our part of this spiritual transfer. Now with Ada here, I was certain the spiritual aspects would be too much for me to handle. I felt in fear and awe of her presence.

In answer to her question about our ride, I simply shrugged that I didn't know. Ada smiled and winked.

"I called them from Florida before I left and set it up."

Then she laughed. Not a giggle, or a chuckle, but a real, honest to God, full blown, goose bump causing, hair raising, laughing cackle. Even the gurney driver looked at her with apprehension.

I felt like an asshole for not considering that possibility. Truly, all this spiritual interaction had me on edge.

I told you I had made Ada for sixty to sixty-five years old. As we spoke, she told me that she was eighty-two. I was surprised. Looking into her eyes, I saw a glint that derided her age. It was the sparkle of a much younger spirit.

I shook my head. There I was thinking spiritual again. I wondered what Ada was like when she was younger. Certainly, if the twinkle I saw in her eyes now was any indication, she must have been a fireball.

* * * * * * * * * * * * *

Wisely, I had picked "Valet" parking. We picked up Ada's bag from the baggage claim area, and walked to the valet area. I gave the kid my ticket, and he went to get the Escort.

"It's chilly," Ada said.

I nodded, "You kinda get used to it after a while."

"I'm originally from Lily Dale, New York," she added. "I never really liked the heat in Florida."

"How come you moved down there?" I asked.

"All the good mediums moved out," she said. "There wasn't nobody for me to talk to but my spirit friends and the four walls."

"I mean, I love 'em and all, but I'm still alive, and I need living folks. Can you understand that?"

I nodded like I did. I thought to myself, me, too. I curbed any other thoughts I had, for fear that she might pick up on them.

I slipped the kid a fin, closed Ada's door and walked around to the driver's side and opened the door. Before I got in, I reached for my pack, and shook out a Red.

Ada stared at me. "Don't light that."

I looked back at her. "What?" I asked.

Ada continued, "That cigarette. Don't light it. It messes up your vibrations," she added. "Besides, you smoke too much, anyway."

I got in. The unmolested Red was temporarily filed in the ash tray for later use.

Normally, that attitude would bother me. For some reason, this time it didn't. I headed for mom's.

"How long have you been a medium?" I queried.

Ada was looking out the window at the snow.

"All my life," she answered, not looking at me. Then turning to face me she added, "I was born a medium, raised a medium. I've been a medium ever since. Had my first trance when I was seven years old. Everyone had me pegged for convulsions, or the loony bin. They took me to court—wanted to lock me up with all those poor souls that really do have mental problems."

"I didn't want to waste my life bein' locked up, so I had a spirit dog come up and bite the judge in the ass. After that, they all left me alone."

There was that phrase again. As I heard it, I really wished that I had never used it. The rest of the ride was without comment. I was relieved to see the porch light of my mother's house. When we finally turned into mom's driveway, Ada seemed to come back to life, as though she had been sleeping, though her eyes were never closed.

"Here already?" she asked for no apparent reason. I presumed that she probably knew exactly when we were going to get there.

Mom had also mentioned that Ada was a tremendously powerful materialization medium.

Ada had shown me a bunch of shit that made me believe that her credentials were authentic. I also thought it was unusual that mom was opening the front door, just as we were turned into the driveway.

Because of my previous experiences with Ada, I wasn't about to ask any questions that I thought might be dangerous.

I got Ada's bag out of the trunk, and came to help walk her to the door.

"Thanks Sean, but I can make it by myself."

I let her walk, but stayed close for support.

Ada greeted mom like she had known her all her life, even though they had never met. Angie settled Ada into the spare bedroom, while mom and I talked. It was finalized that the next session would be on Friday. I told her of the conversation I had with John Stephens.

"Sean, if we are going to be successful, our best chance will be Friday. Ada, is a tremendous force. She has had a number of successful changes in the past. She thinks this one will be easy."

I hoped she was right. Mom didn't seem to be troubled by the timetable I had given John. I was relieved to know that.

I called the Holiday and checked in with Gale. Everything on that end of the phone was A-okay.

"Gale, you've got to meet this lady," I said. "She is strange but nifty."

"What kind of strange," Gale asked.

"I don't know how to describe it. Just strange. I'll tell you all about her when I see you."

"Are you coming back to the hotel tonight?" Gale asked.

"Yeah, I'll be there in a few. I'll pick us up something to drink. See if Jerry and Raven want to get some eats."

"Okay honey," Gale answered. "I'll see you soon."

I hung up.

Then it struck me. "Honey?" Well, well, well. I guess I wasn't the only one that felt the strength of a developing relationship.

I told mom that I would see her at the church on Friday, said my adieus to everyone, and headed for the cold.

The "State Fair Market" sold booze and goodies. I picked up an ample supply of both, and headed for the Holiday.

My plan for the evening included a sirloin, a baked with butter and sour cream, some cold wine, and a sweet woman— all in that order.

Unless I was wrong or sidetracked along the way, it was gonna be a pleasant night!

CHAPTER 36

Friday came a lot sooner than I had anticipated. Even though it was only one day since our last session, the hours flew by. I had hoped the time would pass more slowly.

Gale and I took advantage of the short interlude to rest, recreate, and regroup. Jerry and Raven spent their time sightseeing.

At first, I felt little neglected that they hadn't asked us to be involved in their running around. But, I felt stupid for thinking that when they called us to have breakfast and supper together. I guess I was being overly sensitive.

That's a part of this whole scenario that concerns me. Generally, I'm not a tremendously sensitive person.

Oh, I have my friends, and my moments, but generally I kinda let everyone else do their own thing without being effected by it.

Near as I can figure, this sensitive side, is an outgrowth of my fledgling relationship with Gale. It's nice to have someone to care about, but from a PI's viewpoint, it leaves you somewhat vulnerable.

Gale and I rode in anticipating silence to the church. I can't speak for how Gale felt, but anyone who has ever been involved in athletics knows that on game day, the adrenalin is extra high, the focus is high, and nerves are on edge. That's the way I felt.

Somehow or other, the idea that I was going to be part of an effort to eliminate a human being, didn't seem to bother me in the same way as it had in the past. I had rationalized that Kyle was a slug, and needed to be replaced any way possible.

The one thing that I did still have a difficulty with, was the fact that Cam had been no angel in his last days either. Maybe it was going to be an even swap.

My reasoning said that Cam had a lot more going for him than Kyle did. Also, on the positive side, maybe Cam wouldn't have strayed so far out of line if Kyle hadn't come into the picture.

I pondered on how Cam and Angie would get along after he got back, and whether or not the past would be remembered.

Dealing with the fact that your loved one has been running around is tough enough in the best cases. That much, I knew from experience.

When you add all this other shit into it, well, I didn't know that either one of them would be strong enough to cope with it all.

I hoped the book was right. It had said that after a nights sleep, everyone would forget the past. I knew it would make me feel a lot better if I forgot.

Gale sat quietly as we drove. I presumed her thoughts were as preoccupied as mine.

"Sean?" she asked. "How do we know all this won't blow up in our faces? I mean, what if we all still do remember. I know the book says we won't, but what if we still do?"

I secretly hoped that Gale was wrong, but I had the very same thoughts many times myself. I found myself reciting the part of the book where it talked about the effect sleep would have on our memories after the change was complete. I explained that after the first sleep, all would be forgotten, except for the memories of the concierge. I hoped that part was true.

We didn't have any time to discuss our thoughts in greater detail, because we were at the church. I turned the Ford into the small parking lot, got as close to the sidewalk as I could, and killed the engine. I lit up a smoke and looked at Gale.

"Gale, I don't know how all of this is gonna shake out when it's done, but I want to be sure you and I have something to come home to. Do you know what I mean?"

Gale played coy.

"No, Sean Thomas, I don't know what you mean. What do you mean?"

OK, so I wasn't the best with words, but I was trying to make a point, here. This was my best romantic move. I took a deep breath, and started again.

"I mean," I began, "I want to be sure that you are coming back to San Francisco with me. This thing could be over tonight. With all the shit that has been going on, I sure don't want to hang around any longer than I have to."

Gale laughed and nodded,

"Me neither," then after a moment's thought added, "Yes, Mr. Thomas, if you would like me to accompany you back to your humble scratchings in San Francisco, I would be delighted to do so."

That was a relief. I rolled down the window, and flicked the butt out.

"Gale, I don't know what's going to happen if we pull this off tonight, but I booked reservations for a flight out on Sunday. Jerry and Raven followed my lead, and they are ready to go when we are."

Gale reached over and kissed me softly on the lips. It was time to go.

The church had a different air about it tonight. Not the static of the previous sitting, or the anxiousness of the sitters, but somehow the air seem thicker, if that were possible. Also gone, was the chill in the air.

The basement seemed unusually clean, as though someone had done a heavy duty cleansing job. I had a feeling that this was going to be the night.

Sandy, Angie, mom and Ada arrived and made a pronounced entrance, not by choice or design, but by the sheer fact that Ada commanded a presence, that I never witnessed in a lay-person before.

The type of homage paid to her by the others, was that of a major luminary. I hadn't any idea how important she was.

Lillian announced to all of us, that Ada was one of the founding fathers, or in this case. mothers, of the modern Spiritualist religion.

She was also one of the most renowned materialization and transfer mediums still alive in the world.

I silently attested to the fact that she could also read minds, and that, in addition, I thought she was a little weird.

Just as I finished my thought, Ada looked a look at me that said, "Hey asshole, I know what your thinking, so knock it off." I knocked it off.

Ada had been briefed on Kyle. As we spoke again about him, she pierced her eyes, and looked at me.

"Call the hospital, and be absolutely certain he's still there. Then be absolutely certain that they keep him there." She then turned away from me as though she had just given a queen's command to a subordinate subject. I felt humbled, and without even trying to respond, I headed for the phone.

Going up the stairs, I could hear her say to Angie, "Dear, get me a glass, I've brought my own water. Please be sure the glass is clean."

I thought to myself, Witches brew, no doubt. I instantly dashed the thought, lest she would pick up on it, and dialed Beaumont.

Kyle was still there, and still secure. I relayed the info to Ada.

She simply nodded and said "Good, let's begin."

What happened in the next half hour was like nothing I had ever seen, even with the activity of the past couple of weeks and the book.

I honestly don't think anyone had any control over what was happening in the basement that night, except Ada. I found myself relinquishing control of my body, mind and spirit to her. Ironically, I didn't feel threatened by the thought, or my submission.

In the past, we had gone through a lengthy precautionary period where we had protected ourselves, called guides, and sang songs. Ada chose her position, sat down, and spoke to the group.

"Please be seated. Get comfortable, and focus your thoughts on me. I am the channel."

Right on cue, I found myself thinking of her. Rather than thinking about Cam or Kyle, I could only think of sending my energies to her. I thought to myself, this is probably something like jump starting a car.

Jonathan had turned the lights down, and resumed his seat. That done, Ada began speaking.

"Each of you, picture Cameron Thomas in your presence. Picture him, as though you are with him, can touch him, can speak with him, can picture him."

I did, and from what I could sense spiritually, everyone else did too.

I felt the room begin to spin like a ride in an amusement park. Slowly, I opened my eyes to look around, and the room actually appeared to be spinning, with the lights I had seen in the previous settings spinning in concert, like a well choreographed, laser light show.

I sensed that the room really was spinning, but don't ask me how.

I also felt the rush of air blowing by me, and I had the strongest sensation that I was falling away. From what, I didn't know.

For the first time since this whole process began, I took my hands off my knees, and held on to my chair.

Ada seemed to be enveloped in a cocoon of white light, that began to increase in intensity with each passing rotation. After a few turns, the light was so bright that I couldn't look at her any longer.

Images began to appear around the walls of the basement. It looked like a shadowy family portrait, together with images of other people, that appeared like holograms. Translucent images of people, who I knew, had died long ago.

The next time around I saw dad, standing with grandpa Thomas and a young girl, whom I presumed was my great, great aunt Gabriel who passed away in a buckboard accident in the late eighteen hundreds.

It suddenly occurred to me, that we were really gonna pull this thing off. You might think that thought would make me happy, but there's an old adage that says, "Don't ask for something you're not sure you want, you just might get it".

That's the way I felt. I wasn't sure that I was ready. I don't know why, I just wasn't.

I glanced at the empty chair—nothing. My momentary sense of relief was short lived. Ada spoke loudly over the now rushing noise in the basement.

"Repeat after me. Spirit of Kyle Washington, vile spirit, that you are, be gone from the earth plane for evermore," Ada hissed the words of the statement, finally spitting out the last words.

While I repeated the words, I saw the vision of my friend Fred Kansik who had been killed in Viet Namm. Just as Fred passed from view there was a loud crack, a final rush of air, and then a silence that startled all of us so profoundly, that several of us cried out in surprise.

The room had stopped spinning, yet I still had the intense sensation of motion, much like you might feel after you come off a fast spinning merry-go-round.

I had kept my eyes tightly closed. Though now I wanted to look at the empty chair, I didn't, because I was afraid.

Mom was first to speak.

"Cam," she said.

I squinted, carefully looking over at the empty chair. There, as real as the nose on your face, sat my twin brother, Cam.

This was not a hologram. I arose from my chair, and walked to where he sat, appearing to be awakening from a deep sleep.

"Cam?"

"Sean. Thank you for all that you have done."

Cam, then stood, placed his arms around me, and gave me a brotherly hug.

"I love you, man."

I was still stunned. "I love you too, Cam," I said.

Angie and mom buried Cam in the crush of their love, hugging and kissing him, ensuring that he was really there.

The joy of the moment caught on with almost everyone in attendance, and as so often happens, there was not a dry eye in the house.

I imagine the rest, as they say, is now part of history. We all gathered around Cam and asked question after question, touching him, and finally believing.

Cam, told us of his passing, merely an accident. He relayed the wonders of the realm of spirit, and of his reunion with dad, and the other relatives who had passed on before him.

After a few moments of rest, Cam spent the rest of the night telling us of a heritage that went back to ancient times, filled with people of all races, and all levels of prominence. I was amazed at how much cross-breeding there was in our heritage.

I told you that almost everyone was caught up in the emotions of the moment. Ada seemed totally undaunted, as though she had just taken a walk in the park or something.

Unlike the rest of us, she seemed fresh, and unruffled. That, I didn't understand.

I was concerned that maybe this was all a dream of some kind, but I held Cam, and touched him. He was real.

My thoughts went to Kyle. I wondered if he was really gone. Ada looked at me, as though she had heard my question.

"He's gone, Sean. Trust me."

You can image that after all of this, I did trust her. But vicariously, I wanted to know for sure. I took Gale by the hand, and we went upstairs to use the phone.

"William Beaumont Hospital, may I help you?"

"I'd like the medical custody unit, please", I responded. After a moment, the phone clicked up on the other end.

"M.C.U., Mrs. Nancy."

I tested, "May I have Kyle Washington's room, please?"

The other end of the line was silent for a moment and then, "I'm sorry sir, there's no one by that name in the unit. When was he admitted?"

"I thought a couple of days ago", I lied.

Silence again, and then, "I really am sorry sir, there's no record of a Kyle Washington being in the unit. Are you sure you have the right hospital?"

I felt a sense of excitement.

"Uh, no, maybe not. Thanks for your help."

I hung up the phone and gave Gale a hug.

"Baby, it's over."

Gale kissed me and said, "I sure hope so."

Back downstairs everyone was making up for lost time. It was obvious that it was drawing nearer and nearer to the sleep time, which would mean that we too, would have our memories cleansed.

That thought didn't bother me. I had spent a great deal of time and energy on this caper, and even though I was sincerely happy that Cam was back and our lives were about to move on, I also wanted to have things return to normal as soon as possible.

That certainly wasn't going to happen here, and it wasn't going to happen with everyone remembering what was going on.

Ada asked to be driven to the airport before we slept. I agreed to take her, and so after a few more minutes, Gale and I loaded up the Escort with Ada and her things, and headed for Metro Airport.

We didn't talk much during the ride. When Ada did finally speak, she told me that the day would come when Cam and I would be a great force in the quest.

I didn't debate that point with her, and was anxious to drop her off at the airlines.

As Gale and I pulled away from the Northwest terminal, we both breathed a deep sigh of relief. I turned the escort onto the freeway, and headed for the Holiday. It was finally time for us to go to bed for the night.

****

The rest of the weekend was also unusual. The next day, most of the players had no recollection of the events. Jerry and Raven had no recall, nor did Lillian or Carolyn. I found that to be tremendously intriguing.

Cam and I talked as though we all had just happened to be in town for a visit. Gale also gave no indication that she remembered anything at all.

On Saturday, we ate at the China Star and ran into Susan. She didn't even acknowledge that she knew us. That broke my heart.

At the hotel, I looked for Thelma's number. Even though I had put it where I would remember it, I couldn't find it, and I couldn't remember where I had put it.

However, I did recall my mental note about that being for another place, and another time. Now, I added, and maybe even another life.

I know all of this seems like a lark to anyone not involved, but to us, it was all very real.

CHAPTER 37

It's been seven years since that night at the church. Life has assumed a sort of normalcy.

Cam and Angie had another son, Sean Gerald Thomas. Gale and I, and Jerry and Raven took the big walk, and have lived happily ever after.

The book said, that after the first sleep, all would be forgotten. I figured that maybe they had never done a change with identicals before, because I still remembered some things for a while, and so did Cam.

Mom turned out to be the concierge and when she passed away a couple of years ago, Cam and I shared a sense of relief, knowing that an era of our lives, was finally over.

As much as I tried to remember, I couldn't recall the names or places of the things that led us up to that point, and ma, keeping true to the traditions of her beliefs, never talked with us about it. I guess looking back, all of those things didn't really matter anyway. We had all moved on, to a different level of existence. Cam said that Angie never gave him the slightest inclination that she remembered anything at all, and Gale acts as though that part of her life never existed.

Somehow or other, she believes that she and I met in Detroit while she was visiting a Brazilian family, who were friends of hers.

She says they went back to South America, and I have never told her anything different.

When I first read about how spirit cleanses your thoughts, I believed that it would be virtually impossible to accomplish.

Looking back now, I can see that it was all pretty much true. I guess anything is possible with a little knowledge.

My memory has continued to fade, and I find it very difficult to recall even the faintest details of the entire escapade. I, long ago, gave up worrying about the names, and places involved, because my life has moved forward.

* * * * * * * * * * * * *

My PI business is booming. I took a following to a premonition that I had, and changed the name to "Undercover Associates", hired a couple of young guys to do my biddings and grunt work, and classed up the joint.

My first project when I returned to San Francisco, was to give my phone the four-story, test. That's where you see how well the phone will work after you drop it out of the fourth floor window. Mine didn't. Cheap imported crap.

It took Gale all of about twenty minutes to re-design my office. I should say twenty minutes and the sum total of my next two-month's earnings, but at least it's nice. It's bright, professional, has A.C., and American-made products. It serves our purposes well.

I opted for a window air conditioner so that on the days when it isn't too warm, I can still open the other window and smell the scent of the sea.

And Gale—well, she's almost always by my side. She and I work together now. She pretty much runs the joint, doing the typing, the scheduling, the billing and such. Ours has turned out to be a good relationship for both of us, and I still think it will get even better.

One thing I did find out is that Gale likes leather. No, not the kind you wear. See, she bought this oversized leather couch for my office. When things get slow, well, let's just say, when Gale comes into the office and says, "I love the smell of leather," I know it's time for the answering machine.

I finally gave up the Reds and started back into my martial arts training. Matter of fact, I just made my Second don, a little over a month ago, and I continue to train regularly.

Not too bad for an old guy. I guess to sum it all up, I feel like I have life pretty much by the ass.

* * * * * * * * * * * * *

Today is one of those, not too hot, not too cool, days, and I've got the window open feeling the heavy breeze blowing in from the bay.

Since I don't have anything on the appointment books today, I don't feel guilty sitting here watching the sea gulls flying around and crapping on everything in sight.

The water in the bay is smooth, like glass with ripples. Somewhere, a dog is barking incessantly. I hate dogs.

My hungries told me it was time to look at my watch. Right on cue. It was nearly time for lunch. I thought about calling Gale to come in and see the couch, but before I could do that, Gale buzzed me on the intercom. It was a good strong American sounding buzz.

"Sean, pick up intercom on line one."

I reached for the receiver, and hit the "I.C." button on the console. I hoped that maybe Gale had read my mind, since we have both been active in clairvoyant circles recently.

"What's up, baby?" I asked. Gale's voice sounded different.

"There's a guy here to see you. He says it's personal. He gives me the creeps."

I thought for a minute.

"What's his name?" I asked.

"He wouldn't give it to me," she said.

"He said you'd know who he was." The hair stood straight out on the back of my neck, and somewhere I heard a voice saying, "It's OK Gale, show him in."

I hung the phone up, and pushed myself away from the desk.

After a moment or two, the door to my office cracked, and slowly swung open. I stood up behind my desk as Gale swung the door all the way open and stepped aside.

A tall, good-looking guy walked through the door and strode over to where I stood. I studied his face closely. I had no recognition there. I couldn't place him, but he was smiling a knowing smile.

I wondered if he was a client from my past, or maybe a disgruntled participant in some illicit case we may have been investigating.

Whoever he was, he also made me feel uneasy. I was thankful that I had remembered to pack heat this morning when I came to work. The heavy weight under my arm, bringing a momentary sense of security.

I watched him as he walked across the office. From outward appearances, he didn't appear to be the type to be a trouble maker.

As he neared me, he reached out his hand and I shook it, waiting for an introduction.

"Do I <u>know</u> you?" I asked questioningly.

His smile never wavered. His grin stayed wide. His stare was eye to eye.

"Of course, you know me, Sean. My name is Kyle Washington."

ORDER FORM:

NAME__________________________________

ADDRESS_______________________________

CITY__________________**STATE**____**ZIP**_____

NAME OF BOOK__________________________

QUANTITY___________

An invoice will be sent out with the books for payment...sorry we do not accept credit cards.

Discount 10% on orders over 10 copies.

Free shipping & handling on orders over 20 copies.

Press-Tige Publishing Company
291 Main Street
Catskill, NY 12414
(518) 943-0702 fax